MEN
IN UNIFORM

Courteous, courageous and commanding—
these heroes lay it all on the line for the
people they love in more than fifty stories about
loyalty, bravery and romance.
Don't miss a single one!

MEN
in
UNIFORM

JACQUELINE DIAMOND

BY LEAPS AND BOUNDS

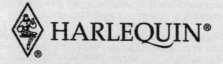

HARLEQUIN®

TORONTO • NEW YORK • LONDON
AMSTERDAM • PARIS • SYDNEY • HAMBURG
STOCKHOLM • ATHENS • TOKYO • MILAN • MADRID
PRAGUE • WARSAW • BUDAPEST • AUCKLAND

Recycling programs
for this product may
not exist in your area.

ISBN-13: 978-0-373-36275-2

BY LEAPS AND BOUNDS

Copyright © 1990 by Jackie Hyman

Printed in U.S.A.

JACQUELINE DIAMOND

Although her own babies are now young adults, Jacqueline Diamond hasn't forgotten the roller-coaster process of having and nurturing them. A former Associated Press reporter, she maintains a keen interest in medical care and technology, thanks in part to being the daughter of a doctor. To keep tabs on Jackie's more than eighty published novels and free writing tips, please check out www.jacquelinediamond.com. You can write to her at jdiamondfriends@yahoo.com.

PROLOGUE

THE SLEET STARTED before they were even out of New York State.

"This is awful." Kerry peered forward between the windshield wipers, which were straining to scrape away the mess. "Maybe we'd better wait."

Beside her in the car, George didn't answer.

She turned to look at him. His famous profile seemed carved out of stone, his eyes focused entirely on the road as if he hadn't heard her. Which wasn't unusual.

"George?" she said.

"We can't wait." So he had heard her, after all. She wished he would acknowledge her more quickly; sometimes, with him, she felt almost invisible. "I start rehearsals on Monday, and you refuse to tell your parents about our engagement over the phone."

"I'm sorry," she murmured. "It just seemed like they ought to hear this in person."

Couldn't he ease up a little? His perfectionism about his work was part of what had made George so successful, but wasn't he carrying things a bit too far?

On the other hand, maybe she had been foolish, Kerry reflected, insisting they set off for Boston late at night. But she had only three days until her next performance with the New American Ballet, and his job as assistant conductor of the New York Philharmonic gave him even less time off, not to mention that he would be flying to Europe next month to make his first recording with a German orchestra.

Besides, she wanted to share the thrill of tonight's triumph with her parents. Maybe when they learned that she was finally a star, finally someone they could be proud of, she would at last break through the polite, distracted fondness with which they usually treated her.

Kerry looked back out the window, hoping that somehow the storm would have lessened. Fat chance. November was a tricky month, and tonight it had decided to play one of its worst practical jokes on them.

Leaning her head against the seat, she wished she didn't feel so let down. Yes, tonight had been important to her career, but right now she and George were embarking on a new life together. Shouldn't she feel more excited? And shouldn't he act as if he cared more about meeting her parents?

It had seemed like an incredible stroke of luck, meeting George Carlisle at a party four months ago and finding that he was attracted to her. Kerry had never considered herself particularly beautiful. She generally kept her honey-blond hair pulled severely back and only put makeup around her light blue eyes when she was going onstage.

George had wined and dined her around New York, showing her off to his friends, toasting her at the finest restaurants. Kerry could never quite believe her luck. He was handsome and a genius, even if he was moody sometimes.

It wouldn't be easy, of course, blending their two careers, but George didn't seem to mind spending time apart. In fact, he obviously liked his privacy.

Kerry sighed. This wasn't the kind of marriage she'd dreamed about as a child, but surely things would change after they were married; they'd talk more about personal things, share their fears and hopes, begin to plan for the day when they could have their own family....

She huddled beneath her coat. In spite of the blast from the BMW's heater, the cold was seeping inside her. To fight it, she tried to revive the way she'd felt earlier in those last, wonderful moments onstage, the feeling of melting into ecstasy, the sense of completion.

In all her years of ballet training, Kerry had never before experienced anything like it—the unfamiliar lightness, the exhilarating flow. She had become part of the air, part of the wind, part of the night. She had been transformed into someone other than Kerry Guthrie, someone free of anxieties and insecurities and the need to please. Someone who knew how to defy gravity.

It had startled her, the applause thundering toward her at the end. She'd forgotten, for a few minutes, that she was a dancer in front of an audience, and she might have stood there in a daze if her partner, Alfonso Carrera, hadn't led her forward to take her bows.

Then afterward, as they retreated backstage, he'd told her quietly that it was obvious this company had a new star ballerina.

Alfonso had said that—Alfonso, a veteran of ten years with the company and Kerry's former teacher; she valued his opinion more than almost anyone's.

"I can hardly see where I'm going." George's cross words broke into her reverie. "This is crazy."

"I'd really like—I mean, my parents would…" Kerry's voice trailed off. She hated disagreeing with George.

"Your parents will understand. Do you think they want us to end up in a snowbank?"

He was probably right. Her parents were terribly rational about everything. Which was part of why Kerry wanted so much to share this high point of her life with them.

Her engagement to George and her professional triumph, both in one night. Surely that would finally impress Everett and Elaine Guthrie, would make up for the fact that Kerry could never follow in their brilliant musical footsteps—her father's as concertmaster of the Boston Symphony, her mother's as first cellist. On the other hand, George had a good point. If only he could be a little more sympathetic about it.

Kerry swallowed the bitter disappointment. "I guess you're right."

"I'll get off at the next exit." George began to edge the car to the right.

"We could go next weekend—no—well, maybe in two weeks," Kerry said. "Just overnight."

He shook his head. "I'm tired of waiting. I want to make an announcement. All my friends are asking questions." After a moment, he added, "Besides, after your success tonight, think how much press coverage we'll get."

"Really? I mean—I guess so." It hadn't even occurred to Kerry that the press would be interested in their engagement. She wasn't sure she liked the idea. Certainly she expected newspaper coverage of the premiere of a new ballet. Her personal life was something else.

She supposed it all sounded like the kind of story the public loved: a ballerina becomes the rising star of her company and simultaneously swears undying love to a brilliant young conductor.

Only, was it undying love?

Startled, Kerry turned to look at George. He was so elegant and assured, so cosmopolitan. It would be an incredible privilege to share his life, wouldn't it? Then why did he seem more concerned with getting publicity than with meeting her family?

The uncertainty that rose up in Kerry scared her. More than anything, she wanted to make this engagement official so there would be no turning back. No more doubts.

Everything would be all right. They just needed more time together, more closeness. After they were married...

"There," George said. "Isn't that the exit sign, just up ahead?"

She would never know where the truck came from. One

minute she was absorbed in quiet thoughts, and the next minute a huge hulk was skidding toward them sideways. It felt unreal, like something out of a movie. Even the terrible jolt and the rending cry of metal didn't register as something that was happening to her.

Kerry felt herself flopping sideways against her seatbelt and then everything turned upside down and crossways. She heard someone screaming and realized it must be her.

The last thing that registered was the intense, crushing pressure against her hips and the searing pain in her legs.

CHAPTER ONE

THE LITTLE GIRL APPEARED smaller than her ten years. She had fine black hair and a slender body that looked as if it would snap in a strong wind.

It was the firmness of her uptilted chin that caught Kerry's eye, and the fierce set of the slim shoulders.

She wanted to say something to reassure this determined little girl in the tattered swimsuit and the tense mother who waited beside her in the dance studio. The mother had the same slender build, although overwork and anxiety had worn premature lines in her face and added early gray to her hair.

But this was no time for reassurances. Not yet.

"Have you had any dance training?" As always, Kerry made a point of standing like a dancer, her arms and legs carefully placed to form a smooth line. The simple black leotard and coordinated skirt were stark, as was her hairstyle, but in a strange way they felt like a refuge.

The little girl shook her head.

Kerry checked the sheet in front of her. "Your name is Suzanne?"

"Everybody calls me Suzie." The child's voice trembled slightly.

"All right." Kerry wanted to soften toward her, but she didn't dare. A ballet teacher had to be ruthlessly objective toward her students. To give them false hope was, in the long run, the cruelest thing of all.

"You can see she would need a scholarship," the mother broke in. Her name, according to the paper, was Vivian Ezell.

"She's been crazy about ballet ever since she saw a program on TV. She reads about it, watches every program she can. She even tries to practice in her bedroom. I'm afraid she'll do something wrong and hurt herself."

"Practicing alone isn't a good idea." Kerry could see the child's eyes fill with tears; she was afraid she'd ruined her chances. "Let me see your feet."

Puzzled, the little girl extended first one foot and then the other as Kerry bent to examine them. They were shaped well and not distorted by bad training. It was a tragic fact that incompetent teachers sometimes put young dancers on their toes much too soon and ruined their feet.

"Good," Kerry said. "Now come to the barre."

Dutifully, the little girl followed her to the waist-high barre that ran along two mirrored walls of the studio.

For one disorienting moment, Kerry imagined herself back in one of the studios where she'd trained in New York. They were all like this one, sparse and unadorned with a scarred wooden floor, a few old folding chairs along the walls and a battered upright piano to one side. From down the hall came the tinkling of a piano from the character dance class.

But this was Brea, California, not New York City; this was the Leaps and Bounds Studio, not the New American Ballet School. And she was Kerry Guthrie, ballet teacher, not ballerina.

Firmly, Kerry forced her attention back to the little girl in front of her. "I want you to make a plié, like this."

Kerry demonstrated how to stand with the toes and legs turned out, and then executed a deep knee bend. As always, she could feel the pain start to tingle through her legs, as if a hundred bits of crushed bone pressed against hidden nerves.

Wordlessly, Suzie imitated her. The child was limber enough, although her movements displayed the awkwardness of inexperience.

"Now, come away from the barre." Kerry moved into the center of the room. "Turn your feet so they're almost reversed—this is called third position. I want you to jump and change feet in the air, like this."

Kerry steeled herself against the twinges. They weren't so bad anymore, not really. Sometimes she wondered if she might dance again, moving through the pain like the mermaid in Hans Christian Andersen's fairy tale, but she knew the agony would erode her stamina. And the doctors said she might do herself permanent harm.

Suzie followed suit dutifully, if a bit clumsily, biting her lip so hard Kerry feared the child would draw blood.

"Now you make a reverence. Like this." Kerry demonstrated the elegant bow. "We do this at the end of each lesson."

Suzie made her reverence and then folded her hands tightly in front of her, waiting.

"We have very few scholarships," Kerry said. The fear in the child's eyes almost overwhelmed her, and she added, "However, you have a good build and flexibility. It's impossible to tell at this point whether you'd make a good dancer, but I'm willing to give you a chance."

A smile transformed Suzie's thin face. "Really?"

"Our first-year students take classes three times a week." Kerry walked to the piano and lifted down some papers she'd left there earlier. "The work is very basic and sometimes boring, but we expect a great deal of dedication and some sacrifice."

"I will!" Suzie said. "Oh, thank you!"

"Just a minute." Kerry handed the papers to Vivian Ezell. "Although your lessons will be free, you will have some other expenses. You'll need a proper leotard and ballet slippers—no toe shoes yet—and some costumes for our performances. You must always be on time, and wear your hair pulled back so I can see every muscle."

"Yes, yes!" The girl's eyes shone.

"Now you'd better go change."

As soon as Suzie left the room, her mother spoke up. "I can't tell you how much this means to us. I could never afford dance lessons on my salary as a receptionist, and it would break my daughter's heart to give up her dream."

Kerry smiled, hoping her own pain didn't show. "I have to warn you that if she doesn't work hard, we'll have to drop her."

"You can see what she's like. She'll do anything you say."

"Yes, but—" Kerry knew she had to give the mother a realistic picture. "At the end of the first year we weed out the class. We get transfer students in the second year, and we need to keep the group small. Some girls simply don't have the aptitude, no matter how hard they try. We have to be honest with them."

Vivian squared her shoulders. It was almost six o'clock, and she'd clearly had a hard day at work, yet her gaze was frank and direct.

"We'll deal with that if and when it happens," she said. "I only wish—my son, Jamie, is sixteen. He's been drifting since his dad left us three years ago, and I'm afraid he's fallen in with a bad crowd. I only wish he'd had something like this, something of his own, to hold on to."

"Adolescence is another problem," Kerry admitted. "Two or three years from now, Suzie's interests could change sharply."

"Well—"

The little girl dashed back into the room, clad in jeans and an oversize T-shirt that made her look even frailer than she was. "I'm ready!"

Her mother put an arm around her shoulders and led her out. "Thank you, Miss Guthrie. So much."

"You're welcome."

After they left, Kerry stood in the empty studio just letting her thoughts wander, letting herself feel and breathe and listen as she'd learned to do in therapy. Through it all came the staccato of the piano down the hall, thumping out flamenco rhythms for Myron's class.

Thank goodness for Myron Placer. He'd been planning to retire from the New American Ballet about the time of Kerry's accident. If he hadn't invited her to help establish this new dance school, she didn't know what she would have done with her life.

Kerry shook her head. That had all been seven years ago. She'd long ago settled into life here, even buying a small house not far from Brea's redeveloped downtown area, where the school was located.

Patting down her skirt, she stepped into the hall. On the way to her office, she couldn't resist pausing in a doorway to watch Myron at work.

He was an older man with an incongruous goatee. That and his longish gray hair made him stand out in conservative Orange County, but the parents and students quickly accepted him once they heard his gentle voice and saw how good a teacher he was.

There were half a dozen advanced students in the class, three boys and three girls. Tom Hadley, Myron's top pupil, was dancing sensuously opposite Melanie Layne.

Kerry wrapped her arms around herself, watching them.

Tom was more of a show dancer than most of their students and would probably use his training on Broadway. He had a flair for presenting himself well, for dramatizing every movement.

Melanie was just the opposite. Despite her fifteen years, she had a mature grace and perfection of line that sometimes took Kerry's breath away.

The flamenco didn't really suit Melanie's light, fluid style, although she had mastered its moves. She was every inch a ballerina, in Myron's class as well as in Kerry's.

The music crashed to a stop. At the piano, Bella Beltran folded her music, her dark eyes still youthful in her creased old face as she nodded in appreciation to the dancers.

The youngsters made their bows and filed out. Kerry stood aside until Melanie reached her.

"Mel? Can I have a moment?"

The girl turned, her face flushed from dancing. "Of course, Miss Guthrie."

Kerry waited until the hallway was empty around them. "I've been meaning to talk to you about next summer."

Melanie looked puzzled. "But it's only September."

"I know, but some things require time to decide." Kerry took a deep breath. "You're our best ballerina and I'd hate to see you go, but I think that next year may be time for you to move on."

A stricken look came into Melanie's eyes. "But I don't want any other teacher! Besides, there's nobody in L.A. any better than you."

"That wasn't what I meant." Kerry knew enough of Melanie's family situation to be aware that this was a ticklish issue, but it had to be raised. "The New American Ballet holds auditions for its school in the summer. In New York."

Melanie stared at her. "New York? Dad would never let me."

"I'm sure a chaperon could be arranged," Kerry said, "if it isn't possible for him to move there himself."

"No, of course not." Melanie shifted restlessly, but even so, her movements were smooth and controlled. "You know, he's a police lieutenant. He can't just transfer. It doesn't work that way. Besides, he hates New York."

"It's just a suggestion." Kerry didn't want to upset the girl. "Something to think about, maybe discuss with him."

"He'll say no." Melanie bit her lip. "Do you really think I'd have a chance? At one of the big companies?"

"More than a chance," Kerry said. "Believe me."

She wanted to pour out reassurances but stopped herself. Going to New York would be a gamble, even for someone as talented as Melanie.

"I—I have to go change," Melanie said reluctantly. "I promised to baby-sit for my neighbor." Despite her busy schedule, Melanie took pride in helping earn the money for her lessons.

"See you tomorrow." Kerry strode away toward her office, wondering how, at twenty-eight, being around Melanie could make her feel so very old.

She picked up her purse and wondered what to do about dinner. Actually, she wasn't very hungry, and she made a point of keeping her weight down anyway. The thought of going home to cottage cheese and fresh fruit didn't hold much appeal.

A swim. That was what she needed.

Nodding to herself, Kerry went out the door. The last thing she saw as she left the studio was Melanie emerging from the locker room down the hall.

The girl looked lost in thought, her mobile face mirroring sadness mixed with determination. Kerry found herself hoping Melanie would win her battle; at least one of them ought to have a chance to see her dreams come true.

THE POOL AT THE HEALTH SPA was especially busy, since the club was running a promotion to draw in new members.

Still, Kerry managed to ease through a few laps and work the kinks out of her muscles. She would have liked a soak in the whirlpool bath afterward, but it was crammed.

Wrapping herself in a towel, she went to check the schedule for the masseuse. There was an opening in half an hour, and Kerry signed up for it.

Some people jostled by her, a man and woman lost in each other's eyes. Kerry watched them go with more curiosity than envy. Sure, she felt lonely sometimes, as if she were missing something, especially after watching a romantic movie on TV. But none of the men she'd met had inspired her with anything more than a mild liking.

As she walked through the club, idly taking in the sweaty bodies laboring over cycles and weights, she thought about George.

He didn't enter her mind often these days, but she'd read an article about him the previous day in the L.A. Times. He had been invited to head a major symphony and to serve as regular guest conductor at another. The promise of seven years ago was rapidly becoming fulfilled.

So far, there'd been no reports of any new lady in his life. That wasn't surprising, considering his schedule.

During much of her lengthy rehabilitation, George had been on a European tour. They'd never announced their engagement, and after a while it had become clear to her that there would never be a marriage.

Neither of them had really wanted it any longer, and yet his desertion hurt terribly. It underscored her fear that she had no value as herself, without the glamour of accomplishment.

Sometimes she missed George, in odd moments. Not him so much as the life-style they'd shared, the whirlwind of sophisticated restaurants and parties, the company of clever, talented people, the feeling of riding on top of an immensely exciting wave.

Kerry gave a mental shrug and strolled onto the bridge overlooking the racquetball courts.

The sharp thong-thong of balls whacking against walls formed a kind of white noise, blotting out some of the tumult in her mind. She leaned against the railing, watching a game being heatedly contested.

From here, she could see only the backs of the two men. One was stocky, clad in jogging shorts and a polo shirt.

It was the other man who caught her eye.

He was about six feet tall, wearing tan twill shorts and a

dark brown T-shirt that clung damply to his back and shoulders, outlining every muscle. And there were quite a few muscles.

He moved with an assurance that impressed her, not only because he was winning the game but because such natural grace was rare. She wondered if he danced or if there were dancers in his family.

Kerry folded her arms on the railing, glad for the privilege of ogling the man without being observed.

She smiled to herself. Ogling. Well, that was what she was doing, wasn't she? And what harm was there, after all?

Sometimes when she took a modern dance class at the gym, she would notice one or two men watching her out of the corners of their eyes. Occasionally they would come over to make conversation afterward, but they seemed more interested in getting her into bed than in finding out what kind of person she was, and that didn't appeal to her.

Now this man in front of her...

He leaped for the ball, pounded it with his racquet and then raced to retrieve it. Terrific eyesight, she decided; it took excellent peripheral vision and depth perception to be a good racquetball player. Or a dancer.

Protected by anonymity, Kerry allowed herself to fantasize. Not that she'd ever really want to get involved with a man just for his body, but it was fun to imagine it.

He had neatly cut, light brown hair, a well-rounded head and terrific shoulders. She wondered what it would be like to dance with him, to feel those strong arms lift her into the air. It would have to be a very private dance, one that could end with her sliding down into his embrace....

This was crazy. She didn't even know what his face looked like!

Amused at her own ramblings, she checked the clock overhead. Fifteen minutes before her massage. Time to start back.

Below, she was vaguely aware of the game finishing. But what difference did it make?

She padded down the steps to the main floor, aware that she instinctively turned her feet out from years of training, as if she wore toe shoes instead of sneakers. All those hard-won muscles had helped her long ago when she had had to learn to walk again, and she was grateful for them.

At the foot of the steps, she spotted the two men coming out of the racquetball courts.

Kerry stopped abruptly. Up close, the broad-shouldered man in the brown T-shirt looked even taller than he had on the court. Although he was sweating heavily, she found the scent refreshingly masculine. It reminded her of the men who had partnered her in ballet.

The pair was about to walk by when, inexplicably, the tall one turned. "I thought it was you," he said.

Kerry blinked. He looked familiar but she couldn't place him. His dark brown eyes had a warmth tinged with wariness; his face was strong, softened only by a clipped mustache. The kind of mustache policemen wore.

"Oh!" she said. "You're Melanie's dad."

He smiled and waved his companion on. "I do have a name, you know. It's Chris. Chris Layne."

"I haven't seen you here before—"

"I'm new." He held out his hand and, feeling a bit awkward, Kerry shook it.

He held her hand a moment longer than necessary before she withdrew it. "I'm—I'm afraid I have an appointment for a massage in a few minutes," she stammered, taken aback by the way he was looking at her.

"Wish I could be there." His smile took the teasing edge off his words.

"You—you were terrific on the court." The breathless catch in her voice surprised Kerry. It reflected a tightness in her chest, an unfamiliar tension. What had she turned into, a bashful teenager with a crush?

Fortunately, Chris didn't seem to notice her discomfort. "I like to work off the tensions."

The relaxed look in his eyes faded, and the creases around his mouth deepened. Kerry was sorry she'd reminded him, however inadvertently, of whatever was worrying him.

He didn't seem to want to move, though, and neither did she. It was as if they both had things to say but couldn't remember exactly what they were. As if they were both intimately aware of each other, wondering how it would be to touch and a little afraid of the thought.

"I was talking to Melanie—" she began.

"I was wondering if you—" he said at the same time.

They both stopped and chuckled self-consciously.

"You were wondering what?" Kerry said.

He twirled his racquet lightly in one hand. "My daughter's baby-sitting tonight and I'm on my own for dinner. I wondered if you'd care to join me."

He probably wasn't going to eat diet food, but on the other hand, Kerry wasn't eager to eat alone. "Sure," she said. "If you don't mind waiting—"

"I need a swim," he said. "Outside in, say, forty-five minutes?"

"Done."

She hurried off, surprised at how eager she felt to be finished with her massage.

THE MASSAGE WAS RELAXING, if mildly painful at times. Unfortunately, it reminded Kerry of the physical therapy she'd endured for so many months, and she had to force herself to let her thoughts float.

Doggedly, they kept going back to Chris Layne.

He was so—sexy. How had she failed to notice it before?

The answer was easy. She'd seen him only in the ballet

studio and only in Melanie's company. He might as well have worn a label pasted over his forehead that said Father of Student.

He'd never felt comfortable at the studio, she could tell, always in a hurry to get somewhere else. Today he hadn't been in a hurry at all.

Had he just asked her out because he didn't like dining alone? Had she imagined that moment of physical awareness between them?

Kerry tried to remember whether she'd ever had such a strong physical response to George. She didn't think so. She couldn't recall ever separating her feelings for him as a man from her awe of him as a musical genius. Even the few times they'd slept together, she hadn't felt much beyond a faint pleasure mixed with uncertainty.

The massage ended. Kerry tipped the masseuse and went to dress.

After applying makeup more carefully than usual, she tucked her hair back into its accustomed bun. As she did so, she glanced around at the other women, who were carefully blow-drying their coiffures, some using a curling iron for finishing touches.

For a moment she wished she'd found some other way to fix her hair. Something more up-to-date and flattering. Well, not much she could do about it now.

Pulling on the jeans and sweatshirt she wore outside the studio, Kerry slung her gym bag over her shoulder and walked out past the reception desk to the parking lot.

Chris leaned against a sporty sedan, his hair still damp from swimming. He wore tailored slacks and a button-down shirt partly open in the front. "Want a ride?" he said. "Or would you rather meet me there?"

"I'll meet you." Kerry preferred having her own car with her. Mobility meant freedom. "Where's there?"

"How about Brea's Best?" She must have looked puzzled,

because he quickly gave directions in case they got separated in traffic.

"Fine." It wasn't exactly in a ritzy area, but the way she was dressed, it should suit her.

She managed to get her battered station wagon started on the second try. It wasn't her idea of an ideal car, but the cargo space was useful for hauling costumes, equipment and sometimes students.

They headed along Imperial Highway through thinning traffic. It was nearly seven-thirty and rush hour had ended.

Brea's Best turned out to be an unpretentious hamburger joint with a glassed-in front and lots of pickup trucks in the parking lot. You ordered and carried your own tray, but the burgers were huge and the servings of fries far more generous than at franchises.

It was a far cry from the posh places George used to take her, Kerry reflected as they made their way between the other diners. The funny thing was, she kind of liked it here.

"Great place," Chris said as they set their trays on a table near two tattooed bikers who ignored them.

"Atmospheric," Kerry agreed, wondering what had possessed her to order such a huge, fattening meal.

"You've never eaten here before? How long have you lived in Brea?" He began slathering his hamburger with condiments.

"Six years." She wondered how much Melanie had told him about Kerry's early career and the accident. It wasn't something she liked to talk about, but she'd seen no point in being too secretive and hadn't objected when Myron told the students.

"Family around here?"

Kerry shook her head. "You?"

"Afraid not." His hamburger was disappearing at an amazing rate. "Makes it hard, raising a kid by yourself."

Kerry nibbled at her fries, fighting the impulse to wolf

them down. She knew that Melanie's mother was dead, but not how or when. It didn't seem an appropriate subject at the moment. "Do you like police work?"

He shrugged. "It's interesting. Beats being tied to a desk, although I don't get out as much as I used to."

"You're a lieutenant?" she said. "What does that mean?"

Chris looked amused. "The guys don't salute, that's for sure."

"No, I mean—"

He finished a draft of Coke. "It means all the reports end up on my desk. In detectives. That's where I'm assigned until the chief decides to get creative and rotate us again."

"Detectives." Kerry ate a small bite of hamburger before going on. "I guess that's not as romantic as it sounds, huh?"

"If they made a movie about me, it would put the audience to sleep," Chris agreed. "Even murder cases—and we do get a few—aren't usually all that exciting. It's not as if we were hanging around when the crime goes down."

Kerry smiled. "Sounds like ballet. Everyone thinks of it as glamorous, but it's mostly doing exercises over and over again. I suppose you know that, from Melanie."

"It's been good for her." He glanced out the window as two motorcycles roared to life and the bikers spun out of the lot. "No helmets. We'll be peeling them off the pavement one of these days."

"Do you always think like a policeman?" she teased.

He looked across at her, suddenly serious. "Not always. Sometimes I just think like a man."

Kerry flushed at the implication.

He was watching her closely. "Are you really—no, that's none of my business."

"Am I really what?"

"As—inexperienced as you seem?"

Darn it, how was she supposed to react? "I was engaged once. Seven years ago."

"And since then?"

Kerry shrugged and bit into her hamburger, wishing she could think of an inconspicuous way to change the subject.

"The men around here must be crazy," Chris said. "I always assumed you'd be too busy to give me the time of day."

"You noticed me before?" From his expression, she could tell she'd said something naive again. "Look, I don't know how to play this game."

"What makes you think it's a game?"

"The way you're looking at me. As if you're surprised I don't know the rules."

He laughed. "Touché. I suppose I can't help wanting to be the one to teach you the rules, but at the same time, I'd hate to spoil that wonderful honesty."

With half her mind Kerry longed to tease him back and find out where this conversation would lead; the other half wanted to bolt from the restaurant.

Darn it, why was she still so vulnerable after all these years? So afraid that if she let herself open up, she might not live up to Chris's expectations, that he might reject her the way George had?

Fumbling with her soft drink, she said, "I've been wanting to talk to you about Melanie."

"Melanie?"

"She's got a rare talent," Kerry said.

"Is this really the time—"

"I don't want to see her waste it, Chris."

He studied her warily. "Meaning what?"

"Meaning—" She knew she was ruining everything, destroying the mood between them, but she couldn't stop herself. "I think next year she'll be ready for one of the top ballet schools in New York."

"New York?" He stared at her as if she'd proposed sending his daughter to Mars.

"I did it myself," Kerry hurried on. "You live with other

students. There are chaperons, of course, and you're so busy with classes that you hardly have time to breathe. And she will be sixteen—"

"That's just the problem," he said.

"Being sixteen?"

"The part about hardly having time to breathe." In Chris's level gaze across the table there was nothing left of the flirtatious man of a few minutes ago. "Don't get me wrong. I'm grateful for how much ballet has meant to her. But there's more to life than dancing, and Melanie hasn't figured that out yet."

"She's got plenty of time," Kerry said. "But the dancing can't wait. You have to make your move when you're young."

"Are you so sure that's the best thing for Melanie?"

"With her talent—"

"Look, Kerry," he said. "You see her as a ballet student, and that's as it should be. But I see her as a young girl, one who's had to take more than her share of blows in this life. A kid who hasn't even gone out on her first date in an era when other girls her age are, well, doing things they shouldn't. Not that I want that for her. But sending her off to New York, burying her in a dance studio—no."

"I did it," Kerry said. "I loved every minute of it."

"You're not Melanie."

"I know, but this time of her life will be gone so quickly." Distractedly, she noticed that he had eaten every bite on his plate. She had barely touched her meal.

"I'm sorry, but until I see signs that my daughter is able to make a truly mature decision about her future, I'm not letting her go anywhere. And especially not to live three thousand miles away with some chaperon."

He looked as if he wanted to recapture their earlier mood, but it was gone irrevocably. Kerry knew she'd shattered it on purpose, and now she wished she hadn't.

After they finished their drinks, Chris walked her to her car. Kerry opened the door, wishing she could think of something to say to restore the warmth between them and finding herself completely tongue-tied.

"I guess we look at things differently," Chris said as she slid behind the wheel. "Coming from different worlds and all."

"I guess." Her voice threatened to catch on the lump in her throat.

"I wish—" He stopped. "Never mind." And he strode across the lot to his car.

Kerry revved her engine and pulled out onto the road.

Why did the first man who'd attracted her in years have to be Melanie's father, anyway? Why did he bring out such painfully conflicting feelings?

She turned on the tape player and let a Mozart sonata do its best to soothe her thoughts. But it didn't make much headway against the turmoil, and she replayed the conversation with Chris all the way home, trying to figure out what she should have said to make it all end differently.

CHAPTER TWO

ON TUESDAY, THOUGHTS of Kerry kept wafting in and out of Chris's awareness. He wasn't sure why. She certainly wasn't the glamorous sort of woman some of his co-workers liked to show off, nor was she the settled, motherly type he'd always imagined would be best for Melanie.

It was the vulnerability that had touched him most, the sense of pain just beneath the surface. He wanted to soothe her, which was a crazy idea, since he'd never been all that good at easing his own worries.

In between reading reports about a robbery at a restaurant and a shoplifting ring plaguing the Brea Mall, Chris pictured Kerry again and admitted to himself that he found her damned attractive.

He'd never met a woman with such an unusual combination of natural, instinctive physicality and something he could only describe as spirituality. Except maybe, in just a little way, his daughter.

Damn it. Was he being unreasonable? Would Melanie resent him in later years for screwing up her chance at the big time?

They'd discussed it this morning over cereal. Melanie had looked like a little kid, her hair pulled back in a ponytail, her eyes huge even without makeup.

She hadn't begged or pleaded; Mel had too much dignity. She'd just let her lower lip tremble, and looked at him in that hurt, pleading way.

His little girl. Maybe he was being overprotective. But he didn't think so.

The phone rang. It was Captain Yarborough.

"Chris? We've had some more problems at the Ahmed house."

All thought of his family problems vanished. "What is it this time?"

"A threatening phone call. Mrs. Ahmed is pretty freaked. I thought it might help if you went out there personally."

"I'll get right on it."

Shuffling through the papers on his desk for the Ahmed folder, Chris strode out to his car. It was a wiltingly hot September day, the middle of a typical late-summer Southern California heat wave, and he turned the air conditioning on full blast as soon as he got in.

The Ahmed house wasn't far away, located in one of the relatively new tracts near the mall.

The problems the family had been suffering weren't serious compared to many of the crimes Chris encountered, but they were delicate. It was one of those situations that could turn nasty.

Gamel Ahmed was a professor of history at Cal State Fullerton. A little over a month before, he'd given a well-publicized speech to a service organization, presenting his insights into some of the issues plaguing the Middle East.

Someone had taken offense. More than offense; they'd begun harassing his family. So far, there'd been only a couple of pasteup letters and some graffiti, but the threats were harsh enough to frighten Mrs. Ahmed and their two small daughters.

Chris hoped it wasn't some weird terrorist sect; he could never figure out the various disputes in the Middle East, but it seemed as if everybody hated everybody else one way or another. And he didn't like to think about somebody planting a car bomb in peaceful Brea.

More than likely it was some isolated nut, or maybe kids who didn't understand how complex these matters were and just wanted to be mean. Whoever it was, Chris hoped he would catch them. Soon.

He pulled up in front of the house, a standard-issue stucco structure with lots of plants hanging from the decorative rafters in front. For once, he wished he were driving a marked police car; he wouldn't blame Mrs. Ahmed if she panicked at seeing a stranger approach.

Chris walked up to the front door and rang the bell. A moment later a curtain was pulled aside in the front window.

He held up his badge. The curtain fell, and the door opened slowly.

Mrs. Ahmed was a small woman with a strong, intelligent face. "Yes?"

"I'm Lieutenant Layne, Brea P.D.," he said. "We're looking into that phone call you received."

"Oh, thank you. I didn't expect a lieutenant." She stood aside to let him in.

Although the house was designed like a hundred others he'd seen, distinctive touches caught his eye—a gold-trimmed Arabic scroll displayed in a glass case, some striking pottery, a lush Persian rug instead of wall-to-wall carpeting in the living room.

Sitting on the couch, Chris accepted a cup of tea. He didn't particularly like tea, but he didn't want to give offense.

Flipping open his notebook, he said, "Tell me about the caller. Was it a man? Woman? About how old?"

"The voice was, um, strange—you know—"

"Disguised?"

She nodded. "I'm sure it was a man. And there was a radio playing. Rock music. I think he must be young."

Chris paused as two dark-haired girls dashed into the room, then halted abruptly on seeing him. Their mother spoke to them gently in a foreign language, and the children raced away.

"What beautiful children," he said. "I have a daughter of my own."

"We're very frightened," Mrs. Ahmed said. "Why would anyone want to do this?"

"That's what we have to find out." He asked her some more questions about the call, but she didn't come up with anything helpful. "Have you talked to the phone company about a tracer?"

"Yes," Mrs. Ahmed said. "We're going to do it. But I hate it, you know?"

"So do I." Shaking his head, Chris stood up. "I'm sorry this has happened. It isn't typical of people around here."

"I know." When she smiled, she was remarkably pretty. "We're new to Orange County but we lived in San Francisco for several years. We like America."

He left feeling a little better, but not much.

Maybe this whole thing would just fade away, but still, it was ugly. The crimes Chris hated most involved violence against innocent victims. Second came racist acts and other types of harassment that were a form of psychological violence against the innocent. Like the Ahmeds.

All they wanted was to live their lives quietly and protect their children. Just like he wanted to protect his own daughter.

Driving back to the police station, Chris felt a twinge of guilt. He hadn't spent much time with Melanie lately. Maybe that was what he needed to do, to get to know her better so he could be sure he was making the right decision.

He'd try to get off early tonight and pick her up at ballet school. It would save her a bus ride and give them more time together.

And if he was lucky, he might even get to see Kerry again.

KERRY TAUGHT two adult classes during the morning. Although none of the students would ever be a professional ballerina, she enjoyed the women's enthusiasm and dedication.

Some of them took class for the exercise. Others had always wanted to dance and were indulging themselves in something they loved.

And quite a few needed the classes professionally. Some actresses and modern dancers drove to Brea from as far away as Los Angeles to study with Kerry. They took show dancing classes elsewhere but wanted the ballet underpinning to keep their technique tip-top.

At three o'clock she welcomed the beginners. Among the dozen new students was little Suzie Ezell.

She and her mother had obviously gone shopping last night. She wore a pink leotard and tights and matching ballet slippers that must have strained Mrs. Ezell's budget.

The child's small face bore its familiar determined air but there was a hint of uncertainty playing around her mouth as she regarded the other girls. They were all larger and more confident; several came from wealthy families.

Well, one thing they would quickly learn: all students were equal here, distinguished only by hard work and talent.

"Line up at the barre, please," Kerry said. The girls scrambled to obey.

Several of them glanced questioningly at the stick she carried in one hand. Kerry smiled. "Don't worry. This isn't to beat you with." Several of them smiled back, but the others didn't look convinced.

"I know you've all seen ballet, either on TV or on the stage," she said. "You probably have visions of going home tonight and dancing on your toes. Well, you're not going to do that for at least another year, and I don't want anyone trying on their own. Understand?"

The little heads nodded.

"Secondly, you're not going to be dancing at all, not for a

while. I know you're dying to, but you have to prepare for it. Muscles have to be strengthened and trained properly.

"All that elegance and speed you see on the stage is the result of long, hard hours of training in technique. Yes, there's artistry involved, too, but that comes later. If you're here to dazzle your friends, then you've come to the wrong school."

No one moved. Kerry had made the same point to their parents, so she hoped there would be no dissatisfaction. This was a serious ballet school.

"Very well," she said. "The first thing we're going to work on is breathing."

One of the girls giggled. At Kerry's sharp glance she said, "But, Miss Guthrie, we already know how to breathe."

"That's what you think," Kerry said.

She spent the next half hour teaching them how to breathe from the diaphragm and giving them exercises to do at home. Then the girls were allowed a short break, sitting on the floor, before they went on.

"Next, we begin working on the five positions," Kerry said. "You thought you knew how to breathe. I'll bet you thought you knew how to stand, too. Well, you don't."

She demonstrated the positions for them. "Today we'll work on the first position. Do you feel your muscles straining? It isn't a natural way to stand, is it?"

Suzie, doing her best to imitate Kerry, shook her head solemnly.

"The purpose of these positions is something we in ballet call turnout," Kerry said. "You have to train your legs and feet to turn out in a way that isn't natural. But it's necessary to dance gracefully."

The girls worked hard, helped by the stick Kerry used to prod knees and elbows into the proper conformation. Before she knew it, the class was over and the little girls had made their bows and dashed away to the dressing room.

She doubted any of them suspected it, but there would be a lot of sore muscles in the morning.

Melanie came in a few minutes later. Her eyes looked larger than usual, as if she'd been fighting tears.

"What's wrong?" After teaching her for five years, Kerry could tell almost instantly what mood Melanie was in.

"My dad," she said.

The pang of anxiety caught Kerry by surprise. "He isn't— isn't hurt or anything, is he?"

"Hurt? No." Melanie crossed to the barre and began warming up. "But he refuses to consider letting me go to New York."

Kerry let out a deep breath. "We've got a few months to change his mind."

"You don't know my dad." Melanie stopped as Tom Hadley bounded into the room.

The air always seemed to crackle and the light to intensify when Tom was around; it was a kind of magic he possessed. Kerry suspected it was what people meant by charisma, and it was going to stand him in good stead when he began his show business career in earnest.

Already Tom had appeared in a couple of commercials and had danced in the chorus for a TV special. In another year and a half, when he graduated from high school, there'd be no stopping him.

The funny thing was that there had never been any sparks between him and Melanie. Most of the other female students had painful crushes on him.

"All present and accounted for, Miss G," he said, executing a grand jeté on his way to the barre.

"Tom!" Melanie was genuinely shocked. "You aren't even warmed up yet."

"When you're hot, you're hot." He winked. "Hey, loosen up, Melissande."

"You won't take it so lightly if you pull a muscle." Kerry

had a hard time maintaining her air of authority around Tom; he was so cocky and engaging, but she did her best.

As the two youngsters warmed up, Bella Beltran padded in, rattling her sheet music. She'd already played for the two adult classes that day and had been assisting Myron for the past hour.

She was a precious find, patient and dependable; Kerry had never heard her miss a note, but Bella had explained once that it was simply a matter of knowing how to cover your mistakes.

When everyone was ready, they launched into a rehearsal of a pas de deux Melanie and Tom were to perform in a few weeks at the school's annual Ballet Fair, a fund-raising event that also gave the students performing experience.

Kerry had choreographed the dance to music by Gershwin. It was a modern ballet with a strong element of show dancing. She'd devised it carefully to emphasize both dancers' strong points.

Rehearsing absorbed her attention so completely that she didn't notice when the boy came to stand in the doorway.

It was a glance from Bella that caught Kerry's attention. Carefully, so as not to distract Melanie and Tom, she turned to see who was there.

The boy was about sixteen, not much younger than Tom, but there was no resemblance between the two.

Where Tom was broad chested and expansive, the newcomer was wiry and guarded. He had dark, brooding eyes and hair of such a deep brown it was almost black. On his navy sweatshirt loomed a deadly looking skull and crossbones, and the same insignia was printed on a band wrapped around his forehead.

What on earth was he doing in a ballet studio?

He didn't seem to notice Kerry, so intent was he on watching the dancers. No, not the dancers; Melanie. The boy stared

at her as if she were some magical being that had material-
ized out of the ether.

Kerry was about to speak to him when a smaller figure
appeared at his side. Suzie sidled up and slipped her hand into
the boy's.

So this was her brother, the one Mrs. Ezell had been so
worried about. What had she said exactly? That he ran with
a bad crowd?

Wonderful, Kerry thought. That was just what Leaps and
Bounds needed, a kid like him hanging around. On the other
hand, he had come to pick up his sister.

She wasn't in the habit of tolerating juvenile delinquents,
but she supposed it wouldn't hurt to give the boy the benefit
of the doubt.

The music ended, and the two dancers swept into their
bows. Suzie and her brother applauded enthusiastically.

Tom took another bow for their benefit, but Melanie looked
confused.

"Thanks," Kerry said. "That was terrific, guys. Can we do
this again Thursday? I'd like you to try a new lift."

Both of them agreed. Tom swept out, tugging teasingly at
Suzie's ponytail on his way and leaving her wide-eyed with
hero worship.

Kerry went to the piano. "I guess he won't do any harm,"
she muttered.

Bella gazed over the music, her dark eyes rimmed with
skepticism. "I'm glad we have locks on our lockers. But who
knows? Kids these days—they all look like rebels."

From where she stood, Kerry could barely make out the
boy's muttered, "Hi. I'm Jamie. Who're you?"

"Melanie." Her always soft voice had faded to a mere
whisper.

"Wanna go out for a Coke or something?"

Kerry didn't need to see the girl's face; she could hear
the panic in her voice. "I can't. I have to get home." Without

waiting for an answer, Melanie dashed by Jamie and raced for the dressing room as if for dear life.

He stared after her and shrugged. To Suzie, he said, "Is she always like this?"

"I don't know," said his sister. "It's my first day, remember?"

Jamie glanced over as if becoming aware of Kerry and Bella's presence for the first time. "See you guys," he said, and ambled out with a show of unconcern.

"Uh-oh," Bella said.

"You don't think he's going to hassle her, do you?" Kerry asked. "I won't allow it."

"A little hassling might not hurt her." The older woman gathered her music. "I'll see you this evening." An intermediate class was held on Tuesday nights.

"Thanks, Bella." Kerry checked her watch. She had two hours, plenty of time to go home for dinner.

MELANIE STUDIED HERSELF in the dressing room mirror, which was ringed with light bulbs. What had that boy been staring at, anyway? She wasn't particularly pretty; at least, no one at school seemed to think so. Her face was too thin, and there was nothing very exciting about light brown hair and eyes.

Maybe she'd seen him at school; it was hard to be sure, with so many kids. But if he went there, he must know she wasn't the kind of girl that boys asked out. The other kids seemed to think Melanie came from another planet, and, frankly, she had a hard time understanding their chatter about rock bands, video games and wild parties.

She wouldn't even know what to do on a date.

Melanie summoned up the dark, intense face in her mind. Jamie, that was his name. His sister was a cute little girl, awestruck about ballet like most of the new students. Melanie wouldn't mind helping her a little, giving her a few tips. But she didn't know what she was going to say to Jamie if he asked her out again.

Well, that wasn't likely to happen, was it?

WHAT HAD BELLA MEANT, a little hassling wouldn't hurt Melanie? Kerry wondered as she walked to her office to change clothes. Was she agreeing with Chris that the girl needed more normal teenage experience?

And was it possible they were right?

Kerry supposed she should have listened more sympathetically to Chris. Then maybe they wouldn't have ended up on such a strained note the previous evening.

The problem was that he kept intruding into her thoughts. He'd made it clear he was interested in her as a woman; why had that intimidated her?

She didn't know much about Chris, really, she reflected as she strolled down the hall, scarcely noticing the posters advertising performances by the New York City Ballet and the Kirov. From what Melanie said, he was a loving father but often had to work long hours.

A policeman. Kerry hadn't known anyone like that when she was growing up. Her parents' friends were all performers or artists of one sort or another, and now that she could view them objectively, she realized it had been a rather rarefied environment.

It wasn't until coming to Brea that she'd gotten to know ordinary people, the folks who sent their daughters and sons to ballet school.

They were a real cross section—truck drivers, engineers, lawyers, fire fighters, secretaries, teachers—some highly educated, some fighting their way through life with what little training they had.

It didn't make sense to categorize them. Each person was so unique, so full of individual quirks and hopes and experiences, that Kerry couldn't imagine how her parents managed to view them in such a limited way.

But then she knew that, despite their effort to keep up appearances, her parents were embarrassed by her own profession. Ballet teacher in a small school in a more or less small town. Not at all the kind of career they'd envisioned for their only child.

During her months of therapy, her parents had tried their best to be supportive. They'd paid for the physical therapy that wasn't covered by insurance, welcomed Kerry into their home, even arranged for psychological counseling.

But underneath she'd felt their doubts and their disappointment, almost as keen as her own. If she couldn't have become a musician, at least she'd been a performer, moving in the same world. Now who would she be?

She felt a surge of anger. Why did they have to be so judgmental?

"You look like you could tackle a den of lions and tigers single-handed." The amused words came from a bare four feet ahead of her, and Kerry halted abruptly. "Somebody tick you off?"

Chris Layne leaned against her office door, his arms folded so that his suit jacket stretched suggestively across his broad shoulders.

Unwillingly, she was reminded of how he'd looked on the racquetball court, an uncoiling masculine figure with energy to spare. Darn it, did he have to be so attractive?

"Melanie tells me you discussed New York this morning." Kerry hadn't meant to bring up the sore subject first thing, but he'd caught her off guard. "I'm sorry if I interfered. This really is between you and your daughter."

"I'm glad you think so." He reached for her stick. "What's this for? Beating off admirers?"

The remark startled a laugh out of Kerry. "Poking errant elbows into place is more like it."

"Does my daughter have many errant elbows?"

"Hardly any." Kerry opened the door and invited him into her office. "Coffee? Melanie's changing, so she'll be a few minutes."

"No problem. She's not expecting me, anyway." He gazed around.

Uncomfortably, Kerry reflected on how small and cramped the office was, the walls plastered with ballet posters between the crammed bookshelves. She had to angle sideways to squeeze past the filing cabinet.

There was hot coffee in the pot on her desk. "I hope you don't mind it strong," she said. "It gets that way after a while."

"Fine." Chris studied one of the posters. Suddenly Kerry wished she hadn't put it there; it was a photograph of her and Alfonso Carrera taken only six weeks before the accident.

"Cream and sugar?" When he shook his head, she poured coffee into a spare cup.

Instead of asking about the poster, Chris settled into a rickety swivel chair and propped his feet on the desk. After sipping for a minute, he said, "How did your parents feel? About you going off to New York at the tender age of sixteen or whatever?"

Kerry had to think for a minute. "They were relieved, in a way."

"Relieved?"

"My parents are classical musicians. They traveled a lot with the Boston Symphony," she said. "I was too old for a nanny by then and they didn't like leaving me home alone. In New York, at least I had chaperons."

He set his cup down. "I've never met anyone like you."

"It's not a background I would recommend." A trace of bitterness sounded in her voice.

"You don't get along with your parents?"

How had they gotten onto such a private subject? "We get

along, at a superficial level. But they're not part of my inner life. They never were."

"I'm not sure any parent is part of his child's inner life, once they reach adolescence," Chris said thoughtfully.

"Melanie doesn't confide in you?"

"Sometimes," he admitted. "But I don't always understand her. I suppose that comes from being a man, or maybe not being in the performing arts myself."

"But you try." It wasn't a question but an observation. "You really want to know how she feels and what she thinks about."

"Of course," he said. "Are you sure your parents don't?"

Kerry wasn't used to analyzing them. "I'm not sure. I guess on one level, they do. But most of the time they just wish I was someone they could be proud of, a big success. Someone to show off."

"Maybe you're being too hard on them," he said.

The door swung open and Melanie peered in. "Dad? Myron said he'd seen you."

Chris stood up. "Hi, babe. Need a ride?"

"Sure." Admiration shone in her eyes as Melanie regarded her handsome father. "How come you got off early? I mean, it's really nice."

"I realized we haven't been spending much time together," Chris said. "I figured the criminals wouldn't run amok if I took off an hour early."

"Could we go out for dinner?" Melanie asked. "I haven't done the grocery shopping yet."

"You're on." They said goodbye to Kerry and ambled out together. She watched them with a touch of envy, but she wasn't sure which one of them she envied. Maybe both.

The phone rang. Pulling her attention back from the departing pair, Kerry answered it.

The caller was Fawn Frye, artistic director of the Brea

Theater Center, a semiprofessional group that sometimes hired Kerry to choreograph its musicals.

"We've decided to put on Romeo and Juliet in January," Fawn said.

"Romeo and Juliet? Is this some new musical version?"

The director laughed. "No. Most people don't realize there's a whole dance scene, at the ball where Romeo and Juliet meet. We'll have eight trained dancers and we'll be updating it to the 1920s. I'll send you a tape of the music we're using. We'd love to have you do it."

Kerry didn't need to consult the calendar on the wall. She had her classes, of course, and the Ballet Fair next month, but that left plenty of free time. "I'd be glad to."

"Fine." Fawn gave her the schedule for auditions. They were set for November; the theater center allowed two months to rehearse its productions.

After hanging up, Kerry closed her eyes for a moment. Romeo and Juliet set in the 1920s! Already, patterns began taking shape in her mind, suited to the theater center's stage and the lively tempo of that period's music.

She enjoyed doing musicals, although she'd nearly exhausted herself one year, taking on Brigadoon and Fiddler on the Roof for two different theaters.

It was partly the excitement of being in a real theater, partly the pleasure of hearing applause for work she'd created, but mostly it was the act of choreographing itself that drew her.

And why not for ballet?

Kerry's good mood vanished. No. She didn't want to be around a professional ballet company. The wounds hadn't healed yet, in spite of the years. Working with her students was one thing; she watched them develop from beginners and had a stake in their progress.

Professionals were another matter. How could she stand by, objective and helpful, as some other ballerina took the dreams from Kerry's heart and soared with them?

She couldn't. Not yet. Maybe never.

A polite tap at the door alerted her only seconds before Myron opened it, but it was enough for Kerry to wipe the distress from her face. "Hi," she said.

He waved an envelope at her. "Some angel just donated ten tickets. Does that take care of your objections?"

Kerry sighed. Money really hadn't been the problem; she just didn't care to go see the New American Ballet, her old troupe, perform at the Los Angeles Music Center next week. They didn't hit the West Coast often, and she'd managed to avoid seeing them all these years.

"Ten tickets?" she said. "Don't you think they should go to the students?"

Myron clicked his tongue. He was wearing a particularly outrageous outfit today, a bright red bandanna and a cowboy hat, which looked downright peculiar above his long gray hair, and an embroidered Mexican shirt that hung down over his rehearsal tights.

"Send our kids without a chaperon?" he said. "Unthinkable."

About to argue, Kerry realized he was right. They'd need not one chaperon but two to handle eight students. The school had to be very careful about its charges.

"All right," she said. "Who are you taking?"

He suggested five of their advanced students, including Melanie and Tom. "And I have two kids in my intermediate class who really deserve it, which leaves you a choice. Do you have a beginner you'd like to encourage?"

Suzie sprang to mind immediately. "As a matter of fact, yes. I have one who couldn't afford to attend with her family."

"Done," Myron said. "It's a date." He went out the door, chuckling.

Kerry shook her head. Well, what harm could it do?

She locked the door and changed into her jeans. As she

pulled on her T-shirt, her gaze fell on the poster of her and Alfonso.

The familiar stab of regret was there, but overlaid with something else, some other blurred emotion that she'd experienced before but had tried to ignore.

Suddenly she knew what it was.

Her life in Brea was full of activity—classes, musicals, occasional platonic outings with Myron. But none of it seemed to be headed anywhere. There was no future promising excitement and challenge; she didn't look forward to the changing of the seasons.

If anything, she wanted to freeze time so she wouldn't have to watch Melanie grow up and move on, so she wouldn't have to grow older herself, so those few glorious years with the New American Ballet wouldn't fade further and further into the past.

For some reason, she thought of Chris. How did he feel, watching his daughter turn into a woman? What did he dream about? Where was he headed?

She wasn't sure why, but thinking about him lifted her spirits as she flicked off the lights and went home for dinner.

CHAPTER THREE

CHRIS STARED IN disbelief at the pile of boxes in Leila Chambers's arms.

Stepping back to let her in the door, he must have allowed some of his dismay to show, because she reassured him as she bustled past. "The store manager said I could bring back whatever she doesn't want. Trust me."

"Well—sure."

Without waiting for directions, Leila disappeared into the hallway. She and her fiancé, Chris's high school buddy Tony Marlon, had only visited here once before, for cocktails, but Leila appeared perfectly at home.

He hoped Leila's experience as a model hadn't led her to pick anything too sophisticated. As she'd said, he would just have to trust her.

Being a single father was a tough job, and even though Chris was up to most of its challenges, picking out dresses for his daughter wasn't one of them.

Only an hour before, Melanie had emerged from her bedroom in tears. Never one to fuss about clothes, she hadn't paid any attention to the state of her wardrobe until it was time to dress for tonight's ballet performance at the Music Center.

Her best dress, a blue shirtwaist with a lace collar, looked much too childish on her; even a tough old cop like Chris could see that. To make matters worse, the sleeves were a good inch too short.

When had they bought the thing, anyway? Two years ago? The changes in Melanie had come so gradually, he'd hardly been aware until tonight that his daughter, at fifteen, looked frighteningly grown-up.

There wasn't time to go shopping, but fortunately Chris had remembered that Leila worked part-time for a Brea Mall department store. He'd called her at Tony's house, given her Melanie's dress size and described his daughter's coloring and hoped for the best.

Now, hearing the murmur of female voices issuing from the bedroom area, Chris wandered restlessly through the living room. He felt like having a drink, but he still needed to drive Melanie to the dance studio to join the others, and he didn't like to have any alcohol in his system when he got behind the wheel.

Too many years as a cop, he supposed.

Why the hell was he feeling so out of sorts tonight, anyway? Was it simply because his little girl wasn't a child anymore?

Chris peered around the living room, realizing it had been years since he'd changed anything in it. The tweed sofa appeared shabby and out-of-date, even to his uncritical eye, and the bookshelves were crammed with volumes he was sure he'd never read again. One of the lampshades still bore faint pink stains from a drink that had connected with it at a long-ago party—he'd meant to replace it, then forgotten—and, frankly, the framed van Gogh prints over the fireplace belonged in some back bedroom.

What must Leila think of the place? What would Kerry Guthrie think if she ever saw it?

He smiled, remembering the crammed unpretentiousness of Kerry's office. It was amazing that someone so sophisticated could also be so uncalculating, so artless. He wished he knew her better. What would she be wearing tonight? He supposed he wouldn't get more than a glimpse when he dropped Melanie off tonight, but at least—

The sharp burr of the telephone made him swing around

and grab for it with instinctive tension. Had something happened at the police department?

"Chris?" Speak of the devil, it was Kerry Guthrie herself. The sound of her voice threw him off-center, as if there'd been an unexplained shift in reality. "Listen, I have an awfully big favor to ask."

"Shoot."

He heard a nervous intake of breath. "Myron's come down with one of those twenty-four-hour bugs. I need someone to help ferry the kids to the Music Center and chaperon. I mean, I've got the tickets and everything. Would you mind?"

His first reaction was that wild horses couldn't drag him to the Music Center, unless it was to investigate a crime. The last time he'd been there, on a date years ago, he mostly remembered wearing stiff, starchy clothes and sitting uncomfortably through a long, boring symphony concert, trying to stay awake.

On the other hand, if he didn't go, the trip might get canceled, which would break Melanie's heart. Besides, Kerry needed his help.

"Sure," he heard himself say.

"Oh, bless you" came the prompt reply. "You'll be here by 6:45, right?"

He checked his watch. Less than half an hour left. "Right."

"Thank you, thank you, thank you," she said, and was gone.

Chris hung up with a sigh. He'd have to pull out his one good suit and hope his dress shirt wasn't too wrinkled.

"Dad?"

He turned, then paused with his mouth open.

Good Lord, was this Melanie? His little gamine, the one whose bangs always hung in her eyes at the breakfast table?

The girl in the doorway was startlingly, captivatingly beautiful. The soft emerald flow of her dress brought out a richness in her skin, and Leila had fixed the dark hair up in some kind of complicated twist. Melanie's brown eyes seemed to have grown, no doubt with the help of makeup, and all the childish roundness had vanished from her face, giving way to dramatic cheekbones and a hint of mystery.

"You look stunning." He moved forward to give his daughter a kiss.

"Is it really okay?" Melanie asked. "I don't look like me."

He glanced up as Leila appeared in the hallway. "You've done a terrific job."

"It was fun." The model, who was wearing nothing more than a sweatshirt and jeans herself, shrugged at him. "Time she grew up. You can't keep your daughter hidden in a closet, Chris."

"He doesn't. It's me. I just never—" Melanie let the words trail away. "I wish you were coming with me tonight, Dad."

"Oh, hell!" How much time had gone by since the phone call? "I am!"

KERRY SNEAKED a sideways gaze at Chris as the ten of them rode up from the Music Center garage in the oversize elevator. They hadn't had a chance to exchange more than a few words in Brea before he set off in his car and she in her station wagon, and then she'd been focused on the dramatic change in Melanie's appearance.

Now she noticed how striking Chris looked in his dark blue suit, but also how uncomfortable. He probably felt about the same way she did, draped in a pink dress spangled with blue stars around the shoulders. As if she was on show.

There was one good thing to be said for the unexpected turn of events this evening: it had taken her mind off the fact that, for the first time in seven years, she would be watching her old ballet company perform.

"Are we going backstage afterward?" Tom asked as they emerged just outside the Dorothy Chandler Pavilion.

"Can we?" asked Suzie Ezell, her dark eyes wide. "Oh, Miss Guthrie, really?"

Kerry didn't answer right away. She'd received a phone message this afternoon from her old partner, Alfonso Carrera, inviting her to visit his dressing room afterward. He'd even extended the invitation to include any students she might want to bring.

How could she ignore such a request without being rude? After all, Alfonso had been her teacher long before she'd joined the company, and he'd encouraged her every step of the way. These past years, she'd sent him Christmas cards and he hadn't pressed for any closer contact, but now...

Darn it, she couldn't skitter away like an injured fawn. She was a grown woman, capable of handling whatever mixed emotions seeing Alfonso might bring out. Besides, her students deserved a special treat.

"All right," Kerry said. "If you all promise to be on your best behavior and stay out of everyone's way."

"We promise!" came a prompt chorus.

Chris's eyes met hers as they shepherded the youngsters through the crowd gathered on the Music Center plaza, toward the pavilion doors. A flash of anguish, almost a plea—but what on earth could he be worried about?

The ballet students, accustomed to discipline, lined up at the door and were checked in as Kerry presented the tickets. Then they all trooped up the broad main staircase to the Founders' Circle on the first balcony.

It seemed safe enough to let the older students, Melanie and Tom, anchor one end of the row, while Chris and Kerry sat together at the other. In between, the youngsters rustled through their programs and whispered to one another in awe at the draped grandeur of the theater, the elegance of the other guests and the muted scrapings wafting from the orchestra pit as the musicians warmed up.

"Was it my imagination or did you have a moment of panic out there?" Kerry murmured.

Beside her, Chris shifted uncomfortably. "Actually, stuff like this really throws me."

"Stuff like what?"

"I have this irrational fear that some matron in a thousand-dollar dress is going to point to me in the lobby and yell, 'Fake! Fraud! How dare you intrude!'"

Kerry chuckled. "That's how Myron feels when he goes to the supermarket."

It was Chris's turn to laugh. "Actually, that's not far off for me, either. I always throw things in the cart as fast as I can."

"Well, you made it through the lobby without getting caught," she reminded him.

"Yes, but now I have to sit here and act interested." Apparently realizing how his words might be taken, he added, "Not that I don't enjoy watching Mel dance. It's just—I mean, that's different. Will you forgive me if I fall asleep while some swan is fluttering out her dying gasp?"

Kerry tapped his arm with her program. "I didn't bring you to Swan Lake. Tonight's program is four short dances, each in a different style. I think you'll like it."

"Maybe." He didn't look convinced.

The lights dimmed halfway, and around them late arrivals scurried for their seats. Then the theater darkened, and Kerry joined the ripple of applause as the conductor made his way into the pit.

A knot of fear formed in her throat. It was ironic that Chris should be worried when she was the one who might—who might—what?

A swell of music cut off her thoughts, and the curtains opened.

MELANIE LEANED FORWARD in the darkness, focusing on the swiftly moving figures below. She'd never seen such lyricism of movement, such extension and elevation. And more than that, the emotion emanating from the dancers. Each was concentrating totally; each had risen above his or her own body, her own frailty, her own individuality. In the dance, they spun a surpassing magic that caught the viewer in its web.

Would she ever be able to dance like that? Was such a thing possible?

Oddly, Melanie found herself distracted, aware of Suzie sitting in enthrallment to her right and Tom nodding to himself on her left.

It was funny, the way Tom had reacted when he saw her tonight. Not with some joking whoop, as she'd expected, but with a moment of startled admiration. The usually unflappable Tom had actually been impressed.

So had Jamie Ezell.

No one else, she was fairly sure, had noticed the intensity with which he stared as he dropped off his sister. He had looked at her as if she were something precious, someone very special.

Why should someone like Jamie, who obviously knew his way around and probably had lots of girls chasing him, be interested in a late bloomer like her?

To her dismay, she realized the music had shifted tempo and new dancers were whirling on the stage. She'd already missed part of the ballet; what on earth was wrong with her?

Frowning, Melanie put her full attention back on the performance.

HALFWAY THROUGH the second dance, Kerry uncoiled her hands and found they hurt from where the nails had dug little moons into them.

No wonder she was so uptight. Every plié, every arabesque and pas de chat reverberated through her muscles as if she were down onstage with the dancers. Her legs and hips throbbed from repeated tensings.

She wanted to dance again. However badly her legs might ache, the pang in her heart was infinitely worse.

The dreams had never left, in spite of her efforts to thrust them aside: someday she would hear of a new surgical technique that could strengthen the fragile joints, mend the frayed bones, put her body back together again. Or the pain would go away by itself, magically restoring her abilities.

But the years passed so quickly. Before long, even a miracle wouldn't be enough. Time never spun backward, not for anyone.

I'm only twenty-eight. Oh, please, let me get my chance before it's too late.

She could feel Chris glance at her, as if sensing her turmoil. Kerry forced herself not to look at him. This was something she couldn't share, not with anyone.

Thankfully, she realized he had returned his attention to the stage. At least he hadn't shown any signs of boredom tonight; if anything, he seemed intrigued.

Kerry stiffened as, below, two new dancers bounded from the wings, instantly eclipsing everyone else onstage.

The man she would have recognized anywhere: Alfonso. He was older now—he must be nearly forty—and not quite as agile as he had been, but his brilliant technique and stage presence masked any weaknesses.

It was the woman, though, who riveted her. Young, as slender as an arrow, spinning with incredible precision and boundless energy. The girl radiated beauty in the spotlight. She took Kerry's breath away.

She's the star I might have been.

A sharp pang of jealousy brought tears to Kerry's eyes. Not that this dancer wouldn't have existed, wouldn't have been just as much a star had Kerry still been with the company.

But I only had that one night to really shine. Not the weeks and months and years that she'll have to perfect her art.

Her heart swollen inside her like a balloon about to burst, Kerry watched the ballerina skim the surface of the stage and float through the air in Alfonso's arms. In spite of herself, Kerry got caught up in the moment, transported by the loveliness of the dancing. This stranger who had stolen her spotlight was capable of bringing joy along with the sorrow.

The dancers vanished, much too soon, and the lights came up for intermission.

"Are you all right?"

Chris's words brought Kerry to her senses. She fumbled in her purse for a tissue to wipe away the tears streaming down her cheeks.

"Y-yes." She managed to nod. "I just—"

"That was amazing." He seemed to accept that her emotional reaction was inspired solely by the performance. "I never thought I'd really enjoy something like this."

Before she could respond, one of the girls called from the center of the row, "I need to go to the bathroom."

Kerry stood up. "Okay, guys," she said. "Bathroom brigade forming here."

It was Kerry the teacher who marched her charges up the crowded aisle, brushing away the last shreds of the brokenhearted girl who had sat in her seat only moments before.

THE DANCERS TOOK round after round of bows. When the lights finally came up, Kerry sat in her seat, stunned.

She'd almost forgotten how dazzling the ballet could be, how it lifted her out of herself. All these years she'd denied herself so much pleasure.

"Miss Guthrie?" asked one of the intermediate girls. "Aren't we going backstage?"

"Oh—yes." Only how did you get backstage? There was no obvious route, and Kerry couldn't see herself and her students climbing through the orchestra pit, even if they could manage it without breaking their necks. "Just a minute. I'll ask an usher."

As it turned out, they had to wade through the crowd all the way out of the pavilion and take the elevator back down to the restaurant level. Then they walked along the sidewalk a short distance to the discreetly marked stage entrance.

Inside, a small waiting area was bounded by locked glass doors and a security guard. After so many years in laid-back Brea, Kerry had forgotten how cautious people had to be in the city.

"Excuse me." She wasn't sure whether she hoped Alfonso had left her name there or whether she hoped he'd forgotten. Obviously they weren't going to get in solely on the honesty of their faces. "My name is Kerry Guthrie. Did—"

The guard checked his list quickly. "Oh, yes." He gave her directions to the elevator, clicked open the glass doors and returned his attention to a magazine.

Upstairs, the dressing room corridors were jammed with dancers and admirers. Kerry was disappointed to realize she recognized very few faces; in seven years, the corps de ballet had changed considerably. Older dancers had moved on—but where? Had they, too, found their dreams fading?

It made her feel a bit ashamed of indulging in self-pity. This was the reality of the dance world. Very few could succeed, and then only for a few years.

Kerry peered sideways at Chris, wondering if he was thinking the same thing. Instead, he was absorbed in watching his daughter.

Melanie's face shone as she inhaled the scents of rosin and flowers and heard the click of blocked toe shoes marking the dancers' footsteps. Around them, voices chattered excitedly and people brushed by.

Aware that her little group was blocking the corridor, Kerry queried her way to Alfonso's dressing room.

A tap at the door brought the familiar sound of his Brooklyn-accented voice. "Come in!"

She peered inside. The clutter of costumes and makeup framed Alfonso's familiar dark face. His hair was grayer now and his jawline less firm, but the smile as welcoming as ever.

"Kerry!" He leaped up to meet her, gathering her close. "I wasn't sure you'd come!"

"I've been such a terrible coward," she admitted, clinging to him.

"But you've survived. That's the main thing."

She stepped back, nearly colliding with Tom. "Oh—Alfonso. I'd like you to meet some of my students." She made the introductions, watching Alfonso's professional gaze travel from one youngster to the next. He shook hands with Chris and commented admiringly on the resemblance between father and daughter.

"So your life is quite full," he told Kerry when the last child had made her reverence. "I've always loved teaching, myself."

"It's more fulfilling than I would have expected." But she wasn't telling the full truth, and she had a feeling Alfonso knew it.

Diplomatically, he changed the subject. "Have you done any more with your choreography? You showed some promise, as I recall." Kerry had created a couple of short dances for student programs.

"I've done some work in musical theater," she conceded. "And with my students."

"No ballet?" He watched her thoughtfully.

"No."

Behind them, the door opened and a woman in a richly embroidered kimono slipped into the room. The luxury of the garment paled, however, before the woman's large eyes and animated face.

"Am I interrupting?" she asked softly.

"Not at all. Larisa Keller, you've heard me speak of Kerry Guthrie."

As the two women shook hands, Kerry tried to mask her mixed emotions. Larisa was Alfonso's new partner, the brilliant dancer who had dominated the stage.

"You were wonderful tonight," Kerry said.

"Thank you. I wish I could have seen you dance. Alfonso tells me I'm not your match, not yet." Larisa's tactfulness helped calm Kerry's nerves. "And these are your students." The doelike eyes fell on Melanie. "A promising ballerina here?"

"I hope so." Melanie bit her lip. "I don't know if I could ever—the way you danced!"

"How old are you?" Larisa asked.

"Fifteen."

The woman smiled. "I'm twenty-three. Maybe someday we'll be rivals. And friends, too, I hope."

You couldn't help liking her; Kerry saw that her students were enchanted, especially Melanie. Even Chris nodded approval, although he didn't look entirely comfortable in his surroundings. Kerry hadn't paid much attention, but she realized now that Alfonso and Larisa were both wearing dressing gowns.

"We'll let you finish changing," she said. "Thanks for inviting us backstage, Alfonso."

"I may be out here again in a few months," he said. "I'll give you a call, Kerry."

"Please do." As they finished their farewells and edged out through the crowded hallway, she wondered why Alfonso would be coming back to Los Angeles. A TV performance, perhaps?

"I'm starved," Tom said as they crammed into the elevator. "Any chance of us getting a bite to eat?"

"Wasn't that a restaurant we passed coming in?" Chris asked. "I'll treat."

"Thanks, Dad." Melanie gave him a hug, but her thoughts were clearly still back with Larisa.

At this hour, they had no trouble getting a couple of tables at Otto Rothschild's, the sophisticated restaurant on the street level of the Music Center. Most of the youngsters settled for soft drinks, although Chris ordered stuffed mushrooms to share with Kerry at the table they wangled for themselves.

She knew that as a dancer she shouldn't eat too much, but the night's excitement had left her ravenous. As soon as the hors d'oeuvres arrived, she dug in.

"Well?" she asked when she came up for air.

"I never thought I'd enjoy an evening at the ballet," Chris admitted. "I'm not sure I really understood it, but it's amazing that people can do those things—takes a lot of athleticism. And I actually felt their emotions."

"Then you understood it perfectly," Kerry said. "Ballet operates at many levels. Sometimes I think the connoisseurs and the critics miss half the fun because they hold themselves back."

"How about you?" he asked.

"How about me what?"

"You weren't holding back." He regarded her thoughtfully over his Coke. "Only I'm not sure all those tears were because of what was going on onstage."

Darn, he had noticed. "I don't know how much Melanie told you."

"That a car crash ended your career." Chris set his glass down gently. "It still hurts, doesn't it?"

"Yes." The simple word was whispered into the air and hung there between them.

"Do you dream of going back?"

"Always."

He made a quick check of the students, who were absorbed

in their chatter. Kerry was grateful; she didn't have the emotional strength to be much of a chaperon tonight.

"How can you do it?" he asked. "Want a career for Melanie, when it's the thing you'd kill to have for yourself?"

"I love Melanie." Kerry had never put her feelings into words before, yet Chris made it easy. "I feel—invested in her. Part of her success would be mine, too."

He looked as if he wanted to comment but thought the better of it. What had he been about to say? That maybe she was putting too many of her dreams onto Melanie's slim shoulders?

Instead, he said, "How do you live with the disappointment?"

"I try to ignore it." Kerry nibbled at another mushroom. "Do you know, it's been seven years since I've seen my old company perform? I kind of avoid the whole ballet world, outside my studio."

"Is there any chance?" he asked. "That you could dance again?"

Kerry closed her eyes for a minute, wanting to find the truth. The real truth. "Probably not," she said at last, meeting Chris's sympathetic gaze. "I have these fantasies but—I'm afraid that's all they are."

"But you can't give them up yet," he said softly. "Because you haven't found anything to replace them with."

His perceptiveness surprised her. "That's right," Kerry said. "I—yes."

"Hey," Tom called over from the next table. "I hate to rush things, but some of these kids are falling asleep here."

"Oh." Kerry finished her soft drink quickly. "I guess we'd better go."

Chris rose quickly and helped her to her feet, his hand cupping her elbow. The touch brought them close. Kerry wished she could lean against him and let his strength absorb some of her own uncertainties.

But there were children to take care of, and then they had to drive back to Brea in their separate vehicles and deliver the students to their respective homes.

Still, through the night, Kerry's mind echoed with Chris's insights. And with something more—with the fact that he, alone of anyone she'd met these past seven years, had seen straight into her heart.

CHAPTER FOUR

KERRY RAPPED HER stick sharply against the edge of the piano. Catching Bella's reproachful look, she knew she risked nudging the venerable instrument out of tune, but the girls were getting on her nerves today.

"Places!" she snapped.

Most of the students scurried to the barre, where Suzie already waited demurely in position. Tiffany was slow to follow, strutting a little to show she wasn't afraid of the teacher as she carefully selected a place as far from Suzie as possible.

Rhea, caught in the middle of a clownish pose that had been entertaining the other girls, lost her balance and stumbled, raising a cloud of giggles before she slunk to the barre. As bad as her unruliness, Kerry noted, was the telltale pudginess beginning to thicken the ten-year-old's waist.

"We will see the five positions," Kerry said. "To the music."

With varying degrees of enthusiasm, the girls complied, then turned and completed the positions on the opposite foot.

There was nothing approaching grace in Rhea's performance, although Kerry was well aware that the girl's love of the spotlight and knack for pantomime could be honed into a genuine stage presence. She still hoped the child might bring herself into line by the end of the year.

More troubling was the way Tiffany kept tossing her head, alternately preening herself and casting annoyed looks at Suzie. Unlike the other girls, including several whose families were quite wealthy, Tiffany had been spoiled since infancy, and Kerry hated to see it already leading her astray.

Parents did their children no favors, she reflected, when they overindulged them. Instead of working harder, Tiffany wasted much of her energy resenting Suzie's dedication.

When the music stopped, Kerry tapped her stick against the palm of one hand.

"I want to see that again," she said. "More lyricism, more extension. Remember, there'll be a lot of people watching you at the Ballet Fair."

The school's annual October fund-raising event was scheduled for the following weekend, featuring performances, sales booths, photography sessions and information for prospective students. Even the beginners had their part to play in performing.

"Miss Guthrie—" Tiffany leaned against the barre insolently "—what's the point? I mean, I know we need to learn this stuff, but it doesn't look like anything. We're not really dancing."

Kerry didn't answer her directly. Instead, she signaled to the pianist. "Bella…"

With understanding born of years of experience, the woman began to play the same tinkling piece again.

Standing in the center of the studio, Kerry lifted her arms gracefully. In time with the music, she segued from first to second to third position, interposing some simple leaps to carry her from one foot to the other in style.

As simple as the movements appeared, they weren't easy the way Kerry did them, with arms properly extended and toes pointed, head carried high, even fingertips quivering with expression.

She stopped when the music did, feeling the pain begin to creep through her thighs and hips. Damn, even that little bit of exercise could stir up her demons.

But it had been worth it. The girls stared at her open-mouthed.

"Wow," Rhea said.

"Now—" Kerry faced the class squarely "—you try it."

There was definitely an improvement this time. Even Tiffany had lost her arrogant attitude and concentrated on her steps.

Suzie especially had learned from what she saw. The girl was a sponge; she seemed to absorb what was around her by instinct. She lifted her torso higher, held her arms farther from her body and appeared lighter on her feet.

Finally the class was over and the girls dismissed, with reminders to bring their tutus with them to the next class. Kerry wanted to be sure there weren't any unsightly sags or dusty old costumes that would detract from the performance.

She leaned against the piano for a moment after the classroom emptied. "Were we ever that young?" she asked Bella.

"You were," said the pianist. "I'm not sure about me."

They chuckled together, then, reluctantly, Kerry paced into the hallway to confront the next set of problems.

It awaited in the main lobby, where Myron, Tom and two of the other senior boys were trying to assemble latticework panels into a gazebo.

"Whoever designed this thing must have had fifteen fingers on each hand," Myron grumbled.

Tom shook his head. "Some of the hardware has to be missing. That's the trouble with ordering stuff by mail."

"Well, we've got a few days yet," Kerry said.

Myron peered at her balefully. "It isn't as if this is the only thing we've got to do. I'm not sure this photography stuff is such a good idea, anyway."

It had been Kerry's inspiration to arrange with a local photographer to come down next Saturday for the fair. Leaps and Bounds would provide ballet costumes from a collection amassed during previous years, and visitors could pose—or, more likely, pose their children—in front of an ivy-draped gazebo for romantic pictures.

The photographer would pay a commission on each order. Even some of the school's own students were likely to take advantage of the opportunity.

But right now, the gazebo looked more like a shack.

"Anybody got some glue?" Kerry asked. All three men glared at her. She shrugged. "Just a suggestion."

"Typical," muttered one of the boys. "And I gave up my Saturday for this?"

Debating whether to reprimand him for rudeness, Kerry was distracted by the jingle of the front door opening.

And then by the sight of Chris Layne's muscular body walking into the lobby.

He wore jeans and a plaid shirt today. They emphasized the masculinity of his well-muscled, long-limbed body in a way no business suit could.

It was the first time Kerry had seen him since the ballet performance the week before, and she felt suddenly shy. As always when she wasn't sure what to say, she chose something practical. "I'm afraid Melanie isn't done yet."

"Oh, I didn't come here just for her," Chris said softly.

Tom, indifferent to the way Chris was regarding Kerry, called over, "Hey! We could use a hand here!"

"Having problems?" Pulling his attention away, Chris studied the mess of latticework littering the lobby. "I'd be glad to help."

"You'd have to be either a carpenter or a magician," Myron said, straightening up to shake Chris's hand. "But thanks for the offer."

"Not so fast," Tom advised. "The guy may know something."

"Thanks for the vote of confidence." Chris reached down

to pick up the assembly instructions, then turned them this way and that. "Who wrote this thing, Genghis Khan?"

"I think it was manufactured in an insane asylum," Myron conceded.

"There seem to be some screws missing," Tom added.

Chris squatted down and began inspecting the parts. Reluctantly, Kerry retreated, taking Tom with her to rehearse his duet with Melanie.

She wished she could stay. Something about Chris's presence soothed her, as if everything became more manageable when he was around. Not that she needed a man to put her life in order, but with the pressure of the Ballet Fair ahead, she'd take all the help she could get.

MELANIE BLINKED against the bright lights framing the makeup mirror as she tried to smooth on eye shadow the way Leila had showed her. She'd put some on this morning, but it had caked into creases during the earlier class with Myron.

She was being silly, really. It wasn't as if anyone was going to watch her rehearsing, and she certainly didn't need to impress Tom. It had become clear years ago that the two of them were friendly colleagues and that neither of them wanted more.

On the other hand, you never knew who might drop by the studio on a Saturday.

The little girls from the beginners' class had all left except for Suzie. The dark-haired child stood angled in the doorway, alternately peering through the curtain into the hall as if waiting for someone and then sneaking awed glances back at Melanie.

"You looking forward to the fair?" Melanie asked.

The girl started as if a statue had spoken to her. "Oh—yes, but—I mean, nobody's going to be much interested in us beginners. Not with you and Tom around. You're so wonderful."

The compliment felt unexpectedly good. There weren't many performances in Melanie's schedule, mostly just hard, hard work, with little external reward. "That's sweet, but I think you little guys are cute."

Suzie traced one toe along a crack in the linoleum. "Tiffany says she's got a tutu with spangles on it."

"It's not that hard to sew spangles on a costume." Melanie had constructed quite a few of her own garments over the years.

"Yes, but hers is from some store in Beverly Hills." The younger girl sighed. "My mom's not much good at sewing. I guess she's too tired in the evening."

"I could help you." Mentally, Melanie ran through her week's schedule of classes and baby-sitting. "You'll be here Friday for the run-through, right? I'll pick up some stuff at a sewing store and maybe we can spend an hour afterward stitching it on. Okay?"

"Wow, really?" Suzie's eyes got so big they seemed to glow. "Thanks!"

"Hello in there?" The masculine voice from the hallway had a young, uncertain edge. "Suzie?"

"Jamie!" The girl threw open the dressing room curtain. "Guess what! Melanie's going to help me fix up my costume Friday night. Isn't that neat?"

"Yeah." Dark eyes studied Melanie, and she was glad she'd fluffed up her hair and tied it back with a ribbon. If only her tights didn't sport a flamboyant run just above the ballet slippers!

"Oh, it's not hard." She tried not to stare at him. Jamie must be a few years younger than Tom but he seemed more sophisticated somehow. There was something tough about the way he carried himself and yet his eyes had a wary, vulnerable look.

"Maybe I could help, too." To Suzie's giggle, he quickly

added, "I don't mean sewing, but I could bring you guys some Cokes while you're working."

"You aren't going out with your buddies Friday night?" Suzie asked.

"They're getting kind of boring." Jamie met Melanie's eyes. "You know. Sometimes the kids you hang out with, they fool around too much. Not your friends, I guess."

"My friends are all dancers," Melanie agreed, although she didn't really have any close friendships. Not since last year, when her best pal, Elaine, had moved with her family to Seattle.

"Anybody home?" Tom's head appeared behind Jamie's. "Kerry's waiting, Mel. Get a move on."

"Okay, okay." Gliding forward with a coolness that belied the thumping of her heart, Melanie stepped past Jamie into the hall. "See you guys Friday, then."

She wondered if this qualified as a date. She didn't suppose so, but it wasn't as if she had a vast amount of experience to judge by.

EVERY TIME SHE WATCHED Tom and Melanie dance together, Kerry marveled at the quirks of nature. Here were two gorgeous, supremely talented young people, thrown together by circumstances again and again, raising sparks on stage that could ignite the building. And yet the moment they stopped dancing, they settled back into what might best be termed a brother-sister relationship.

No chemistry. She thought about Suzie's brother and the way he'd looked at Melanie that day in the studio. Not to mention how Melanie had responded. Definitely chemistry there, but why? As far as Kerry could see, the two had nothing in common.

Just like her and Chris. On the outside, anyway. She couldn't imagine any two lives more different than theirs. Ballet, which formed almost her whole world, was an exotic mystery to him, whereas she had only the vaguest idea of what real-life cops did.

Yet seeing him today had set her blood racing, an experience she hadn't had in years. Even now, focusing on the little nuances of Tom and Melanie's performance, she found her thoughts wandering back to the lobby. Back to Chris.

He'd said that he hadn't come here today just for Melanie. She hoped he meant that.

She snapped back to the present as Tom and Melanie flung themselves into the final moments of the dance, a series of dramatic lifts and turns that were even harder than they looked. Tom handled his part with assurance and power, giving Melanie the appearance of floating.

How delicate she looked. Ethereal, even. Funny what an illusion talent could create, even in a ratty old leotard and tights that had a run in them.

"Wonderful." Kerry clapped lightly as the music ended, then switched off the tape recorder. They'd decided to use a recorded version of the Gershwin piece rather than live piano accompaniment for the actual performance. "We'll give it a run-through Tuesday and Friday."

"Are you sure that's enough?" Melanie, ever the perfectionist, brushed a strand of damp hair off her forehead.

"I don't want to overrehearse," Kerry said. "Anything you might gain technically, you'd lose emotionally."

"That felt really good." Tom nodded. "Miss Guthrie, could I talk to you for a minute?"

"Sure." She watched Melanie run lightly from the room. "Nothing's wrong, is there?"

"No." He shifted from one foot to the other. "You know, I'll be graduating from high school next spring."

"I know." Kerry waited. They'd already discussed, the previous year, the possibility of going to New York, but at that point Tom's parents had nixed the idea.

"Well—" It wasn't like him to be this hesitant. "I've got this friend in L.A. He's a dancer, too. Anyway, he finds out about auditions for all sorts of things. TV stuff and musicals."

"There'll be plenty of time after you graduate," Kerry said. "I don't see how you could go to school, take classes and—"

"I didn't think so." Tom smiled ruefully. "It just seems like such a terrific opportunity. I thought maybe you could speak to my parents."

"They're not going to stop casting TV shows and musicals anytime soon. They'll still be there a year from now." Kerry kept her tone light. She didn't want Tom to exhaust himself and dissipate his talent running all over Los Angeles, and possibly risk failing in school, as well. "What's the big hurry?"

"My folks have been pressing me to apply to colleges," Tom said. "It seems like a waste of time."

From a dancer's perspective, Kerry had to agree. A career in ballet was very short; college could come later. Although she supposed that if she were a parent, she might see things differently.

"I'll tell you what," she said. "You keep your eyes open for a really terrific opportunity—a chance to join a major dance company or a big role that could open doors for you. Especially if it can wait until next summer. Then I'll be glad to back you up with your parents. But get those applications in anyway, just to be on the safe side."

"Thanks." He nodded thoughtfully. "You see things in perspective. I mean, my parents do, too, but they're not dancers. Thanks, Miss Guthrie."

He bounded away, his spirits obviously undaunted. Kerry had a feeling he'd float to the top, no matter when he began his career.

The sound of hammering drew her out into the hallway. It sounded as if progress were being made on the gazebo.

Sure enough, she found when she entered the lobby that the structure was almost in place.

"This man's a wizard," Myron told her.

"Yeah," added one of the teenagers, "and he thought to dig around in the box to make sure we hadn't overlooked any pieces. Turned out we had."

"Sheer genius." Chris paused in his hammering to grin at Kerry wickedly. "Hey, think you guys can take it from here?"

"We'll manage." Myron accepted the hammer with a nod of gratitude. "May the bird of paradise lay eggs in your nest."

"I think it already has." With a broad wink, Chris escorted Kerry back into the corridor. "How about joining Mel and me for lunch?"

"As long as it's salad," she said.

They stopped outside her office, Chris standing so close she could feel the murmur of his breath. "You still watch what you eat as if you were going onstage next week, don't you?"

Did she? Kerry had never questioned her old habits. "Lots of women watch their weight."

"I'm sorry. It's really none of my business." He ducked his head but didn't move away, his body forming a question mark around hers.

"Okay, you're right," she admitted. "I try to stay in condition. Even so, I'm rusty. I don't work out enough because it hurts."

"I wish I could do something to help." He shook his head. "For once in my life, I wish I were a surgeon instead of a cop."

"Then you'd be even more frustrated, because you still couldn't help." Kerry managed to keep her tone light. "Listen, it was really nice of you to come down here today and give Myron a hand."

He touched a stray lock of her hair so lightly it felt as if a breeze had blown by. "I suppose I could say I've been neglecting my fatherly duties and want to spend more time around Melanie, which isn't entirely untrue."

"But?"

"Are we fishing for compliments?"

"Needing reassurance, maybe," Kerry said.

"You?" He looked startled. "The way you move, it's as if you own everything in sight."

"Really? Me?"

"My daughter does the same thing, so I suppose it's a characteristic of ballerinas." His breath felt warm against her cheek. "Now, about lunch. There's the Soup Exchange, or..."

A high piercing beep sounded from his shirt pocket.

"Damn." Chris took out his cell phone. "Okay if I duck into your office?"

He returned a few minutes later, his expression grim. "I'm afraid there's been an incident. It's a nasty harassment case, a Middle Eastern family that someone's trying to intimidate. I need to check this out myself."

"No one's hurt, I hope?" Kerry swallowed her disappointment.

"No, but somebody took a shot at their dog on the front lawn. Whoever's doing this is packing a gun and I don't like it." There was a cold fury in Chris's eyes that made Kerry glad she wasn't the target of his anger. "They've got two little girls and—well, I don't need to spell it out."

"Good luck," she said.

His expression softened and he touched her shoulder. "Give my regrets to Melanie, will you?"

She watched him stride down the hallway and knew his thoughts were already flying ahead to the task at hand. She supposed police work was as all-consuming in its way as conducting an orchestra, and even more important.

She hoped it didn't mean relationships had to be kept at an arm's length. For some reason, the idea bothered her a lot more with Chris than it ever had with George.

"THERE WERE FOUR OF THEM, I'm sure of that," the silver-haired lady told Chris.

She was standing on the sidewalk in a knot of neighbors, not seeming to mind the heat of the October sunshine. The faces around her displayed concern and outrage.

"Can you describe any of them?" Chris knew the patrolman had already gone over this territory, but sometimes witnesses recalled things later that slipped their minds initially.

"I'm not sure I would recognize any of them. I wasn't paying much attention until I heard the shot, and then they were speeding away," the woman said.

"Anything at all," Chris said. "Race, clothing, distinguishing characteristics. Gang colors, something like that."

"Gang colors?" asked a younger woman.

"All of them wearing red or blue, for instance," he said.

"I don't think so," the silver-haired lady said. "They looked like they could live around here."

Chris made a note to have one of the detectives nose around the area high schools. Kids liked to brag about their exploits. If these jerks really were local, it would make things easier.

"Thanks." He handed the onlookers his business card. "If any of you remember anything, even some minor detail, please give me a call. And keep your eyes open. They may be back."

A man glowered. "Those little punks. I'd like to get my hands on them."

"Don't forget, they have a gun," Chris warned, although he'd already learned the caliber of the weapon was too small to have done much damage. Still, you could never tell, especially if a stray bullet hit an eye. "Don't try to play hero. Call us. That's what we're here for."

The appreciative looks from the neighbors buoyed him on his way to the Ahmeds' house. He was glad he worked in a city that supported its police department. In so many areas, he'd heard people resented authority figures, but not here.

A lot of his friends and family had wondered why he wanted a job like this, anyway. In fact, Tony, Leila's fiancé, was the only school friend he'd retained, but that might be more because of the drifts of time than due to his occupation.

Inside the Ahmeds' house, a patrolman was gravely inspecting the lap-size white dog under the solemn gaze of two little girls.

"No bullet holes here," the policeman said. "Doesn't look like so much as a graze."

"Are you sure?" The older child spoke without any trace of an accent. "She was sure scared."

"Well, I'd keep her inside for a few days," the officer said. "Play with her a lot."

"Oh, we will," the younger girl said solemnly.

Behind them, Mrs. Ahmed sat sipping tea with her husband, a distinguished-looking man with graying temples. His neatly pressed slacks and collegiate cardigan testified that he'd been called away from campus duties. He stood up to shake hands.

"I'm afraid no one got a good description of the car," Chris told them. "Or the boys in it. All we know is it was a midsize vehicle, gray or blue, California plates, which doesn't tell us much."

"We are grateful for your concern," the professor said. "It was only a dog, after all, and not really harmed."

His courtesy touched Chris more than any amount of fuming could have. "Yes, but this whole business is highly disturbing. These guys are turning ugly. Please, Mrs. Ahmed, don't let your children play in front. When you go out, check the street first, then get in your car while it's still inside the garage. And check again when you back out, all right?"

She nodded, clearly alarmed but not panicky.

Chris stayed a few more minutes, offering further tips

but wishing he could do more. Like catch the creeps before somebody got hurt.

After he left, he swung by the dance studio again, but it was midafternoon and everyone had gone.

That was the other thing about being a cop; it had a way of interfering with your private life. Sometimes it didn't leave you much of a private life at all.

By now thoroughly out of sorts, Chris steered his way to the health club and took out his frustrations on the racquetball court.

CHAPTER FIVE

MELANIE CLOSED HER EYES, trying to relax against the strain. She'd forgotten what close work it was, sewing on sequins, and the light in the dressing room wasn't geared for needlecraft.

Next to her, Suzie reached out to touch the stiff netting of the tutu. The girl had tried sewing on sequins earlier, but after half a dozen finger pricks, Melanie had relieved her permanently.

"Did you see Tiffany's costume?" Suzie asked. "At rehearsal tonight?"

"I'm afraid not." Melanie wasn't even sure she knew which girl Tiffany was.

"Well, her dress has these neat straps in the back and the whole material sort of ripples when she moves." Suzie held out the scissors to Melanie, who thanked her and snipped off some thread.

"This may not look quite that fancy," she warned the younger girl.

"But it's special." Suzie placed the scissors back on the counter. "Because you did it. Maybe some of your talent will rub off on me, too."

Melanie smiled wearily. "I hope so." She stretched her shoulders, wondering why she felt so tense. The practice with Tom had gone smoothly, and although she'd had a long day, it was still only nine o'clock. From outside in the halls, the clack of hammers testified that work was still under way in preparation for tomorrow. Lots of people would be staying here for hours yet.

But of course, she did know what the problem was. Jamie hadn't shown up. And she wasn't about to ask Suzie whether he was coming.

"There." Melanie held up the little dress. "How's that?"

Suzie fingered the sequins carefully. "They won't fall off?"

"I hope not."

"It's so beautiful."

Actually, the addition of sequins had only marginally brightened up the inexpensive tutu, but Melanie knew that lights and distance could turn paste and cheap sparkle into magic. Besides, the change would boost Suzie's confidence, and that was worth more than a ton of glitter.

"Well, I guess we're done." Melanie began putting the materials back into her sewing kit. There was no point in delaying; if a guy couldn't show up by nine o'clock on Friday night, he must have found something better to do.

"I'll go get Jamie." Suzie slid off her chair.

"You mean he's here?"

"Myron put him to work," the little girl said. "Be right back." She darted out.

Melanie snapped the kit shut, surprised at the wave of relief she felt. It scared her that a boy could make her feel so vulnerable.

Maybe she was being foolish to encourage him. After all, her schoolwork and her dancing didn't leave much time for having fun. And something about Jamie made her wonder whether her father would approve.

On the other hand, one of the reasons Dad had argued against her going to New York was her lack of experience with dating and other so-called normal teenage experiences. So she supposed getting to know Jamie could be chalked up as educational.

Yeah, right.

All Melanie's rationalizations flew out of her head the

moment Jamie walked in the door. As usual, he wore jeans and a sweatshirt, but he'd dropped the skull and crossbones for a picture of U2. His hair bore signs of having been carefully washed and blow-dried; all this for her benefit?

"Hi," she said.

He jammed his hands into his pockets. "You guys all finished?"

Melanie held up the tutu. "This should look cute on your sister."

Instead of merely glancing at it, Jamie eyed the costume for a moment. "It catches the light," he said.

"That's the idea."

"I'll bring my camera." He moved aside to let Suzie in. "Get some pictures of her tomorrow. And you, too."

"Jamie takes great pictures." Suzie produced a hanger swathed in plastic and angled the tutu inside. "There." She hung it on the costume rack. "Hey, Jamie, you promised us Cokes."

"Yeah. Come on, you guys."

The car was a practical, late-model Chevrolet that must have belonged to his mother. Melanie made room for Suzie in the front, but the girl diplomatically opted for the back seat.

"You want a hamburger?" Jamie asked.

"Maybe some fries." Despite the amount of exercise she got, Melanie watched her weight carefully. Still, she was hungry.

The fast-food restaurant was nearly empty. The three of them took a table by the window, where Jamie wolfed down a full meal while the girls nibbled their fries.

"You coming tomorrow?" Melanie asked. "Oh, yeah, what a dumb question. You said you were going to take pictures."

"Don't expect much." Jamie sipped his orange soda. "I mean, the lighting in the studios isn't so hot and I can't afford lights of my own."

"You mean like professionals use?"

"Yeah. I mostly like to shoot outside in the daytime. But I'm working on my mom."

"Our uncle's a photographer in Marina del Rey," Suzie said. "Jamie thinks he might sell Mom some of his old equipment, you know, for Christmas?"

"Is that what you want to be?" Melanie wondered how many girls went on their first date accompanied by the boy's ten-year-old sister, but actually, Suzie's presence made it easier to talk.

Jamie shrugged. "Not exactly. I don't want to stand around in some studio all day taking pictures of brides and babies. I've been thinking about film making, reading some stuff about it, but that takes a lot of money."

"Mom thinks it's just a phase he's going through," Suzie added. "You know, to impress his friends."

"Leave those jerks out of this," Jamie said.

"If they're jerks, how come they're your friends?" Melanie asked.

Jamie spread more mustard on his hamburger. "We used to have a lot of fun. Lately they've gotten kind of weird."

"Mom calls them punks," Suzie volunteered.

Her brother shot her a dirty look. "She doesn't know them very well. And neither do you."

"What's weird about them?" Melanie said.

He grimaced. "Let's not spend all night talking about me, okay? What about you? Who do you hang around with?"

Feeling awkward, she admitted she didn't have much time for friends. "My Dad and I try to go out one night a week. That's because he works such long hours, sometimes we don't see much of each other."

"Your dad's a cop, right?" Jamie frowned. "Wouldn't you know it? He'd probably punch me out if I came to pick you up for a date."

"No, he wouldn't," Melanie said. "He wants me to go out. Or at least, that's what he says."

"Not with me." Jamie rested his elbows aggressively on the table. "He'll figure I'm a punk, too."

"What makes you so sure?"

"I've seen him at the dance studio. He gave me a funny look, like I'd crawled out of a hole somewhere." Jamie finished his fries and wadded up the wastepaper. "This is crazy, you know?"

"What is?" Melanie wished she could follow his moods. Why had he suddenly turned resentful?

"You. Me." He picked up the tray and deposited its contents into the nearest trash container. "I don't know why I'm wasting my time."

"Don't listen to him," Suzie said. "He's just being dumb."

Melanie stood up, not sure how to react. "Nobody forced you to take me out. This isn't even a real date."

"That's right." Jamie held the door. "Maybe we should keep it that way."

"If you like." Melanie stalked out of the restaurant. "I can walk home from here."

He strode ahead of her and unlocked the car. "Get in. I don't want somebody mugging you."

Melanie considered arguing, but he was right. Late Friday night was no time to go for a solitary stroll. "Well, okay. If you insist." She slid onto the seat.

Suzie climbed into the back. "I wish you guys wouldn't fight. Jamie, you're being pigheaded."

"Stay out of this." He twisted the key in the ignition and shot the car backward out of the parking space.

"Don't worry, Suzie," Melanie said. "You and I are still friends."

Except for giving directions, she didn't say anything more on the drive home, and Jamie kept his eyes focused straight ahead, as if she weren't even there.

"Good night," Melanie told Suzie when she got out. "I'll see you tomorrow."

"Okay." The little girl's eyes were wide with misery as the car drove away.

Melanie stared after them in dismay. What on earth had gone wrong? Was it something she'd said?

It just went to prove that she'd been right in the first place, that she ought to stick to her dancing until she got older. Then she'd know how to handle guys like Jamie.

But the thought didn't make her feel any better.

"HI. GLAD YOU COULD MAKE IT." Kerry nodded to a woman and her three daughters as they came through the lobby door, joining the throng browsing through the booths.

"Is she a real ballerina, Mommy?" asked one of the children.

"I guess so." The woman smiled at Kerry, who tried not to feel self-conscious in her costume with its below-the-knee netting, satin bodice and puffed, see-through sleeves. "We've been wanting to talk to someone about ballet lessons."

"Here's an information sheet and an application." Kerry handed them out. "We'll be having a beginners' class demonstration in a few minutes, if your kids would like to watch. Studio B. We've already begun classes for this fall but we'll start a second class after Christmas if there's enough interest."

"Thanks." The woman shepherded her small flock toward the gazebo, where a line was forming for photographs.

Only ten o'clock, and by Kerry's count at least two hundred people had shown up—more than they'd had in the entire day four years ago, when she and Myron first cooked up the Ballet Fair.

Although the studio could function without the extra revenue, it allowed them to offer scholarships, provide occasional field trips and hire an auditorium for their end-of-the-year recital—all nice touches that the students appreciated.

With one last glance around to make sure everything was

functioning smoothly, Kerry glided back into a corridor to check on her dancers.

Chaos reigned, but that was to be expected. Youngsters in leotards dashed through the halls, ignoring the shouted last-minute instructions of their parents. Inside the girls' dressing room, frantic last-minute hunts were under way for missing slippers, while mothers bent over their daughters, decking their fresh young faces with rouge and lipstick.

"Beginners, five minutes," Kerry called.

She hurried out just as Melanie arrived, her own costume draped neatly across her arm.

"We've got quite a crowd," Kerry said. "I'll get Myron to squeeze a few more chairs around your studio."

"Fine." Melanie kept her face averted.

"Are you okay?"

"Yeah, sure." The girl brushed past her into the dressing room.

About to follow, Kerry spotted Chris at the end of the hallway and went to him instead. "Is it my imagination or is Melanie upset about something?"

"I was hoping you could figure it out." His brown eyes studied her in perplexity. "I thought I knew my daughter but—she was out till nearly ten last night and just muttered something about practice, and at breakfast she hardly spoke two words. I think they were, 'Not hungry.'"

For some reason, Kerry immediately thought of Jamie. She'd seen him here last night, helping hammer a booth together, but had figured he was merely waiting for Suzie.

"I know she helped one of the younger girls with her costume," Kerry said. "Listen, I have to go get ready for a demonstration. If I learn anything, I'll let you know."

"She's always talked to me before." Chris sounded hurt. "I really appreciate your help, Kerry."

She hated to leave him, but duty was duty. "Later." Kerry hurried away.

People overflowed the chairs and lined the walls in Studio B. Kerry had to wangle her way through them. "Please keep a path clear for the girls," she called.

"Excuse me." It was a long-haired young man draped with cameras. "I'm from the local paper. Okay if I take some pictures?"

"We don't like to use a flash during a performance." Kerry hated to discourage him, though. "A dancer might slip and hurt herself. I'll tell you what. If you like, we can set up all the poses you need afterward."

The man nodded. "That's fine. I'll just watch, then."

Kerry scurried out to summon the beginners from the dressing room. They followed her as directed, walking primly and without chattering.

When the girls entered the studio, the audience fell silent. Kerry could feel the children's nervousness; this was, after all, their first performance. In one corner, Vivian Ezell sat with her hands clenched tightly. Beside her, even Jamie looked a little tense.

She noted abstractedly that Chris had entered, too, and was leaning against the wall. Was he watching her, or merely passing the time until Melanie's duet?

"To the barre, please," she said, and turned to the viewers as the students obeyed.

"This is our beginning class," she said. "They are learning the fundamentals of ballet. At Leaps and Bounds, we take our dancing seriously. In the beginning, there's lots of hard work, and it isn't very glamorous.

"We stress the basics—learning the five positions, developing the muscles and flexibility and arm movements needed to master more complex choreography. You won't see young children in toe shoes here. That can ruin their feet. Nor will you see ten-year-olds trying to dance junior versions of Swan Lake.

"The girls will be demonstrating the five basic positions.

Emphasis is on correct position of the feet, legs, arms, torso and even the head, on creating an elegant line and what we call turnout, opening the body to the audience.

"Please, if you have to use a flash, wait until after the demonstration and we'll have time for pictures then."

She nodded to Bella, and the music began.

Watching critically, Kerry noticed that three of the dancers stood out, for different reasons.

The one who caught the eye first was Tiffany, resplendent in an expensive pink tutu made of material that practically glowed. The girl herself hammed it up at every chance, adding flourishes to her hand gestures, tossing her head, practically crying out, "Look at me!"

Otherwise, her technique wasn't bad, but it suffered from too much attention to ego and too little to ballet.

Rhea was having problems keeping the rhythm. She always seemed to be half a beat behind the other girls and then, hurrying to keep up, would push ahead. There was nothing approaching grace in her movements, even though she was obviously trying hard.

The third dancer who stood out was Suzie. Solemn, highly focused, the child executed each movement with as much extension as she could muster. Technically, she was a shade above the other girls, but what distinguished her even more was an intangible quality that Kerry could only call stage presence, an inner magnet that drew eyes to her.

The music ended and applause rippled through the room. The girls made their bows.

"Please remain at the barre." Kerry stepped forward. She noticed individual faces in the crowd, proud mothers and fathers whom she'd met before. Vivian Ezell beamed as her eyes remained on Suzie.

There was a thoughtful expression on Chris's face, as if the sight of the young girls had taken him back to Melanie's first days as a dancer. How strange it must feel, seeing his little girl grow up so quickly.

"We're going to take some photographs now," Kerry said. "The rest of you, thanks for coming. Our intermediate dancers will be performing after lunch. But first, in half an hour, a special treat. Our two star pupils, Melanie Layne and Tom Hadley, will perform a duet in Studio C. I hope you'll all be there. They'll repeat the performance at three o'clock."

She posed the girls at the barre as most of the viewers filed out, Jamie losing himself among them while his mother stayed behind.

Cameras clicked and flashed. When the parents had finished, it was the newspaperman's turn. He took his time, lining up a number of shots of the row of girls.

"I'd like to get some individual shots of one of the dancers," he said at last. "That one." He pointed to Suzie.

The child's face lighted up, even as Tiffany's mouth formed a pout.

"I don't see why!" Tiffany blurted. "That ugly old costume—you can see her mother bought it at a thrift store."

To Kerry's relief, one of the other girls leaped to Suzie's defense. "You're just jealous because Melanie helped her sew on the sequins," the child said. "I think it looks nice."

Suzie, on the verge of tears, managed a timid smile. "Thanks, Eileen."

A tall woman wearing a designer jogging suit caught Tiffany's arm. Kerry expected her to reprimand her daughter, but instead the mother regarded Suzie with disdain. "Come on, Tiff," she said. "We're going to have some real pictures taken of you."

They marched off together, backs ramrod straight.

"The rest of you can go and change," Kerry said. "Thanks, girls. You did a splendid job."

Eileen waited while the photographer posed Suzie and took several pictures. When he was done, the two girls skipped off together. From the back of the studio, Vivian Ezell followed some distance behind.

Kerry felt like apologizing to Vivian, who must have overheard Tiffany's rude remark, but sensed that it would only make matters worse.

"Guess the kids get jealous of each other." Chris ambled forward through the empty room.

"Usually they're a little more discreet about it," Kerry said. "But it does happen."

"There isn't anything like that troubling Melanie, is there?" Chris said. "I've certainly never skimped on her ballet expenses."

Kerry debated briefly whether to reveal her thoughts and decided Chris had a right to know. "I think she might be interested in a boy."

"A boy?" He sounded as if she'd named some exotic object. "I mean—but—I thought she was here last night."

"She was." Kerry began turning off the lights in Studio B. "You know that little girl, Suzie, the one who got her picture taken? She has a brother who's about sixteen. He was here working on the booths last night and I thought I saw the three of them leave together."

Chris digested this as he followed her toward the door. "Nice kid?"

"I don't know," Kerry admitted. "He's been very responsible about picking up his sister from practice."

"Have you seen him around today?" Catching her querying look, Chris added, "I wasn't planning to interrogate him. But obviously something upset Melanie. I'd just like to—to—"

"Wring his neck?" Kerry paused at the door of the studio.

Chris grinned wryly. "All right. Just get a look at him, then."

"Actually, he was sitting with his mother in that corner." Kerry pointed. "You didn't happen to notice him?"

A shake of the head. "Damn it, no."

"What are you planning to do when you find him?" she asked. "Other than look?"

"Talk—"

"Chris," she said. "I know I'm not a parent, but can you take a little advice?"

He cocked his head and studied her through half-closed eyes. "I can listen to it. Whether I take it or not is another story."

"Stay out of Melanie's business." Kerry tried to ignore his deep intake of breath, hoping it didn't spell anger. "Let her work this out for herself."

"You may not be a parent, but you are a woman." To her relief, he was smiling. "I suppose you've got a point. Don't I get to play Superman to the rescue?"

"Macho nonsense," she retorted.

"But that's part of what I like about being a cop." His eyes were wide open now and fixed on her. "Old-fashioned values. Getting to be a hero. Or at least that's how I thought it would be."

"You are a hero," Kerry said. "To most of us. But nobody's a hero to his own daughter. Not when it comes to interfering in a romance."

His expression darkened unexpectedly. "And it isn't as if I've been such a big success in that department myself."

She guessed that he referred to Melanie's mother, but what could he mean? His wife had died. What did that have to do with failed romances? "Chris—"

"This kid," he said, "he isn't from one of those snobbish families, is he? He isn't snubbing my daughter because she doesn't drive a Porsche and run with a country club set, is he?"

"On that point, I can assure you," Kerry said. "Absolutely not."

"Still, I'd like to get a look at him."

Obviously her advice wasn't going to be taken, or at least not swallowed whole. "Your next best bet," she said resignedly, "will be Studio C. During Melanie's performance."

"Then let's go," Chris said, and escorted her out.

THE LITTLE GIRLS RUSHED into the dressing room, chattering and giggling. Melanie, jerked out of her introspection, looked around.

"Where's Suzie?" she asked one of the youngsters.

"Getting her picture taken for the paper" came the reply. "You should have heard what Tiffany said! Insulted her costume..." The girl stopped, realizing that she might offend Melanie.

"Eileen said she was just jealous because you helped with it," another girl piped up.

"Ballerinas get jealous of each other sometimes, but they need to be polite like anybody else," Melanie reminded them, feeling like a mother hen.

Thoughtfully, the girls scattered to their dressing tables, except for one slightly pudgy child. Rhea, that was her name. "Melanie?" she said.

"Mmm-hmm?" She checked her makeup in the mirror and added another dusting of powder.

"How do you—I mean—stay on the beat? I know we're supposed to count, but then I lose track of what my feet are doing."

"Try to feel the music," Melanie advised. "The counting should come as second nature. Practice at home with a metronome if you have to."

"Okay," the girl said dubiously.

Beginning to feel claustrophobic in the crowded room, Melanie slipped out into the hall. She still had half an hour before her duet, so she headed for the inappropriately named Green Room, a lounge for the older dancers that was actually painted beige and blue.

Just outside it, she spotted Jamie talking to Tom. Melanie paused in midstride, uncertain whether or not to retreat.

It was too late. Jamie's head came up and his eyes swept over her, dark and unreadable.

"Hey, Mel." Tom gestured her over. "Listen, Jamie's brought his camera." For the first time, she noticed the large Nikon hanging from Jamie's shoulder. "He'd like to get some shots of us before we start dancing. Studio A ought to be empty. What do you think?"

"I need to warm up some more," Melanie said.

"Oh, come on." Tom gave her a playful nudge. "I saw you going at it earlier. You're fine. Besides, I really could use publicity photos and Jamie's offered to give me some. Help a guy out, will you?"

She could hardly refuse, even though Jamie's presence was having an odd effect on her. She felt clumsy and self-conscious and at the same time wanted to stick her chin up as high as it would go and flounce away like a Spanish fandango dancer.

"Yeah, all right," she grumbled. "A couple of poses, I guess."

Studio A was the largest rehearsal area, set aside for this afternoon's demonstrations by the intermediate and advanced students. Just last year, Myron had installed new track lighting, and at the flick of a switch the mirrors reverberated with brilliance.

With more poise than she'd seen in him before, Jamie set about arranging them, querying Tom and her about their duet and the different moves involved. She was impressed to note that he spoke with the quiet authority of a professional.

They struck a classic attitude, Melanie half-supported by Tom as she rose on point and extended one leg.

"Your face," Jamie said. "Tilt a little this way. I want to highlight your bone structure. Tom, can you put your hand on your hip? Like that. Good."

He shot several frames in quick succession. "Okay. Can

you guys manage one of those—what do you call it, when the guy picks up the girl?"

"Lifts." Tom's eyes met Melanie's. "She's heavy as a horse, but sure."

"Thanks a lot." His teasing helped dispel her anxiety, although Melanie always hated being photographed. She liked to lose herself in fluid motion, and in front of the camera she felt stiff and awkward.

She stepped back slightly then glided forward, and Tom boosted her overhead. Jamie circled them, shutter clicking, and she realized he didn't want them to strike some stiff attitude. He wanted them to dance.

Tom whirled her gently around, using great care. He was a terrific partner, never endangering her in order to show off.

As they moved, Melanie felt the familiar harmony of muscles, the blending that helped Tom and her work so well together. Instinct took over, the passion of the dance, the exhilaration of being held aloft. Her body arched, her hands wove designs through the air, and unexpected disappointment surged through her when a shift in Tom's stance told her it was time to slide down again.

Earthbound, she paused, remembering Jamie's presence. He was staring at her.

"Got enough?" Tom asked. "We have to go."

"Thanks." Jamie slid on his lens cap. "I'll get some prints to you next week and a disc with the files, okay?"

Tom waved and walked out. Melanie would have followed, but Jamie caught her arm.

"I wanted to apologize for last night," he said.

The touch of his hand on her bare elbow gave her a funny feeling. "What was that all about, anyway?"

"Insecurity," he said.

"You? Insecure?"

"Why not?" Jamie's fingers stroked her arm lightly. "You

may have noticed, I'm not exactly president-of-the-class material."

"Well, neither am I."

He stared at her in disbelief. "You're a ballerina. A star."

"A big fish in a small pond." She knew she ought to hurry to her performance, but she couldn't seem to move. "Who knows if I'll make it in the big time? If I ever even get there."

"Yes, but—" Jamie searched for words. "You're somebody. You matter."

"And you don't?"

"Not really." He let go to shift the camera higher on his shoulder. "But it doesn't matter. Or maybe it does. Oh, hell, sometimes I'm not sure what I want."

"Me, either," Melanie said softly. "Listen, I've got to do this duet, you know?"

She could see his mind working quickly. "I'm tied up this weekend, but I can clean up the images by next Sunday. Maybe I could come over and show them to you?"

"Sure," Melanie said. "I'd like that." About to leave, she added jokingly, "Does this count? As a real date?"

A smile lighted up Jamie's dark face. "You bet it does."

Wanting to skip, Melanie strode away to her performance.

As MANY TIMES as he'd seen his daughter dance, Chris never got over the transformation. She seemed older, remote, a rare species of bird that had nothing to do with him. How could he and Lou ever have created anything as wonderful as Melanie?

Those overhead lifts made him a little uneasy, but he'd seen Tom dance often enough to trust the boy. This duet they were doing was really striking, different from anything he'd seen before. More daring, more original. He remembered Melanie commenting on how much work Kerry was putting into it.

Chris glanced across the rows of rapt onlookers to where

Kerry leaned against the wall, her eyes fixed on the duet. He had the feeling she saw things that he couldn't, that there were nuances and hidden meanings in the dance for which he lacked any appreciation.

Funny, he'd never thought about what it would be like to get inside Melanie's head. He was proud of her dancing, but it wasn't something he needed to understand. Until now. Until Kerry.

How did she feel, this lovely woman who seemed so unaware of her own attractiveness? How could she be so confident at one moment and so touchingly young the next? Was it painful for her, watching Melanie fly through the air as she used to do, and could no longer?

Yet on Kerry's face he saw only pride and a teacher's wariness, not envy. It was hard to imagine how, after so many years, her yearning for a lost career could still burn so bitterly. But he'd seen it, unmistakably, the night they went to the Music Center.

Chris tried to imagine what it would have been like if he'd had to give up police work. Not that his family and friends hadn't tried to talk him out of it. Talk wasn't even the right word; pressure was more like it.

Now, after nearly fourteen years on the force, he'd lost a lot of his early idealism, but not all of it. He certainly had no desire to take some meaningless job in a company that made high tech disposable gadgets.

Restless and immature, Dad had called him. Wanting to play Superman. Well, what was wrong with that? Being an engineer in the aerospace industry like his dad had its value, but Chris had wanted to make a difference in people's lives. And, sometimes, he had.

Guiltily, he snapped to attention as his daughter whirled above Tom's head in a grand finale, and he joined eagerly in the applause. Beautiful, that was his daughter.

Darn it, was he wrong to stand in her way over this New

York business? Was he acting just like his father, trying to impose his own outdated values on another generation?

But she was so young and so inexperienced. He didn't want her going that far away. Not yet.

Chris stood up as the audience began to filter out. About to approach his daughter, he saw her head swivel toward the back of the room and her whole body come to quivering attention.

Turning, he saw a young man lounging against the wall, a dark-haired boy who even in repose managed to look tightly strung. His sweatshirt and jeans had a rumpled, defiant air and Chris felt himself tense instinctively in response.

Could this be the guy Kerry had mentioned? Why did Melanie have to pick somebody like that instead of a fellow like, well, like Tom?

Except that, deep inside, Chris knew Tom was safe. He and Melanie had an easy, brother-sister relationship that was completely nonthreatening. Kerry was right. Chris was responding irrationally just because he was a parent.

He tried not to react as his daughter glided forward to speak with the boy and they went out of the room together. There was nothing wrong with Melanie talking to a boy, for heaven's sake.

When he looked up, the room was empty except for Kerry, and her eyes were fixed on him.

"Well?" she said. "How'd the look go?"

"Lousy." He managed a rueful grin. "Couldn't she pick somebody tamer?"

Kerry chuckled. "As in, about twelve years old?"

"Or younger," Chris admitted. "A kid who hasn't reached puberty would do nicely."

Kerry collected the oversize tape recorder. "Hey, I have mixed feelings, too." They walked out together. "Ballet takes tremendous concentration. A lot of girls get sidetracked when they hit their teens. I hope that doesn't happen to Melanie."

"You really care about her career, don't you?" He closed the door behind them. "It doesn't make you just a little bit jealous?"

"Not Melanie." A shadow flashed across Kerry's face and vanished as quickly as it had come, as if she were remembering something. "Other dancers, maybe, but not my students. I'm invested in them. When they succeed, I succeed, too."

"I liked that dance they were doing." He took the heavy recorder as they strolled toward her office. "Those steps you worked out—that was clever. More than clever. I wish I understood how you do it."

"Next time you catch me nabbing a crook, we'll be even." Kerry unlocked the door and slid the recorder inside.

It occurred to Chris that the few times he'd spent with Kerry had come about by chance—at the health club, at the theater. He knew she'd be busy the rest of today with the fair, and he didn't want to leave further meetings to chance.

"Do you ever go bowling?" he asked.

She blinked. "Bowling?"

"You know, they have these heavy round balls with holes in them for your fingers and you throw them at the pins."

"Oh, that kind of bowling," Kerry teased. "Not in years. Why?"

"My departmental bowling team gets together Sunday nights." Chris wondered how she'd react to the earthy types he worked with; they weren't much like dancers, that was for sure. But he'd have to take the plunge sometime. "I'd like to have you join us, if you're not busy."

"As a matter of fact, I'd love to, if you don't mind me fouling up your averages," Kerry said.

"Pick you up at six? We usually get a pizza while we're playing."

"Sounds fine." She barely finished giving him her address before a couple of intermediate students flurried up, begging for help in subduing their new toe shoes. "Tomorrow, then."

Watching her go, Chris realized Kerry hadn't even protested about the high-calorie menu. He chose to take that as a good omen.

CHAPTER SIX

KERRY HADN'T BEEN in a bowling alley since she was a teenager, when her aunt and uncle came to visit. They'd been avid bowlers and had spent some time showing her how to aim with her thumb, but she recalled their instructions only vaguely.

The noise hit her first, the rumbling thunder of heavy balls rattling down wooden lanes, mingled with the ping-ping of video games from one side. The next thing she noticed was the tantalizing smell of fast food cooking at the snack bar.

"I hope I'm dressed all right." She'd chosen slacks and a cotton sweater.

"You'll fit right in," Chris assured her as he steered the way toward a group of people occupying two adjacent lanes.

Kerry wasn't sure what she'd expected a group of policemen and their wives to look like. Clean-cut, that certainly fit, but otherwise there was plenty of room for individuality. The men ranged from young and debonair to middle-aged and tubby. As for the women, one wore a chic designer jumpsuit; another had opted for jeans and a T-shirt that read Beautify Brea—Clean Up Your Act.

Probably the mother of teenagers, she decided.

They headed for one small knot of people and were quickly engulfed. Kerry tried to keep their names straight, although it wasn't easy, meeting so many people at once.

Captain Yarborough, she gathered, must be Chris's superior. A stocky man with graying hair, he welcomed her with a warm smile.

Then there was Sergeant Daryl Rogers and his wife, Jane.

Daryl, Chris explained, handled robbery-homicide. It was hard to imagine such a mild-mannered, slim man confronting dangerous criminals; definitely not Hollywood casting. Jane, the woman with the Beautify Brea T-shirt, had the knowing confidence that came with turning forty and, as Kerry had guessed, raising three kids.

The only person in the group who made her uncomfortable was the traffic sergeant, Ken Oakland. About thirty, he radiated after-shave lotion and scrutinized her from top to bottom, his eyes lingering on her bustline and legs.

"Recently divorced," Chris told her as they picked out balls and bowling shoes. "An occupational hazard."

Rejoining the group, they added their names to the score sheet. The others had been warming up; the real game hadn't begun.

"We play for fun," Jane told her. "None of that league stuff."

"Good." Kerry's arm already ached a little from hoisting the heavy ball. "I'm totally out of practice."

"Want to warm up?"

"Not much point." Kerry sighed. "You play every week?"

"On Sundays, if we don't have a Little League game," Jane said. "Daryl and I coach."

"Oh." Kerry didn't know what else to say. Even though she taught children all week, she had little exposure to the other side of their lives, to the normal things that families usually did.

As the game got under way, to the accompaniment of a round of beers, she let the conversation eddy around her without trying to join in. There were jokes about people in the police department, references to the upcoming basketball and football seasons, comments on city council members and their sometimes impenetrable policies. Kerry found it interesting, even though she couldn't follow everything.

Chris was a terrific bowler, she could see from the start, when he rolled a spare and then a strike in succession.

"You have to get your whole body into it," he explained on her second turn, following a meager four points the first round.

"If I put my whole body into it, I might loft the thing into the ceiling," she admitted.

"I guess that was putting it a bit strongly." He stood behind her, adjusting her shoulders. When his hands moved to Kerry's waist, she had to fight the impulse to lean back against him.

What would his friends think?

"Swing your arm smoothly from the shoulder. And you need to work on your stride." It seemed to Kerry that he touched her more than was absolutely necessary, but she didn't mind. Actually, this mini lesson was probably the best part of bowling.

"Here goes," she said at last, and heaved the ball straight into the gutter.

A groan went up from the sidelines, accompanied by a few cheers.

"That's the spirit!" Jane called. "Don't let him intimidate you!"

Kerry managed a weak smile. "That's me. Proud and defiant."

Chris surveyed the untouched pins with a shake of the head. "For somebody as graceful as you are..."

"Dancers are the clumsiest people on earth when they aren't dancing," Kerry told him.

"Really?"

"Besides, my muscles are in my legs, not my arms." Before anyone else could comment, she added, "Or my head."

"Atta girl!" Jane called. "Dump another one!"

Maybe it was a desire to show she wasn't entirely a failure, or maybe it was just luck, but on her second try Kerry managed to knock down a respectable eight pins.

"Well?" she asked Chris, feeling proud of herself.

"Mmmph." He looked up at the score display. She knew her total of twelve points must seem pathetic against his spare and strike. "Well, it's a start."

"Does Melanie bowl?" Kerry didn't suppose her prize pupil had time for any other activities than dancing, school and baby-sitting, but who could tell?

"Let my precious daughter loose among these wolves?" Chris draped his arm around Kerry's waist. "Not on your life."

"Who's a wolf?" Ken Oakland strolled by.

"Not naming any names."

"Eat your heart out, Layne." Ken posed with his bowling ball, his back to them. It seemed to Kerry that he strutted more than necessary as he moved forward to bowl.

The ball zoomed straight down the lane and pins shot everywhere.

"Strike!" Ken crowed as he walked past them. "Like me to give your friend some lessons?" He looked pleased with himself, as if his success somehow diminished Chris.

It was Ken's second strike in a row. Chris glared at the score, and Kerry was surprised to realize that he took his game seriously, or at least his rivalry with Ken.

Her playing improved only mildly, but from then on the two men didn't seem to notice. They were out to beat each other, and it was a close game.

"Are they always like this?" she asked Jane.

The older woman shook her head. "I think it's called macho madness."

"You mean it's because of me?"

"I've never seen Chris like this with a lady," she said. "He doesn't bring many women around, and then he isn't posses-sive. I'm not sure why Ken is needling him."

The game ended with Ken ahead by two points. Announcing that he'd won a beer, he dispatched a grim-faced Chris to the snack bar and took a seat beside Kerry.

"Hi." Ken slid over until his leg touched Kerry's. "You sure are a pretty lady."

"Thanks." She would have scooted away, but it would be too awkward; the rest of the group, while pretending to busy themselves with other things, were paying close attention.

"How'd you meet this loser, anyway?"

"Are you referring to Chris?" She wasn't going to tolerate hearing him insulted.

"Hey, lighten up. It's a joke, all right?" Ken laid his arm along the back of her seat, just touching her neck. "You two aren't engaged or anything, are you?"

"No, of course not." Kerry didn't feel like explaining that she taught Chris's daughter. Somehow she wanted to tell this pushy guy as little about herself as possible. "So—you're in traffic. Does that mean you investigate accidents or what?"

Ken ignored the question. "So if you're not engaged, how about going out with me sometime?"

"Thanks, but—"

He leaned closer. "I could show you a real good time. Old Chris is a great guy, but kind of a stick-in-the-mud. You like sports cars? Wait'll you get a load of—"

Kerry sensed rather than saw that Chris had returned. Ken stiffened slightly, then shrugged and moved away.

"Nice chick," he said. "Maybe I'll take her out sometime."

Without answering, Chris tossed him a can of beer. "We'd better be getting back," he told Kerry without meeting her eyes.

No one else objected, although it was obvious the evening had barely begun. Kerry wished she knew what to say. She'd never had to cope with anything like this before. "Okay. I'm ready."

They exchanged their rented shoes and walked out together,

Chris moving stiffly. Kerry felt eyes burning into their backs until they were through the door and into the parking lot.

"What's going on?" she asked as they approached the car.

"You tell me."

"You can't think—" She studied him in dismay. "Chris, I'm not responsible for that guy's obnoxious behavior."

"I didn't see you doing anything to discourage him." He jerked the car door open for her.

Momentarily at a loss for words, Kerry slid inside. Intellectually, she knew this was a display of jealousy, but it made no sense.

"Why are you so angry?" she asked as Chris took the wheel. "I didn't do anything."

"That's the point," he growled, staring straight ahead but not turning on the ignition. "You helped Ken show me up as a fool in front of my friends."

"I thought he was the one who looked stupid," Kerry said.

"Oh? Maybe he thought you were interested. Maybe they all did." Chris's frown might have melted the dashboard if he hadn't finally transferred his glare to her. "Why didn't you just tell him where to get off?"

"How?" Kerry asked.

"Oh, come on. A guy practically drapes himself on top of you, and you don't know what to do? How old are you, Kerry?"

"Twenty-eight." She hated his accusing tone, but she hated even more feeling that she'd let him down.

"From Melanie, I'd expect something like that. Not from you." He paused. "Are you serious?"

"About what?"

"That you didn't know how to tell him off?"

Kerry nodded slowly. "I figured it would just embarrass everybody if I made a scene, and I knew you'd be back soon."

"Guys like Ken need to be embarrassed." But he didn't sound so angry anymore. "Come on, I know you're no social butterfly, but you used to be engaged. Surely you've got enough experience with men to know how to put one in his place."

"It never came up," Kerry admitted. "Dancers may get involved with each other, but we also have to work together. Guys aren't usually that blatant."

"Was your fiancé a dancer?"

"No." She welcomed the change in subject and the softening of Chris's tone. "He conducted an orchestra."

Chris whistled. "Talk about esoteric occupations. But prestigious."

"Conductors are like movie directors. They think they were chosen by God." After holding George in awe during their entire courtship, Kerry was pleased to find she saw him now with all his flaws, and it no longer stung. "I was more of an ornament than a real equal to him."

Chris stirred the engine to life. "I'm sorry. I shouldn't have come down on you like that. It's just—Melanie's mother, Lou—well, she used to enjoy flirting. It drove me crazy." He exhaled deeply. "I'm the one who made a fool of myself, aren't I?"

"Let's not go home yet," Kerry said.

His fingers tapped against the steering wheel. "How are you at miniature golf?"

"No worse than at bowling."

With a chuckle, he headed toward the freeway.

The golf center in Anaheim sprawled around a mock castle that housed an enormous video arcade. Circling to the back, the two of them rented clubs and balls and set out to defeat gravity, water traps and windmills.

Chris won by an overwhelming margin. Kerry didn't mind,

especially not after he put his arms around her several times to demonstrate the proper way of holding a club.

"It would really be a shame if I got good at this," she joked as they strolled back to the cashier's booth. "Then you couldn't show me how to swing."

The overhead lights glinted off his teeth as he smiled. "You've got a point there."

They turned in their equipment and retreated to the castle snack bar for a pizza.

"Since I cheated you out of one at the bowling alley, it's the least I can do," Chris explained as they dug into extra-thick layers of cheese and crust.

"I don't usually eat like this." Mentally, Kerry reminded herself to spend an extra hour at the health club tomorrow.

"Do you good. You're too thin." He hesitated. "I know you dream about dancing again, but, Kerry—"

She held up her hand. "Don't. Please. It might happen. I've got a few years yet, and medical science is making tremendous strides."

He looked as if he wanted to argue but held back. "Okay. I hope you're right."

They ate in silence for a while.

"Kerry," Chris said, "was it really a drag for you tonight? Hanging out with my friends—bowling, stuff like that?"

"Not at all." She scraped a strand of cheese from her cheek. "I enjoyed it. Except for Ken."

"But it's not—" He searched for words. "It's not like an evening at the ballet. It's not stimulating—artistic—whatever you're used to doing at night."

"Actually, I rent a lot of videotapes in the evenings," Kerry said. "I'm a little embarrassed to admit it, but I like kung-fu movies."

Chris nearly choked on a bite of pizza and had to take another sip of his soft drink. "You do?"

Leaning across the table, Kerry said, "You have this idea

that I'm some rarefied specimen who can't abide ordinary life. Chris, it's not that way. I have my work the way you have yours. I didn't understand everything you guys talked about tonight, any more than you understand everything at the studio. So what?"

"It's not the same thing," he said. "It's not just ballet—your whole world is different from mine. In fundamental ways, Kerry. Oh, hell, what am I talking about? We have a good time together, and that's what counts."

He wouldn't be satisfied for long just having a good time, and neither would she. But Kerry didn't know him well enough yet to push the matter, so she let it drop.

"You'll be pleased to learn that the Ballet Fair raised three thousand dollars for the studio," she said. "Thanks for your help."

"I didn't do much, but Melanie deserves a lot of credit." He beamed with pride. "She amazes me." Then he stopped, his mouth tightening as if something troublesome had occurred to him.

Was he thinking about New York? Kerry hadn't brought the subject up recently, and as far as she knew, neither had Melanie. There was no need to press the matter, not this early in the school year, but it obviously concerned Chris.

She didn't want to say anything now. Maybe she'd guessed wrong about his thoughts. In any case, it was sure to be a sore subject.

Would there always be gaps between them, no-man's-lands where neither dared to tread?

"Melanie's wonderful," Kerry said gently. "She means a great deal to me." She pushed the rest of the pizza toward him. "Take it home. But don't let her eat more than one piece, okay?"

"What makes you think there'll be any left by the time she gets done baby-sitting?" Chris asked as he picked up another slice.

THE WEEK WAS A ROUTINE ONE at the police department. Chris felt a bit embarrassed walking in Monday after his display of jealousy at the bowling alley, but no one commented. Fortunately, he and Ken worked in different divisions, so they weren't thrown together.

Putting the incident in perspective, he could see how off-base he'd gotten. Ken was nothing but a bantam rooster; there was no reason on earth why Kerry would be interested in him.

But the sight of another man with his arms around her had sparked a fury in Chris. Damn it, the guy had no right to touch her, none at all—although it seemed almost funny now, as he remembered how stiffly she'd sat there waiting for Chris to return.

She hadn't been stiff at the miniature golf course; she'd practically melted into the curve of his body as he helped her swing. Maybe he should have pursued his advantage further, invited himself in when they reached her house, but he hadn't wanted to move too fast, for either of them. He and Lou had jumped in both feet first and lived to regret it.

He didn't know why he put so many obstacles in his own way. Kerry was nothing like Lou. Except—

Except that, in the end, they had moved in different worlds, too. There had been gaps neither of them could bridge, not even when a cruel twist of fate threw them back together again.

He felt sometimes as if he'd failed with Lou, as if, had he been a different person, he might have saved her. Which was nonsense. But at least they might have given Melanie a more joyful childhood.

How did you ever know for sure if you were doing the right thing with a child or with a woman? Maybe if he were some artistic type—but then, that conductor fellow hadn't come out so well, either.

Overwhelmed by paperwork, Chris spent Saturday in his

office and didn't reach home until nearly suppertime. When he walked in the door, he headed straight for the kitchen.

Melanie had laid out a supper of cold cuts and a relish tray. Unlike her usual flourishes, the items had been tossed randomly into the serving dishes.

"Mel?" he called, moving through the modest house toward the bedrooms. "You here?"

"Yes, Daddy." Her voice came from the bathroom, but the door was open and he peered inside.

His little girl—not-so-little girl—stood in front of the mirror putting on makeup. She'd pulled her hair free of its usual ponytail and curled it so it fell loose around her shoulders, and she was wearing a new glittery top over her jeans.

Damn, but she looked grown-up. Too grown-up for fifteen, but he could hardly ask her to wipe off her makeup and pull her hair back, could he?

"Got a date?" He hoped he sounded casual.

"Jamie's coming over with some pictures he took of Tom and me." Melanie applied lipstick carefully to her mouth, a darker shade than she usually used.

"Looks like you did some shopping today."

"I had that money left over from my birthday." She blotted the lipstick lightly on a tissue. "You don't mind, do you? I should have enough saved up by the end of the year for my recital costume."

"Hell, no, I don't mind. I want you to enjoy yourself." Realizing his words were more forceful than necessary, Chris drew back. "Thanks for fixing dinner."

"I already ate," Melanie said.

"Right." He went to the table and began slapping bread and meat together, wondering why nothing looked as appetizing when you had to eat it alone.

The doorbell rang.

"I'll get it!" Melanie sang out as he stood up, and she raced through the living room to the door.

It struck Chris in the split second before the door opened that maybe she had a date with someone other than Jamie. Some respectable-looking boy, some—

"Hi." Good Lord, why was the punk wearing a headband with a skull and crossbones on it, not to mention the matching sweatshirt? The symbol didn't belong to any gang that Chris knew of, but it certainly wasn't the kind of image he wanted his daughter associating with.

Still, he tried to look pleasant as his daughter made introductions, and he shook Jamie's hand firmly. The boy met his eyes with a brief, hostile glare and then turned to Melanie.

"I've got my laptop with the pictures out in the car," he said. "Let's get going."

Naturally, the kid had no manners.

"Where are you headed?" Chris asked.

Jamie shrugged.

"Nowhere special," Melanie said. "Are we?"

Jamie shook his head.

It was like swimming against the stream, but Chris couldn't abandon his job as a parent. "What time do you think you'll be back?"

When Jamie didn't answer, Melanie said, "Not late, Dad." She stood on tiptoe and kissed his cheek. "We'll be fine."

"Have a good time," he forced himself to say, although he didn't see how that was possible.

As the door closed behind them, he realized he wasn't used to questioning Melanie that way. She managed her life well, and he never worried about her when she was at the studio or baby-sitting. He hoped she wouldn't think he was treating her like a baby, but this dating business was a whole new ball game.

If that little creep laid a hand on her...

Angry at himself, Chris stalked back to the kitchen. Jamie was just a kid. A mixed-up kid, yes, but nothing Melanie couldn't handle.

Right?

Sitting down with his sandwich, he thought briefly about calling Kerry, but he was in no mood for company. In no mood to do anything but slouch down in front of the TV and wait for his daughter to come home.

"YOUR DAD DOESN'T LIKE ME."

They were sitting in a hamburger restaurant, photographs spread across the table. The pictures were terrific, although Jamie didn't seem satisfied with them. Unlike the stiff images she'd come to expect of herself, Melanie found that these captured the vibrant spirit she felt while dancing.

"He doesn't know you." She toyed with the straw in her orange soda. "He's not used to me dating, either."

"He took one look at my headband and wanted to throw me out," Jamie said. "I know what he'd like. Some guy in designer duds driving a Porsche."

"My dad's not status-conscious," Melanie protested. "But you have to admit, a skull and crossbones isn't likely to reassure him."

"You don't like the way I dress?" he demanded.

"Hey, can't we just talk about this?" Melanie didn't like the surliness in his tone. "What do I have to do, watch every word I say for fear of offending you?"

"Oh, to hell with it." Jamie stood up and scraped the pictures carelessly together. "Come on. I'll take you back to your safe little house and Daddy the cop can keep all us criminal types away."

"Great," Melanie snapped, but didn't say anything more until they were in the car. There were too many people hanging around, some of them kids she recognized from school.

As he started the engine, she said, "Does this remind you of anything? Like the last time we went out?"

Jamie glared down at the steering wheel for a minute. "I guess it just goes to prove we don't have much in common."

"What're you so touchy about?" she said. "I'll bet you dressed that way deliberately tonight. Like you were testing my dad to see how he'd react."

Startled, he met her gaze. "I don't know. I didn't think about it."

"I like you," Melanie said. "I think we could have fun together. But I don't want to be on trial all the time. If you don't like what I wear, I expect you to say so, and I want the same freedom with you. Okay?"

"What about your dad?"

"What about him?"

"How am I supposed to act when he looks at me as if I'd crawled out of a hole?" Jamie said.

"You planning to go out with my dad?"

Unexpectedly, he smiled. "Not hardly."

"Well, then, I think you're tough enough to stand up to him for two minutes at the door, don't you?"

"Yeah." He stretched behind the wheel. "You want to go to Knott's Berry Farm? They've got a rock band tonight and I love roller coasters. How about you?"

Melanie had been to the amusement park with her father a number of times but never at night when it turned into a teen haven. "Sure."

"Well, then, let's go."

CHRIS MUST HAVE FALLEN asleep in front of the TV, because the scrape of the door woke him up. Grumpily, he shifted, his back aching from the unfamiliar position.

On screen, a bunch of Hollywood cops were chasing fake robbers with a squeal of tires and a recklessness for bystanders that would have gotten them hauled up for disciplinary action in real life.

Through the doorway, he heard whispers and then the unmistakable sound of a kiss. It was a good thing he hadn't come fully awake yet or he might have leaped up and sent Jamie packing.

Fifteen. Wasn't that a little young to be kissing on the first date?

Finally the door closed and Melanie came in.

"Have a good time?" he asked.

"Wonderful." Why did she have to bounce around like that? How could she have so much energy at—at—good heavens, it was nearly one o'clock in the morning!

"Mind my asking where you went?"

She told him. "That parachute ride at night is really exciting. You can see for miles! And look." She handed him a CD.

Glancing through them on his computer, Chris was grudgingly forced to concede the kid had talent. "You look terrific," he said. "I always wondered why nobody could capture you on film."

"We're going out again next week." Melanie sailed toward her bedroom, then paused. "And, Dad, he promises not to wear that silly headband again. Maybe I'll get him one of the Leaps and Bounds sweatshirts, too. What do you think?"

"Great idea," he said.

She was gone. Wearily, Chris wrenched himself out of the chair and turned off the TV.

He didn't know how many more of his daughter's dates he could survive.

CHAPTER SEVEN

IT WAS ONLY TWO-THIRTY on a Saturday afternoon when Kerry arrived at the Brea Theater Center, half an hour before auditions were scheduled to begin, but already more than two dozen dancers sprawled across the lobby, filling out application forms. Some of them were warming up, as well.

All had come attired for dancing, mostly in leotards with a few in stretch tops and pants. Kerry herself wore a leotard and tights with a matching skirt, the same outfit she'd worn to conduct her classes earlier.

"We've had quite a few phone calls," the artistic director, Fawn Frye, told Kerry as she entered the auditorium.

The stage lights reflected off the set for Private Lives, the theater's current production, but at least the furniture had been pushed out of the way to make room for the dancers.

"I was hoping we'd get a good turnout, and it sure looks like it." Kerry selected a seat halfway down the aisle. "How much acting do these people have to do?"

"Not much." Fawn, a thickset woman in her fifties with upswept silvering hair, sat beside Kerry and pulled out some papers. "As you know, we'll need four men and four women."

"You must be planning to pay them," Kerry said. "There's a lot of people here already."

"We do have a small budget for salaries, but it's not much more than pocket money." Even though it strove for professional standards, the theater operated on a shoestring.

"Frankly, several of the people who called said they want to work with you."

"With me?" Kerry's choreography for musical theater had drawn some critical praise, but she didn't suppose many people read reviews that closely.

"Your reputation has apparently spread by word of mouth," Fawn said. "As a teacher and a choreographer. You really ought to do more ambitious work, Kerry. Not that I want to lose you, but you should aim higher."

Although the compliment felt good, it troubled her, too. "I like my life the way it is. Who needs the pressure?"

"I don't think that's it," Fawn said. "Forgive me, but sometimes I think—no, it's none of my business."

"What?"

"That you're scared of something. Of failing, perhaps. Or of making such a big commitment."

A group of dancers trekked in, handing Kerry their applications along with résumés and composite photographs. She thanked each of them, grateful for an excuse not to reply to Fawn's remark.

She didn't think she was afraid of failing, not as a choreographer. But commitment—yes, that rang true. Committing herself to anything other than being a dancer meant giving up her dream once and for all. And she wasn't ready to do that.

Would she be when she turned thirty or thirty-five? Kerry couldn't be sure.

Still the fact that people had come here specifically wanting to work with her was tremendously flattering. In turn, she sympathized with these young people and regretted that she wouldn't be able to use all of them.

Dancers had a hard life, particularly gypsies like these, who weren't part of a regular company. They devoted long hours to their craft and more long hours to auditioning for jobs that brought minimal pay and little chance of wealth or fame. All the time they struggled with injuries and the need to juggle part-time jobs.

It might not make a lot of sense to an outsider, but Kerry understood. Needing to dance was like needing to fall in love. If people operated from a purely rational point of view, no one would ever do either.

She leaned back in her chair, scrutinizing the applications. Some of these people had impressive experience, major touring shows, TV work. Had they really been drawn by her reputation?

Excitement prickled across her skin. She liked being here, sitting with the director, wielding the power. Most of all she couldn't wait to begin working with her dancers. She'd spent much of her spare time these past few months listening to the music Fawn had sent and letting her imagination sparkle.

Not that there'd been as much spare time as usual. She and Chris had gone out several times, casual dates to the movies. He hadn't invited her to any more bowling matches, which bothered her a little, although she wasn't eager for another confrontation with Ken, either.

She wished Chris didn't seem so distracted, although she knew he had good reason. While matters had quieted with the Middle Eastern family, he'd been tied up with a string of liquor and convenience store robberies.

On top of that, Chris was clearly uneasy about Melanie's new social life. She and Jamie were together almost constantly, at the studio and apparently outside it, as well.

Kerry smiled. Not that she didn't respect Chris's concern, but he seemed oddly cast in the role of anxious father, like a character from a sitcom—pacing the floor, fearing his daughter might elope in the middle of the night.

At least Melanie's dancing hadn't suffered. Jamie spent quite a bit of time at the studio, taking pictures and helping out with odd jobs. Although he rarely spoke to adults and hadn't lost his rebellious air, Kerry was coming to like him.

With a start, she realized more dancers were handing her their applications and she hadn't even gotten halfway through her stack yet. Time to get down to business.

After reading through them, Kerry mounted the stage. Instantly, the theater quieted.

She gazed out at the dancers, perhaps forty of them. "Thanks for coming all the way to Brea," she said. "I've been looking at your résumés and they're impressive. I wish I could use all of you, but we only have eight parts—four men and four women."

A young man raised his hand.

"Yes?" Kerry said.

"Would it be possible to understudy?" he asked. "For no pay?"

Surprised, she glanced at Fawn, who shrugged. "I don't see why not," Kerry said, "but there are only a dozen performances. The chances of your going on aren't very good."

"That's okay," he said.

"Well, after I make the final cut, those of you who came close can let me know whether you'd be willing to understudy," she said. "Now, Fawn has updated the play to the 1920s. The Capulets and the Montagues are rival Mafia families, so we'll be doing dance steps of the period.

"We can't all fit onstage at one time, so I'm going to divide you into four groups. Count off from one to four, starting with the front row."

Within minutes, the first group had climbed onto the stage behind Kerry. When everyone was in position, she ran through a sequence of steps that incorporated movements of the Charleston.

Once she'd finished, Kerry stepped back and signaled the dancers to begin. They ran through the steps with varying degrees of proficiency.

"You and you and you, stick around," she said. "Everybody else, thanks for coming."

She tried to ignore the disappointment on the losers' faces, but she couldn't, not completely. This was something Kerry had never had to deal with; her own career might have been short, but at least it had been successful.

Soon the second group was running through its paces, then the third and the fourth. At the end, she had chosen fifteen dancers, seven more than needed.

"Let's try something different," she said, and demonstrated another sequence. This time she looked not only for dancing ability but for the physical proportions and styles of the individuals and how they fit together.

One man was a terrific dancer, but at six foot three he towered over the others.

"I'm sorry I can't use you," she told him. "You're very good but you're too tall for the ensemble. However, if you don't mind, I'll keep your name in my files in case I need you for another show."

"Thanks." He met her gaze levelly. "I really would like to work with you sometime."

"Great," Kerry said. "Thanks for coming."

Soon she had her eight dancers, plus a male and a female understudy. The whole audition had taken a little over an hour.

Fawn helped her double-check everyone's names and phone numbers and hand out a rehearsal schedule. Although some directors and choreographers set their schedules at the last minute, Kerry felt that was unfair to the dancers, who were already balancing commitments to work and classes.

"Pleased?" Fawn asked as the dancers trooped out.

"Impressed," Kerry said. "What a talented bunch. But they do need refining. Did you notice all those superfluous arm gestures? And some of them seemed to be working from the outside in, instead of the other way around."

"That's why they want you to direct them," Fawn said. "So they can learn."

"I guess I didn't realize how much I knew." Even as she spoke, Kerry realized something startling. Not once during the auditions had she envied the dancers up there. Not once had she wished to change places with them.

Was that because none of them was a really top-notch ballet dancer? Or was it because she enjoyed being the choreographer more than she'd realized?

She stepped down from the stage before spotting a masculine figure at the back of the theater, leaning against the doorway.

"Chris!" Kerry went to join him. "What are you doing here?"

"Do you mind?" He straightened. "I got tired of working six days a week and decided to take Saturday afternoon off. Melanie said you'd be here."

"Did you get to see much of the auditions?" In contrast to the dancers, he looked solid and self-assured.

"Most of it." Chris escorted her out, waiting while Kerry collected the résumés and notes into her portfolio. "That must be hard on the kids' egos."

"It's awful," she agreed as they exited the theater. "Actors and dancers are so vulnerable, and then we put them through this torture. But I can't think of any way to avoid it."

"Will Melanie have to go through this?" he asked.

"Yes and no," she said. "She won't be auditioning for individual shows but for a school. Once she's admitted, the director of the company can observe her in class. She won't be put through cattle calls like this."

"How would you feel," he said, "about helping me shop for furniture?"

"Furniture?" The sudden switch of subject left Kerry disoriented.

"I need some." He unlocked his car. "And my taste is rotten. Normally I'd ask Melanie to help but she didn't come back after class. I presume she's out with what's-his-name."

Kerry made herself comfortable in the front seat. Chris's sedan had accumulated its share of years and scratches, but at least the seats weren't splitting like the ones in her station wagon.

"You don't call him what's-his-name in front of Melanie, do you?" she asked as Chris took the wheel.

He flushed guiltily. "Maybe once or twice. Not too diplomatic, I guess. Jamie. What kind of name is that?"

"Short for James," Kerry said.

He shot her a look. "I knew that. I mean—why not Jim?"

"Is it my imagination or are you searching for things to dislike about the boy?"

Steering out of the parking lot, he didn't answer immediately. When he did, he said, "Okay, I admit it. I'm biased. I don't think he deserves my daughter."

"Who does?"

"If I meet him, I'll let you know."

"I won't hold my breath."

In comfortable silence, they headed north on the freeway to Puente Hills, where stores sprawled for miles around the hub of a mall. Chris pulled to a halt in front of a row of furniture shops.

"Surely we can find something here," he said. "Look at all these places."

"What exactly are we looking for?" Kerry swung out into the brisk November breeze, glad for the warmth of her tights and the long sleeves of her leotard. The air crackled with a faintly smoky tang, and alongside the parking lot a liquid-amber tree punctuated the landscape with brilliant golds and oranges.

"A new sofa and a couple of lamps," Chris said.

"What's your color scheme?" They strolled through a chiming door into a vast showroom.

"What's a color scheme?"

Kerry studied him to see if he was joking, but there was no hint of a smile. "What colors are in your living room?"

"Browns, I guess," he said. "Beiges. Stuff like that."

A saleswoman approached, but Chris waved her away. "Let's just look. Maybe I'll get inspired."

Acres and acres of furniture unrolled before them. Kerry, who had inherited her furnishings when her parents redecorated their house, found herself dazzled by the selection. There were Art Deco pinks, Chinese reds, Danish-modern tans, whole suites of sofas and end tables and coffee tables and sideboards.

"See anything you like?" she asked Chris.

"What do you think of that?" He indicated a display replete with stuffed leather, heavy woods and mock animal trophies on the wall.

"Kind of macho," Kerry said.

"Oh." He looked disappointed, like a boy told he couldn't sleep in a Batmobile bed. "I guess you're right. Melanie wouldn't like it."

"You need something neutral," she advised. "How about that?"

He studied the rust-colored couch and matching recliner with coordinated brass floor lamps. "Not bad. Let's look around some more, though."

They prowled through the store, and then through two others in the shopping center, but ended up back at the same display. "Okay." Chris fingered the price tags and winced. "What are these things stuffed with, dollar bills?"

"We offer financing." The saleslady seized her moment to approach.

"No, thanks. I hate owing money." Chris tapped one of the lamps. "I'll take two of these and the sofa and chair. And, what the hell, the coffee table, too. Do you deliver?"

"Certainly." Fifteen minutes later, he'd finished the paperwork and they were done.

"Satisfied?" Kerry asked as they emerged into deepening twilight.

"Just glad I could get all this done in one trip," he admitted. "I hate shopping."

"I would never have guessed."

Chris paused. "Would you take it the wrong way if I invited you back to my house?"

"What's the wrong way?" Kerry said, a little surprised at her own boldness.

He regarded her with amusement. "Forget I said that. Come on."

They stopped by the theater, where she picked up her car. A short time later they met in front of a modest stucco home in one of Brea's older neighborhoods. Kerry had seen it before when she picked Melanie up because it was raining, but she'd never been inside.

"It's not much—" Chris opened the front door for her "—although it'll look better with the new furniture."

As he'd warned, the couch and other appointments had a weary look to them, but the place felt homey all the same. Framed photographs hung over the fireplace—Chris and Melanie, Melanie alone, an older couple who must be grandparents. From the way the paint had faded, she gathered they'd recently replaced some other pictures, no doubt part of the new redecorating plan.

Oddly, there were no pictures of the late Mrs. Layne. Did reminders of her hurt too much?

"That's a beautiful shot of Melanie and Tom." Kerry pointed to a picture in a shiny new frame.

"Jamie took it," Chris said. "I have to hand it to the kid, he did a good job."

Although she'd noticed Jamie carrying a camera on several occasions, Kerry had never seen any of the results. "I'm impressed."

"Like a beer?" Chris headed for the kitchen. "Soft drink? Melanie probably has some diet junk in here."

Kerry relaxed onto the sofa, her muscles reminding her that it had been a long day. Classes in the morning, auditions in the afternoon. "Beer," she said.

"Really?" Chris peered through the doorway. "Never mind. One beer, coming up."

When he joined her, they sipped the brew for a few minutes. It struck Kerry that in the months she'd known George, even when they were unofficially engaged, they'd never simply sat around and enjoyed each other's company.

Looking back, she couldn't imagine what it would have been like to marry him. At the time, she'd naively thought he would change, that they would learn to communicate. Now she could see it would have been a marriage in form only, without real intimacy.

On the other hand, it was a little scary having thoughts like this when she hardly knew Chris. What made her think life with him would be any better? Different, sure, but—

"This place must look really tacky to you," Chris said.

"Rumpled, but so what?"

"It's just that—" He paused to reflect a moment. "I think of you as having grown up in a wealthy family."

"Me?" Kerry set down her glass. "No, we weren't rich. Although you'd be right if you're thinking my parents were— and are—very fussy about their home. They bring back art from their travels. The whole place is like a museum. I wasn't allowed to use the living room until I was twelve."

"Melanie was very impressed when she found out they play with the Boston Symphony," Chris said. "Why didn't you follow in their footsteps? Or should I say, footnotes?"

Kerry would have smiled if it hadn't been such a painful subject. "No talent" was the best she could sum it up.

"Is this a topic you'd rather avoid?"

"Why do you ask?"

"You got tense all of a sudden." He leaned forward from his chair, his fingers brushing Kerry's wrist. "You have a bruised look around your eyes. Sometimes you look so fragile, I'm afraid you'll break."

"I already did that…" Kerry's voice caught. "And all the king's horses and all the king's men couldn't put Kerry Guthrie back together again. Not entirely."

To her relief, he didn't express pity. She might have cried or gotten angry. Instead, he simply watched her for a moment. "You couldn't be a musician so you became a dancer, and a hell of a good one, and then in one shattering moment you lost your career and your fiancé and something else. Your identity. And you've never quite replaced them."

Damn, maybe she was going to cry anyway. Kerry thrust her chin out. "It's not so bad. I could have been crippled or killed. I have a satisfying life, all things considered."

"How did your parents take it?" he asked.

It wasn't an easy question to answer. "On the surface, they were very supportive. They paid for my physical therapy, let me move in with them, even arranged for some counseling."

"But?"

"I disappointed them. I guess I was always disappointing them." Kerry twisted her hands together. "If I'd married George, that would have thrilled them. And my being a dancer—at least I was doing something related to music. But they never wanted to see inside me, to see things from my perspective. The only perspective that mattered was theirs. And I don't fit into it anymore."

"A mere dance teacher in Brea, California, doesn't qualify?" He pried her fingers gently apart and held one of her hands loosely in his. "They don't feel you're accomplishing anything important, so you don't, either?"

"Not exactly." She wasn't sure she liked having someone

read her so perceptively. Kerry retrieved her hand and reached for the beer glass. "I'm just not accomplishing enough."

"You want my advice?"

"Chris—"

"You enjoyed those auditions today, didn't you? Except for having to reject people. You like being in charge, and I have the feeling you're good at what you do."

It was true. "Okay. But it's not a big deal, choreographing a small-time production."

"Then why not try the big time? Surely ballet companies need new works, too."

"I don't see them beating down my door." Kerry's defenses sprang up instantly. Don't push me. I'm not ready.

"Have you applied? I don't know how the system works, but maybe you need to put the word out." He leaned forward. "You've been through some tough breaks, but it's time to stop feeling sorry for yourself."

"Thanks for the pep talk, coach." Stiffly, she replaced the glass on the table. "I think I'm capable of making my own decisions, thank you."

"Hey—" Chris held up his hands playfully "—I know that, but sometimes an outsider sees things more clearly. You aren't happy. I know all about wallowing in self-pity because I've done it a few times myself."

"I'm not wallowing in self-pity." Kerry stood up. "Thanks for the beer."

"Kerry..." He moved toward her. "Look, I didn't mean to step on your toes. It's just so damn frustrating, watching you eat yourself up wanting something you can't have."

"Who says I can't have it?" Kerry turned to face him. "I'm only twenty-eight. There's time yet for some new—some new medical technique or something. I could still dance. I could still be somebody."

"You're somebody now."

"You don't understand!" To her alarm, tears threatened to

well from her eyes. "Dancing isn't just something I do. It's what I am!"

"I don't think you know what you are," he said quietly.

Angrily, Kerry bit back her tears. "How would you know? Maybe I'm being stubborn and wishful, but I'm not a quitter. I haven't given up yet and I'm not going to, not for a long time! No matter what you and my parents think!"

"Hey, wait a minute—"

She didn't wait to hear the rest. Instead, she swung around and stalked out the door.

Chris strode across the living room. "I didn't mean to upset you. Kerry—"

"I'll talk to you later." She half ran down the walkway to her car, praying that he wouldn't follow. He didn't.

As she put it into gear, she glanced up and saw Chris watching her from the doorway. "I don't give up easily, either," he called just before she pulled away.

Somehow that thought reassured her, and by the time she got home, Kerry didn't feel like crying anymore.

ON SUNDAY MORNING, Kerry's mother called.

Although they talked on the phone occasionally, it was usually at Kerry's initiative, so she heard her mother's voice with concern.

"Is anything wrong?" she asked.

"No, of course not." Elaine Guthrie made it sound as if she and her husband were impervious to bad luck. Which, it sometimes seemed, they were. "I wanted to let you know we're making a trip to the West Coast in two weeks. We have some recording work in Los Angeles—a movie score—and it looks like we'll be there for Thanksgiving, so we thought perhaps we could take you out to dinner."

Naturally, her parents wouldn't suggest anything like spending a lot of time together. Their only other visit had been for a weekend, and they'd chosen a hotel over Kerry's small wood-frame house. Still, Thanksgiving dinner in a restaurant sounded too impersonal even for them.

"Let's eat here," she said. "I'll make the turkey."

"That's so much trouble." Her mother had never cooked a Thanksgiving dinner in Kerry's memory; usually they went to someone else's house or had it catered, or her parents were away on tour.

But that wasn't all. Fine-tuned to her parents' unspoken thoughts, Kerry understood her mother's hesitation. Eating out took only an hour or so, but dinner at her home meant half a day at least. She and her parents hadn't felt really comfortable together these past few years, not since two years ago when her father expressed disdain for the school and demanded to know why Kerry couldn't at least teach in New York.

Her loyalty to her students and to Myron, her enjoyment of the slower pace of life in California hadn't meant anything to him. In New York she could have top students, could achieve something meaningful.

She'd blown up at him for the first time in her life, accusing him of being domineering and elitist. Relations had been strained ever since.

"I'll invite some people over," Kerry said quickly. "People you'd enjoy. How about it?"

With the possibility of other guests as a buffer, her mother didn't sound so reluctant. "I'm sure we'd enjoy that. Thanks so much, dear. We're looking forward to seeing you."

"Me, too," Kerry said. It was partly true. She just wished the anticipation of seeing her parents weren't mixed with apprehension. Yesterday Chris had accidentally pushed her buttons, but that was nothing compared to what her father could do.

A short visit. Surely that would be all right.

Kerry pulled out a pen and paper and began mulling over who else to invite.

"DON'T FORGET, these are upper-class characters." Kerry, hands on hips, surveyed the sweating dancers on the Brea Theater Center stage. "I know it's hard to perform a dignified Charleston, but watch those head and hand movements."

One of the women surveyed her dubiously. "I don't understand. I mean, I'm trying, but the music is against us."

"That's true." Most of the dancers were experienced in a wide variety of styles but masters of none. Typical show dancers. "You have to work from the inside. You have to feel like nobility. Better yet, a prince or a princess. Now let's see it again."

Kerry stepped backward down the aisle, watching as the dancers took their positions and the rehearsal pianist started up. Already she could see a marked difference in their performance; the reference to nobility must have struck home.

"Very clever," murmured a voice behind her.

Turning, she felt a moment of disorientation. What on earth was Alfonso Carrera doing here?

The music stopped, and she pulled her attention back to the stage. "Much better," she called. "Okay, take five, guys."

"I hope I'm not intruding." It was definitely not an illusion; mirages didn't have Brooklyn accents.

"I'm delighted to see you. Just surprised." Kerry stood on tiptoe to plant a kiss on his cheek.

Her former partner had aged in the intervening seven years, something she hadn't really noticed when she'd seen him backstage in makeup. Silver laced his black hair, and the lines around his eyes and mouth had deepened. Otherwise, though, he remained in splendid shape.

"I think I mentioned I might be back on the coast." He walked beside her to the lounge, where she bought them each a Coke from the machine.

"Going Hollywood?" she asked.

"In a sense."

The dancers swirling around them, chatting and sipping

coffee, seemed to inhibit him. At Kerry's suggestion they retreated to the theater's lobby, a plush, empty space where they sat on the padded bench that ran along one wall.

"The fact is, I'm starting my own company," Alfonso said.

"That's terrific!" She hated to throw cold water on his plans, but she added, "You know, ballet companies haven't done terribly well in Los Angeles."

"That's why I'm not basing it in L.A.," he said. "I've done my research. Orange County is where the audience is these days. The Performing Arts Center, South Coast Repertory—and your dance studio."

"You're going to be right here in Orange County?" Kerry could hardly believe it.

"Fullerton, as a matter of fact, which is right next to Brea." Alfonso managed to bring grace even to such a simple act as drinking Coke from a can. "I like what they've done with renovating their downtown. All those art galleries and restaurants. I've found a building that can be converted into a theater inexpensively. Well, so to speak. I do have some backers."

"What dancers are you bringing?" Kerry asked.

"Larisa is coming, and some of the others." His fingers moved restlessly across his knee, still keeping time to the 1920s music. "I hope in some of the larger productions we can draw on your students for the chorus."

"Of course!" Still, they both knew the center of the ballet world was New York. "Do you mind my asking—why would Larisa come out here?"

"Many of the dancers are tired of touring all the time, of the dog-eat-dog environment," he said. "Some of them are married, some want to pursue acting. Here, the pace will be less hectic. They'll be able to have more of a normal life."

"That still doesn't explain Larisa."

He smiled. "You're too sharp for me. Very well. They've changed management at the New American Ballet. They're bringing in their own pet dancers from Europe, plus we have a ballerina joining us who defected from the Soviet Union. No better than Larisa, but easier to publicize."

"So rather than let yourselves be pushed into the back seat, you're striking out on your own." Kerry admired Alfonso's courage. "That's terrific. Anything I can do to help, please let me know."

"I was hoping you'd say that."

With a sinking feeling, Kerry hoped he wasn't going to ask her to dance. Surely Alfonso knew that was impossible. "Oh?"

"We'll be staging a gala grand opening in June," he said. "Three short works—a traditional ballet, a Balanchine and something entirely new. Kerry, you always showed a flair for choreography, and I hear you have something of a reputation in Los Angeles. I want you to create a centerpiece for us."

She clutched her soft-drink can so hard she put a dent in it. "I've never choreographed classical ballet."

"It can be in any style you like," he said.

"I don't think I could—I mean, I'd hate to fail you. So much depends on it." But that wasn't what really held her back.

"Kerry..." He caught her hands, stopping their restless movement. "Do you think I don't know you, even after all these years? Do you think I don't understand how painful it will be, day after day, watching Larisa dance? But it's a step you're ready for, and we need you. You have the talent. We don't have a lot of money to pay you, but we can provide a showcase. It's time to stop hiding from the world."

They both knew which world he meant: the only one that counted, the world of the ballet.

"Can I let you know?" she asked.

Alfonso released her hands. "Of course. I'll be out here for another week or so. Larisa is joining me to look for an apartment. We have to dance the Nutcracker for Christmas in New York, and then we'll be moving here permanently in January. Can you let us know by then?"

"Won't that be too late for you to find someone else?"

"I don't want someone else," he said. "I want you." He stood up. "I think by now your dancers have absorbed their caffeine."

"Oh—yes." Kerry bounced to her feet, realizing guiltily that she'd let too many minutes slip by. "Alfonso, thanks for the vote of confidence. I will consider it very seriously."

"Don't run away, Kerry." He tapped her nose playfully. "We all have to modify our dreams sooner or later."

After a brief hug, he was gone. Kerry stood in the lobby a moment, her heart going out to him. After all his years with the New American Ballet, Alfonso was being thrust aside by new management.

She admired his initiative. But he'd had his years of glory. Still, did working with his company as choreographer have to mean giving up all hope of dancing again?

Maybe Chris had been right, that she was eating herself up wanting something she couldn't have. Now it wasn't even a question of her seeking assignments; a plum offer had come unsolicited. How could she ever turn it down?

Her thoughts in a muddle, Kerry headed back into the auditorium.

CHAPTER EIGHT

"ARE YOU SURE THERE aren't some extra pieces on this bird? A turkey can't possibly be this complicated."

Chris stared down in dismay at the slippery pink fowl that defiantly slithered this way and that whenever he tried to slip it into the roasting pan.

"I've never fixed one before," Kerry admitted, eyeing the less than helpful directions she'd found in a magazine. "Maybe we ought to sneak up on it."

"I could use my handcuffs," Chris said dubiously, and they both laughed.

"Okay, let's try again." Kerry slid her hands into the fray, brushing lightly against his side. Chris tried not to reveal the shudder of pleasure that raced through his nervous system. This was no time to get amorous; not at nine o'clock on Thanksgiving morning, with company coming and an incredible array of cooking to do.

It didn't help that Melanie had gone off for the morning with Jamie instead of helping out. She'd said Jamie wanted to photograph a motorcycle rally. Bikers! Chris hated the thought of Melanie even getting near people like that, but he was trying hard not to smother her. Wasn't this what he'd been wanting, for Melanie to experience dating and so forth? If only he'd known what it was really like, he wouldn't have been so eager.

"Now for the stuffing." Kerry lifted the pan of sausage, raisins and bread crumbs that she'd prepared the night before. "I guess you just push in as much as will fit."

Chris couldn't remember a time since childhood when his hands had felt so mucky, but he gamely joined in, grateful that Kerry had invited him not only to the feast but to the homey, intimate task of preparing for it.

He'd been pleased when she called to learn that she wasn't really angry at him. He supposed he had overstepped his bounds, trying to influence her career decisions. But it was hard for him to maintain a distance when more and more he wanted to be included in everything she did.

At the same time, an inner voice warned him to maintain some distance. She wasn't like Lou, not by a long shot, and yet there were similarities. He couldn't count on her sticking around. Kerry had the kind of talent that was sure to rise to the top sooner or later, and the top wasn't likely to be found in Brea, California.

"There." Kerry checked her directions again. "Now we have to truss the thing and make a tent with aluminum foil. Did you preheat the oven?"

"No." Chris wasn't even sure what preheating an oven involved.

"You tie up the chicken, Lieutenant." Kerry washed her hands. "I'll turn the oven on."

Somehow they managed to get the turkey laced, tented and baking contentedly. "What's next?" he asked.

Kerry examined her list. "We can't make the gravy yet— hmm. We have to peel the potatoes, get the sweet potato casserole ready, fix a salad…"

Flexing his shoulders, Chris sighed. "I never imagined it took this much work to fix one meal."

"Count your lucky stars. The pilgrims didn't buy their cranberry sauce in cans." Then Kerry relented. "I guess we both need a break. Want something to drink?"

"I'd kill for a cup of coffee."

"Thank goodness we have some." She filled a cup for him and gestured toward the front room.

Although he was pleased with his own newly arrived furnishings, Chris had to admire the antique-style sideboard, table and chairs as he passed through the dining room and the old-fashioned coffee and end tables in the living room. For all its uprightness, the sofa even managed to be comfortable.

The Degas prints of ballerinas blended in smoothly, and the wall of photographs of Kerry, the New American Ballet and the Leaps and Bounds students had a timeless aura.

"How are things going at work?" Kerry asked as she settled into a chair with her coffee. "They've certainly been keeping you busy." In the two weeks since their shopping expedition, Chris had put in overtime almost every night.

"We've had a new development with our robber." He slipped his shoes off and leaned back, luxuriating after the frustrating wrestling match with the turkey. For some reason he felt as much at home here as in his own house. "Apparently he's got a new accomplice, a woman."

"Did they pull another holdup?" Curled in a chair, Kerry didn't look much older than Melanie.

"Apparently she's as vicious as he is," Chris said. "They robbed a convenience store in Norwalk and she kept waving her gun at the customers."

"Anybody hurt?"

He shook his head. "Fortunately, no. But neither of them has any self-control. I feel like time is running out."

Kerry rested her chin on her hand. "Would it frustrate you if one of the other police departments caught them?"

"I just want them locked up." He thought about her question for a minute. "That's how real cops are different from movie cops. We're not interested in playing hero. We just want to get the job done."

"No ego trips?" Kerry asked.

"I won't say never. But this is a team sport."

She mulled over his comment for a minute. "Don't you ever want to shine? To stand alone in the spotlight, so to speak?"

"I'd rather stay alive," Chris said.

Kerry frowned, as if she hadn't given much thought before to the dangers of his job. How delicate she looked, honey-blond hair tumbling around her heart-shaped face. He was touched that such a special woman was concerned about him.

It amazed him that one person could be competent in so many areas: a dancer, a choreographer, a teacher, even a cook. She'd organized that Ballet Fair like a pro, maintaining her patience in the face of endless questions and demands on her time. A woman with boundless self-discipline and determination. Maybe too much, though, come to think of it.

Did she ever let go? The moments when laughter slipped out, when her blue eyes softened into dreaminess, were so rare and so brief. Underneath, Kerry Guthrie was strung as tight as a rubber band.

It was a dangerous trait to combine with his own nerve-racking profession. Both of them were under tremendous pressure; he hoped the stress of being involved with a policeman wouldn't destroy this relationship as it had the marriages of some of his friends.

"Maybe it's because we don't have to dodge bullets, but we dancers are terrible egotists." Kerry was talking mostly to herself, he could tell. "Ballet is a team effort, too, but we don't think of it that way. We want everyone to admire us. Sometimes I felt like a little kid."

"Maybe that's because your parents paid so little attention to you," he guessed.

Kerry's forehead creased. "But they did pay attention to me, in a way. When they weren't on tour, I felt as if they were always watching me. Analyzing everything I did. Appraising, looking for things to criticize."

"That may be attention, but it's not the same as acceptance."

"No," she admitted. "How about you? I picture you leading the normal, all-American life. Baseball in the vacant lot, barbecues in the backyard."

"Not far off," he conceded. "Mom was a housewife, Dad was an aerospace engineer."

"They're both dead?"

"I'm sorry to say, yes. They were older when I was born—it took them a long time to have a child," Chris said. "Maybe that's why Dad felt so invested in me. He didn't necessarily want me to be an engineer like him but he had his heart set on one of the professions."

"Being a policeman didn't qualify?" she asked gently.

"He thought I'd lost my mind," Chris said. "He insisted I could go on to graduate school, even though I was married and had Melanie by then. Well, I suppose I could have, but I hated school. I've never liked sitting indoors for long periods. I might not have minded being a doctor. I wanted to make the world a better place, naive as that sounds. But all those years of medical school were more than I could face."

"What made you choose police work?" Kerry had finished her coffee but made no move to refill the cup.

"Nothing dramatic," he admitted. "I just looked into the future and didn't like what I saw. Much as I applaud a lot of the progress in our society, there's been a lot of degradation, too. Drugs are widespread, people don't take responsibility for their own actions anymore—well, I figured I owed it to Melanie to help make this a safer world."

"Ever regret it?"

It was a question he'd never asked himself, and Chris had to think for a minute. "There are some things about it I don't like. The long hours, the paperwork. The frustration when a criminal gets off on a technicality. But no, I can't imagine doing anything else."

Kerry shifted position in her chair. "So here we are. Two people who've found out that life isn't always like the story-books."

"Did that come as a surprise?"

"Fairy tales are a ballerina's stock-in-trade," she said.

"Even when your feet hurt and your ankles have to be taped?"

"Even when. We rise above it, like Hans Christian Andersen's mermaid," Kerry said.

"And spread magic around you." Even here in her cozy living room, Chris could feel the sparkle that radiated from Kerry. She must be mesmerizing onstage. "We hardheaded cops need to be reminded that there's a world out there worth protecting."

Her gaze met his, and he felt his body respond instinctively. Without thinking, Chris moved forward and lifted Kerry from the chair. She rose lightly, as in a dream.

His mouth came down over hers as his hands cradled her face. He felt her tense for a moment and then relax as the kiss deepened, as his fingers stroked gently down her neck to the proud, straight shoulders and the strong contours of her back.

A moan welled from deep within Kerry and she trembled. Chris tightened his grip on her, pulling her closer, feeling her body mold itself instinctively to his and then grow rigid, resistant.

"Am I scaring you?" He lifted his head. "I assumed—you were engaged—"

"I haven't been close to anyone for a long time." Her voice emerged in a hoarse whisper. "I can't—I can't let go, Chris."

Damn. What happened between a man and a woman who cared for each other ought to be so simple and natural, but he knew by now that it hardly ever was. Even if things went smoothly at first, they got complicated later.

"No hurry." Reluctantly, he let go of her and stepped back. "Anyway, I hear some sweet potatoes calling from the kitchen."

She managed a smile. "Then let's go teach them what's what."

Together, they went back to work.

WHY COULDN'T SHE GIVE IN to her instincts? Kerry wondered as she stirred flour-and-water paste into the gravy. Just enjoy the spontaneous attraction she felt to Chris and not worry about where it might lead?

The emotion that had brought her up short could only be described as sheer panic. She wasn't even sure what she was afraid of—that he would leave her like George?

No, it was more basic than that. She couldn't separate sex from love, and love meant commitment, bondage, the loss of her freedom and her identity. It meant trying to please a man the way she'd tried for so long to please her parents. She wasn't ready for that; maybe she never would be.

"Melanie should be here soon." Chris, setting out rolls on a baking sheet, scowled at the wall clock. "It's nearly three and she promised to be here before the other guests."

About to make excuses for the girl, Kerry stopped herself. After all, she didn't know what Melanie and Jamie got up to when they were alone. If she were a parent, she'd worry, too.

"Did I tell you who else is coming?" she asked, to distract him.

"You said seven people." He paused. "That leaves two un-identified."

"Remember the two dancers you met at the Music Center? They're in town, so I invited them." She'd been disappointed to learn Myron had other plans for the holiday, until she thought of Alfonso and Larisa. Once the idea had popped into Kerry's head, it made perfect sense. Here were people her parents could relate to.

Besides, she might be working with them next spring. The possibility appealed to her more and more, but there remained one large stumbling block: Kerry hadn't the faintest idea what kind of dance she wanted to create.

She'd spent so long pushing away any possibility of working in classical ballet and now the ideas wouldn't come. Always before she'd had the music given to her, and the parameters: a wedding dance for Fiddler on the Roof, or her current challenge in Romeo and Juliet. Not total and complete freedom.

Perhaps she'd already reached the peak of her ability, working out clever dances within narrow confines. Maybe she didn't have the kind of originality it took to create a centerpiece for the Carrera Ballet.

"From the thunderclouds gathering on your face, I wonder why you invited them." Chris began counting out silverware.

"Oh. That wasn't because of them exactly." Kerry turned down the heat under the gravy. "Alfonso wants me to choreograph a ballet for his new company. I'm not sure I can do it. I'm not sure I'm good enough."

"I think you're your own worst enemy," Chris said. "You'll worry yourself into a catatonic state."

If she hadn't been afraid of burning the gravy, Kerry would have turned around and thrown something at him. "I'm not that bad!"

"Worse," he observed, and made his getaway to the dining room.

When the doorbell rang a few minutes later, Kerry set the gravy aside and took off her apron. She'd changed earlier from jeans into a blue silk shirtwaist, the sort of understated elegance her mother would appreciate.

"Shall I pretend I just arrived or am I playing host?" Chris looked up as she passed through the dining room; he was placing silver candle holders along the center of the table.

"You deserve credit for all your hard work." Kerry smoothed her skirt nervously. "Besides, Melanie's sure to spill the beans and it would look like we were hiding something."

"Maybe that's her at the door," he said. "That would simplify everything."

But it was Kerry's parents, standing on the porch holding a bottle of wine and a spray of roses as if they were visiting a stranger's house.

"Mom...Dad. Boy, I'm glad to see you." Kerry kissed them each on the cheek and stepped back to make way.

"We really appreciate your going to all the trouble." Elaine Guthrie wore an Italian-tailored suit of dove-gray silk. With her upswept hair, it gave her an air of nobility that Kerry's dancers would have done well to study.

"Smells wonderful." Everett Guthrie handed her the wine and the flowers. A tall, thin man, he looked intently around, although the room hadn't changed in the two years since he'd visited. "I see we're not the first."

"Mom, Dad, this is Chris Layne," Kerry said. "I've told you about his daughter, Melanie. She'll be here soon. And you remember Alfonso—he'll be joining us, too, with his new dance partner."

She wished she didn't feel obligated to reassure them that the company would be compatible. She wished they could all feel comfortable together and let the moments take care of themselves. Maybe it was all her own imagination, her own overreaction.

"Pleased to meet you." Chris strode over and shook hands. "So you're in town to make a recording?"

The business of providing drinks, putting flowers in water and exchanging chitchat occupied the next quarter of an hour, to Kerry's relief, until the doorbell rang again.

It was Alfonso and Larisa. Their toned dancers' bodies and striking faces looked oddly out of place in this humdrum small-town setting, but the smiles were broad and genuine.

"Come in!" Kerry thanked them for the bottle of wine they proffered. Thank goodness there were enough guests to drink it all! "Alfonso, I think you've met my parents—"

Introductions were made and drinks poured. Basting the turkey, she heard with relief the steady hum of conversation from the living room.

When she joined the others, her father was saying, "You really think this area can support a ballet company?"

"Not in Lincoln Center style." Alfonso leaned forward intently. "I've been studying the operation at South Coast Repertory. They have a touring troupe for schools, with corporate funding, and I plan to do the same. Lots of special events, maybe some master classes in conjunction with Kerry's studio."

"Still, I'm surprised you'd leave the Northeast," her mother said. "Especially you, Larisa."

"I've never lived anywhere but New York." The ballerina's longish face was offset by wide gray eyes and an endearing smile. "I'm tired of all the pressure. Last season I danced much too often with injuries. I was afraid I wouldn't get cast in the best roles if I took too much sick leave."

The conversation buzzed along steadily until it was time to serve the food. Four o'clock and Melanie still hadn't arrived.

"I'll wring her little neck," Chris muttered as he carried the sweet potato casserole to the sideboard. Underneath, Kerry sensed real worry.

This wasn't like Melanie. She'd always been so dependable before. And so dutiful.

Alfonso, who professed to expertise in such matters, was carving the turkey when the doorbell rang.

"Finally," Chris said, and went to answer it. Kerry saw her parents exchange glances. They probably thought there was more between her and Chris than really existed; well, let them think so.

Melanie apologized several times for her lateness. "There was a horrible jam in the parking lot and we couldn't get out. We must have sat there for an hour."

"Rock concert?" Alfonso asked.

"Bike rally." Seeing the puzzled reactions around the table, she said, "My boyfriend's a photographer. He thought they'd make a neat series."

"Shall we say grace?" Kerry's father asked.

After the blessing, plates were loaded. Kerry found herself taking much bigger helpings than usual, although she noticed that Larisa restricted herself to a mere taste of everything except the salad.

At the table, her father regaled the group with anecdotes of the last concert tour—the assistant conductor caught in bed with a chambermaid; the cellist with a horror of rodents who had to play through fifteen minutes of a concert with a field mouse sitting attentively not five feet away; the trombonist whose missing luggage turned out to contain stolen hotel towels.

The conversation shifted and eddied, but at its center were music and dance, art and theater, with an occasional dash of political commentary, especially about the government's inadequate arts funding.

Witty remarks flew between Alfonso and Everett Guthrie, while Larisa and Elaine compared the health and beauty hazards of touring. Melanie listened in fascination.

At last everyone finished eating. Melanie and Larisa cleared the table, while Kerry and Chris served coffee and the pumpkin pie she'd bought the previous day.

"Marvelous," Alfonso said as he dug in. "Of course I'll have to starve myself tomorrow, but it's worth it."

With a start, Kerry realized that, unlike Larisa, Melanie had eaten a normal meal instead of her usual small portions. Well, it was Thanksgiving, after all.

She only hoped this didn't mean Melanie was losing some of her dedication to the dance. Or worse, that she'd begun purging herself like a bulimic. Eating disorders ran rife among dancers. But surely Chris would have noticed anything like that.

Finally the guests began excusing themselves. At the door, Alfonso gave Kerry a hug. "You're thinking about my offer, aren't you?"

"I'm not sure I can come up with the right idea," she admitted. "Maybe you should think of someone else."

"From what Alfonso's said, you'd be terrific," Larisa put in. "Please, Kerry, you'd really be helping us out."

Kerry looked at the beautiful young woman, only five years her junior. She liked Larisa and wished her well, but the thought of watching her whirl and leap and fly made Kerry feel like a caged bird.

"I am considering it," she said. "But please don't hope for too much."

After them, it was Everett and Elaine's turn.

"Delicious food," her mother said. "Thanks so much, Kerry."

"Maybe you can come back to Boston to visit this summer." Her father shook hands with Chris. "Nice to meet you."

Then they were off to Los Angeles in their rental car.

Watching them out the window, Kerry was only vaguely aware of the clatter of dishes in the kitchen, where Melanie was washing up. Mostly she noticed how empty the road looked in front of her house, and how empty she felt inside.

"Did I miss something?" Chris murmured.

"What?" She looked up.

"I thought you guys hadn't seen each other in two years," he said.

"We talk on the phone."

"Still—no questions about the dance studio? Or how you're doing otherwise? They hardly said anything personal to you all evening."

That was what she'd been missing, Kerry realized. "I know they love me. They just don't know how to relate to me."

"I've never met people like that," he admitted. "Most parents, if anything, are too nosy and too eager to mix into their kids' lives. It's as if your parents live in some other dimension."

"I know," she said. "I've been trying to break into it for twenty-eight years and it hasn't worked. Right now I'm just relieved that we got through the evening and everyone had a good time."

He reached over to rub her shoulders. Kerry leaned back, luxuriating in his touch.

"No wonder," he muttered.

"No wonder what?"

"No wonder you're afraid of getting close to people," he said.

"You thinking of any people in particular?"

He nipped at her earlobe before stepping away. "Who, me?"

"I—" Kerry stopped as Melanie came in from the kitchen. "Did you have a good time, Mel?"

"Sure. Your parents are fantastic." The girl jammed her hands into her jeans pockets. "Dad, can I go now?"

"Go where?"

"Jamie's driving down to his uncle's tonight to develop the pictures, and he invited me to go. I'd like to learn how to work in a darkroom."

Chris hesitated. From where she stood, Kerry sensed his conflicting feelings. "It is a holiday, you know. People usually spend those with their family."

"Oh, Dad!" About to argue, Melanie paused and apparently thought the better of it. "Well, I am kind of stuffed, and he said he'd be there real late. I hate to cancel on him in a text. I'll go call from the other room. If that's okay?"

Getting assent, she returned to the kitchen.

"Enough is enough," Chris said.

"You can't blame her for pushing a little," Kerry reminded him.

"It's time she got her priorities straight."

"What was it you said a minute ago?" Receiving a blank look, she explained, "About parents mixing into their kids' affairs too much?"

"I was referring to grown children." But his glower softened. "Do you think I was wrong?"

"No," Kerry said. "Just that—don't expect her to be perfect, Chris. This whole business of having a boyfriend is new to her. It'll take a while to put her life into perspective."

"I hope I survive the process," he said, but when his daughter came back into the room, he gave her a big hug.

"What was that for?" Melanie asked.

"Being the most beautiful, wonderful, talented kid a man could ask for," he said.

"Oh, is that all?" But she was smiling as they left.

"YOU WON'T BELIEVE THIS." Tony's voice still had a boyish lilt over the telephone, the way it had in high school. "Leila and I finally decided to tie the knot."

"You've only been engaged for, what, three years?" Chris realized his irony might be mistaken for sarcasm. "Actually, I'm thrilled. She's a wonderful girl."

It was just like Tony to call on Thanksgiving night; he had an impulsive, childlike side that never dimmed. Leaning back on his new, rust-colored sofa, Chris wondered whether the workers at Tony's restaurants ever saw this aspect of him.

"Write this down." Tony gave him a date. "And New Year's Eve."

"You're getting married twice?"

Tony chuckled. "The first is a cocktail party at my place, in lieu of showers and all that nonsense. No presents, please. We haven't got room for any more stuff. Then we're getting married New Year's Eve. Sound romantic?"

"You won't have any trouble remembering your anniversary." Chris wondered if he could still fit into his good suit. Tony and Leila liked to do things up fancy; Tony's "place" was a Mediterranean villa in the city of Orange that resembled a hotel more than a house.

"Good old Chris, always the practical one." A woman was speaking in the background, probably Leila. "Well, I've got to go. My helpmate reminds me we've got a lot of other people to call. Oh, and she says the formal invitation will be in the mail one of these days, but she wants to be sure you keep the dates clear. Got that?"

"Got that," Chris said. "And tell Leila thanks again for helping out with Melanie's dress."

After they hung up, he sat staring at the telephone for a minute, glad that Melanie was busy watching TV in her room and he didn't have to answer any questions right away.

It might not make sense, feeling so ambivalent about his old friend's marriage, but then, that wasn't exactly what bothered Chris.

It was the cocktail party that disturbed him. Chris hadn't seen most of his old schoolmates since graduation. The ones Tony kept in touch with, he knew, were successful businessmen and professionals. Some of them probably made as much in a month as Chris did in a year.

Why was that troubling him now? he wondered irritably. He didn't regret deciding to become a policeman.

But it wasn't as if his life had been such a brilliant success in other areas, either. These people had known Lou when she and Chris were high school sweethearts. They didn't really understand what had gone wrong. He wasn't sure he understood it himself.

Impulsively, Chris picked up the phone and dialed Kerry's number.

"Hello?" She sounded—not sleepy, but languorous. A radio played in the background.

"Chris here."

"Hi." He could picture her stretching like a cat. "What's up?"

"I need a sounding board." He told her about the upcoming events. "It's ridiculous, feeling this uneasy. I don't want to miss Tony's party, but I'm afraid I'll feel out of place."

"Hmm." The radio quieted behind her. "I'm a bad one to ask. My tenth high school reunion is this summer and I haven't got the least intention of going. The ones who weren't dancers, I didn't know, and the ones who were, well, I'm not too eager to see them."

"It's irrational," he mused. "For some reason, I'd like to impress them. Think they'd come out to the practice range and watch my target shooting? I've won a couple of medals."

Kerry laughed. "And I could go back to New York, line everybody up and teach them the five positions. In both cases, I'm sure we'd be as popular as poison ivy."

He felt better just talking to her. "I suppose I'm uncomfortable about personal questions. At events like this, people always want to catch up on your private life, right? What am I going to tell them? My daughter's growing up and my feet are getting flat and that's all I have to report?"

"If you think it would help, I'd be glad to go with you," Kerry said.

The idea appealed to him instantly, but his cautious side warned not to leap before he looked. Would it bother Kerry if the conversation turned to Lou? Or would she find, seeing him in the company of wealthy, high-powered people, that she preferred their world to his?

"I appreciate the offer. Okay if I let you know?"

"Sure," she said.

Melanie wandered in from her bedroom. "Dad? Can I use the phone? I want to see if Jamie's back yet."

He stifled a groan. "Sorry, Kerry, I'm being displaced by you-know-who. I'll talk to you soon."

"Good night."

When she hung up, Kerry found she couldn't concentrate on her book anymore or relax despite the mood music wafting from her radio.

Why didn't Chris want to take her to the party? Was it because she wasn't really a part of his life? Yet these past few months, even though they'd deliberately kept things casual, they'd been growing closer a little at a time. Or so she'd assumed.

On the other hand, he might simply want to protect her from nosy people. Or from his own dissatisfactions with his life.

They were both going through major changes, she realized—Chris having to face his daughter's newfound independence and with it the realization that he himself was getting older; she, in turn, having to deal with approaching thirty, with offers to choreograph, with the reality that miracles were in short supply and the time for them was running out.

Not a good time to start a relationship. On the other hand, they both needed the support and understanding of someone who cared.

Darn it. She didn't want to be shut out of Chris's life. Or to shut him out of hers, either.

Her thoughts scared her a little. Maybe she was just reacting to seeing her parents again and experiencing the disappointment that she never grew hardened against.

If she and Chris ever got really close, he wouldn't let her down. Somehow Kerry felt sure of that. The only question was whether that intimacy would ever come.

CHAPTER NINE

FAWN FRYE SLIPPED INTO the theater and took a seat beside Kerry, watching silently as the dancers exploded through the ballroom scene.

"Wonderful," she murmured. "Such energy. You're going to set the house on fire."

Kerry smiled her appreciation as the music ended. "Okay, guys," she called up. "You're doing great. Tomorrow we'll work on some new lifts. You're really coming along."

Cheered, the dancers waved as they wandered offstage. Several of them had improved dramatically in the few weeks they'd been rehearsing, Kerry noted silently, and hoped they were aware of it, too.

"Kerry?" The young woman understudy approached hesitantly. She and her male counterpart had stepped in several times when other dancers were late or had to miss a rehearsal because of conflicts. "Jim and I haven't had to substitute this week and I was wondering if you could critique us."

"Sure." It was a reasonable request, especially considering they were donating their time. "Let's try it again."

Kerry was vaguely aware of Fawn wandering out as she rewound the tape and played it again. Afterward, she gave the couple some notes.

"Thanks," the girl said. "You know, I've learned more these past few weeks than in all the dance classes I took this year."

"I find that hard to believe, but thanks," Kerry said.

"What she means," Jim said, "isn't so much that we've

learned more steps or more techniques but that we've grown as artists. We understand better why we're doing things."

"Thanks, both of you." As tired as she was from the long rehearsal, the praise restored Kerry's spirits. "You both have lots of talent and I wish you luck."

After they left, she pulled on her jacket and wandered out of the theater, turning out lights and locking the doors. By the time she finished, hers was the only car in the parking lot.

The expanse of blacktop looked bleak in the dim moonlight, and a cold wind bent the tops of a row of evergreens. Winters in southern California might be short and mild, but they brought no softening snowfalls, no romantic, cozy retreats around the fire while sleet pinged at the windows.

Why did she feel so let down? Was it because she hadn't heard from Chris in a week? Or because her parents had gone back to Boston without seeing her again? Or simply because, in the interval between holidays, her students at Leaps and Bounds chattered and goofed off more than usual and it took extra energy to get them motivated?

As she walked across the pavement, another car pulled into the lot. Kerry hesitated until she recognized the sedan.

"Guess I'm too late to watch." Chris rolled down his window. "Want to ride on a Ferris wheel?"

"Is this a riddle?" she asked.

"It's Friday night, in case you hadn't noticed." He opened the passenger door. "There's a carnival at Hillcrest Park. I know because Jamie and Melanie are going."

"You weren't planning to spy on them, were you?" Kerry folded herself into the seat.

"Of course not." His mischievous glance belied the indignant tone. "If we happen to run into them, I'm sure they'll understand."

"Naturally." Despite her skepticism, Kerry felt immensely warmer here in the car, and it wasn't just because of the heater. "Oh, what the heck? Let's go."

The carnival turned out to be crowded but not overwhelmingly so. Parents were departing with small children draped in their arms and over their shoulders, leaving the rides to teenagers and young couples.

Music of the oom-pah-pah variety added gaiety to the flashing lights and the drifting smells of popcorn and cotton candy. "Reminds me of my childhood," Chris said. "How about you?"

"I think we went to a carnival once." Kerry couldn't remember clearly. "Oh, yes. I bet a nickel and won a stuffed dog, to my mother's amazement. I named him Lucky."

"There's the Ferris wheel." Chris steered her between packed bodies. "Let's go."

When they got in line, Kerry noticed Melanie and Jamie three couples ahead of them. Realizing they'd been spotted, she called out a hello. Melanie waved back but studied her father and Kerry for a moment before turning away.

"You know," Kerry said, "Melanie might be as interested in your social life as you are in hers."

"Maybe. I haven't dated much." Seeing her questioning glance, Chris added, "Don't get me wrong. I haven't exactly been living in a monastery, either."

"I'd guess you've kept people at arm's length nearly as rigorously as I have."

"I've been busy raising a daughter." As the line inched forward, he conceded, "Okay, you might be right. But I'll deny it with my dying breath."

"Two emotional cripples," Kerry joked. "We make a great team."

"Why not? We can lean on each other."

They climbed into a gondola, and the wheel cranked forward a notch. Kerry knew the teenagers were a few cars above them, but they were invisible from this angle.

Slowly the gondola ascended as more and more passengers

were seated until Kerry and Chris sat at the top of the circle, surveying the nighttime glitter of Fullerton.

"It looks like magic from here," she said.

"I used to imagine that something fantastical would happen when I went to a fair." Chris rested one arm around her shoulders. "A fortune-teller would transport me to a mythical kingdom, or I'd discover a genie in a bottle, or—who knows?"

"All I ever wanted was to dance better," Kerry said. "My dreams were all about performing, being a star."

"And they never came true," he murmured.

"Oh, yes, they did. For one night." Kerry closed her eyes, remembering the exhilaration of applause rolling toward her. "I suppose I should be grateful. How many people get even that much?"

His arm tightened around her. "There are all kinds of dreams, Kerry. Maybe this is one of them, right now."

As she opened her eyes and saw the lights twinkle below, heard the rumble of music and felt the warmth of Chris's body against hers, Kerry's head swam. A dream. She liked the sensation of not quite being in control, as long as Chris was here beside her.

The wheel churned into action. Slowly they circled around, every now and then glimpsing Melanie and Jamie. It looked as if they were kissing. Chris frowned and turned away.

They rode for a while in silence. His expression gradually softened, to Kerry's relief.

"By the way," he said as they reached the top again. "Did you mean what you said, that you were willing to go with me to the party?"

"Yes."

"I'll take you up on it, then."

Kerry hoped the Ferris wheel would never stop. It was turning out to be magic, after all.

LATER THAT NIGHT, home again, she riffled through her closets wondering whether she had anything suitable to wear.

He'd said the party would be dressy. Hesitantly, Kerry lifted out a designer gown she hadn't worn in seven years.

Reaching to midcalf, the dress glittered even in the modest light from the overhead fixture. The silhouette was simple, a boat neck and squared-off sleeves, the bodice formfitting until it flared around the knees.

But the design delighted her now as much as when, intimidated by the price but determined to impress George, she'd bought it in a New York boutique. Shimmering geometric blues and greens had been worked into a glowing golden background, the entire design created in bugle beads.

She wasn't sure why she'd kept it all these years—because it was a work of art in itself, perhaps, and also because, having paid so much for it, she couldn't carelessly toss it away.

Gliding over to a mirror, Kerry held the dress in front of her. It looked as if it would still fit; she hadn't gained any weight.

How would she wear her hair? Loose across the shoulders, the way she'd chosen seven years ago?

It was time to make a change, Kerry realized. Not because she was getting older, or moved in different circles, but simply because she was ready for a new stage of her life.

A new hairstyle. Yes, and she'd have a beautician show her how to put on makeup, too, beyond the minimum she usually wore.

I'm not the same girl I was seven years ago. There's no use pretending.

Changing her hairstyle meant leaving part of herself behind, admitting she was no longer a ballerina who lived only for the stage. No more sticking her hair into a bun for classes or running out in the morning with it still wet.

Did she really want to do this?

Resolutely, Kerry put the dress back in the closet. Yes, she was ready. And after all, if she did choreograph a piece for Alfonso's gala, she'd have another occasion to show off her new image.

Immediately, her thoughts turned to his proposition.

More and more, she liked the idea. Working with the Romeo and Juliet dancers was turning out to be more stimulating than she'd expected. The only frustration was that, although they were skilled show dancers, the performers weren't up to top ballet standards. Also, the limitations of time and music were beginning to chafe.

If only she knew what it was she really wanted to do.

In the kitchen, Kerry poured herself a cup of decaf and sank into a chair. On the subject of Alfonso's centerpiece, she was finding herself totally and completely blocked. A classical work? Jazz? Something offbeat?

Defiantly, her thoughts floated back to the carnival earlier tonight. She and Chris had ridden a roller coaster and taken turns in a shooting gallery, where he'd won three stuffed animals, all of which they'd donated to sleepy but grateful children.

Secretly, Kerry had had to fight back the urge to keep one for herself. Not that she collected stuffed animals, but she wanted a souvenir. Except that nothing tangible was needed. She would never forget tonight.

What was it about wandering hand in hand down a midway that brought back the carefree feeling of youth? Time had stood still for one evening.

Where would it lead, this growing sense of belonging with Chris? Where could it lead? Much as she loved Brea, Kerry had never intended to spend the rest of her life here. But right now she was satisfied with moments.

If only there was some way to capture onstage the excitement the fair sparked. Some way to put into dance the soaring ups and downs of the roller coaster, the heights of the Ferris wheel, the youthful exuberance of skipping—might as well admit it—hand in hand with someone you cared about. And the unabashedly gaudy lights, the cheerful thumping music, the surge of the crowd.

Kerry sighed and finished her coffee. If she could accomplish that, Alfonso would have a brilliant gala indeed.

THEY STOPPED THE CAR in the driveway outside Tony's villa, which Chris had visited a couple of times on less public occasions. Tonight, two valets waited to assist the guests while the entire complex sparkled with all-white Christmas tree lights that cycled on and off in random patterns.

"Wow," Kerry said as he handed her out and they walked toward the entrance.

The interior courtyard was packed with cars. Chris noted one Rolls-Royce and a sprinkling of Mercedes, Porsches and Jaguars. His own sedan made a sorry picture as the valet steered it into place.

"Tony's not exactly poor," he said.

Kerry's face lighted up in a smile. "If there were a prize for understatement, I think you just won."

He couldn't think of anything to say, mostly because her appearance was so bewitching. That incredible dress had caught his eye when he picked her up, but it looked even more spectacular here.

It set off her glowing face and regal neck, her lustrous eyes—how had she managed to make them look even bigger than usual?—and the mass of hair curling down from the crown of her head. He might make a poor showing in his department-store suit, but there couldn't be another lady here who could hold a candle to Kerry.

Well, maybe Leila, but she was a model and a bride-to-be. Other than her, nobody.

A uniformed maid ushered them into the sprawling modern living room, which opened seamlessly onto a terrace. The rustle of dozens of voices rolled toward them, along with the clink of glasses and the effervescent smell of champagne. In the far corner, a bartender deftly mixed drinks for a crush of partygoers.

"There." Chris pointed to Tony and Leila, standing near the glass doors that opened onto the veranda.

Tony didn't look much older than when they'd graduated from high school seventeen years before, except for a tracing of gray in his longish hair. Narrow-rimmed glasses gave him a sophisticated air, matched by a suit that, even to Chris's inexperienced eye, looked Italian and hand-tailored.

Beside him, Leila radiated contentment. Her upswept blond hair was sprinkled with glitter picked up by the shiny dark blue fabric of her gown.

"She's beautiful," Kerry said.

"She's a model," Chris explained. "Although she's going to be devoting herself full-time to helping Tony with his restaurant business after they're married."

"A partnership." Was that a touch of envy in her voice? "It's nice when people have so much in common."

Before they could advance halfway across the room, a balding man with a slight paunch confronted Chris. "Hey! Layne the Brain! Remember me?"

Out of the distant mists of memory came an image of the high school's resident jokester, a pudgy youth with a ready quip for any occasion. "Buster! Buster Duster—no, that's not your real name, is it?"

"Buster Destry, actually." The man pumped Chris's hand. "What've you been up to? You didn't really go off and become a cop like you threatened, did you?" He laughed heartily.

"Actually, I did," Chris said quietly.

The laughter subsided. "Really? I mean, that's terrific." Buster shifted from one foot to the other. "I'm in banking, myself. It's a good field if you ever get tired of playing cops and robbers."

Chris realized that, despite his roly-poly appearance, Buster was wearing a silk suit and a watch that must have cost a thousand dollars. "Great. Good to see you again."

He excused himself to pay his respects to Tony and dragged Kerry off without an introduction.

Two steps farther and they were accosted by a woman with the leathery skin and deep facial lines that came from too many summers spent baking in the sun. Nevertheless, she'd maintained a slim figure and wore some delicate, flowing thing that Chris guessed must have designer labels fluttering inside.

"Chris Layne!" The throaty rasp was accompanied by the smell of tobacco, even though there was no cigarette in sight. "Nadine Franks, remember me?"

"Prom queen," he said promptly. "Of course."

"And—" She looked at Kerry questioningly. "I'm sorry. I didn't realize you and Lou weren't—"

"Lou died ten years ago," he said.

Nadine's mouth opened and closed. After a moment she said, "I'm really sorry. I had no idea. You and Lou were so wonderful together. I used to envy you, all the fun you had. Oh, I'm sorry. Is this a touchy point?"

"Not at all," Kerry said smoothly. "I wish I'd known her."

To Chris's vast relief, Tony spotted him and came barreling over. "Chris! Welcome! You'll excuse us, Nadine?"

Chris found himself and Kerry piloted to where Leila and a handful of guests stood making introductions and trying to remember names. Thank goodness not everyone here had gone to high school with him and Tony.

The others, he learned, were a real estate broker, an insurance executive and the president of a computer software company. All exuded affability and wealth.

To his dismay, he couldn't help wishing he'd gone out and spent more than he could afford on a really good suit. Not that it would fool anybody once they learned what he did for a living.

What was wrong with him, anyway? He didn't want some desk job shifting money from one pocket to another, some meaningless occupation where the sole measure of success was charted on a profit-and-loss statement.

Yet he couldn't help but wonder what Kerry thought of all this. As he'd expected, she put every other woman but Leila in the shade. That dress was amazing. He hadn't really appreciated before how unique it was, the very essence of sophistication.

Although her field was the arts, Kerry obviously belonged among people like this, people of wealth and taste. Most of the men were giving her the eye, and the women studied her with a mixture of admiration and raw envy. Did she feel let down to be on the arm of a guy wearing the cheapest pair of shoes in the room?

Chris glanced at Kerry's face, but he couldn't read anything there except polite interest in conversation, which focused on the latest developments in the stock market.

In a way, he wished he hadn't brought her. This was a world he entered only as Tony's friend. It was a life his father had wanted for him—visible success and prestige. But it wasn't the life he'd chosen.

He didn't belong here any more than he fitted in with Kerry's parents or her ballet friends. He'd much rather be at the bowling alley right now, even if he did end up getting trounced by Ken Oakland.

KERRY WISHED SHE COULD figure out why Chris wore a grim expression whenever he thought no one was looking.

Wasn't he enjoying the party? The hors d'oeuvres were exquisite, there was plenty to drink, and everyone else seemed to be having a good time. Besides, Chris obviously liked Tony and Leila, and they clearly felt the same way about him.

So what was the problem?

She clutched her champagne glass tighter and wondered if it was because some of these people had been friends of Lou's. Nadine's comments played over and over through her mind. What a lot of fun Chris and Lou had had together. What an ideal couple they'd been.

Was he missing his late wife? Was he wishing he and Kerry had more carefree fun together instead of being preoccupied so often with their work?

Or did he envy these people their money, their expensive cars and clothes? It would be a perfectly natural response, but Kerry hoped that wasn't the problem.

Although, when she was dating George, she'd moved among even more worldly circles than this one, she'd never really been a part of them. Ballet didn't pay very well except for the biggest stars. Instead, you got lots of long hours, touring, time lost with injuries and unending expenses for classes and toe shoes.

She'd never really cared. Her work was what mattered, not how much she earned at it. She liked the fact that Chris shared her attitude.

No, more likely he was being forcibly reminded of Lou, and missing her. Kerry couldn't exactly blame him, but it was an unsettling notion that he still mourned his wife.

"Is something bothering Chris?" Leila had drawn Kerry aside.

"You noticed, too? I thought maybe—well, one of the women didn't realize his wife had died, and—I thought he might be missing her," Kerry blurted out.

Leila gave her a strange look. "He hasn't told you?"

"Told me what?"

"About him and Lou? I guess not. Ask him." She turned to greet some new arrivals, and Kerry wandered back to Chris's side.

What had the hostess meant? Kerry wasn't sure she dared

raise the subject, since Chris hadn't broached it himself. But then, he'd felt free to ask questions about George, hadn't he?

When they were finally alone together in the car, heading along a nearly empty freeway and fighting yawns as the dashboard clock edged past midnight, Kerry decided to risk it.

"Leila suggested I ask you about Lou," she said.

"What about Lou?" At least he didn't sound annoyed, merely puzzled.

"Well, I thought…" She gathered her courage. "You seemed rather pensive tonight, and I thought after what Nadine said that you might be missing her."

"Missing Lou?" He took his eyes from the road for a moment to stare at Kerry.

"It does seem logical," she told him. "She was your wife. And she died so young. Why shouldn't you miss her?"

He inhaled deeply. "I see. You didn't know that Lou and I were divorced?"

She sat stock-still. "Divorced? But Melanie told me once that she remembered you driving out in a storm to buy some grapefruit juice for her mother when she was going through chemotherapy and couldn't tolerate anything else."

"She remembers that? She was only five." Chris veered left to pass a slow-moving truck on the steep grade. "Lou moved back in with me when she got sick. There was no one in her family to take care of her."

"You nursed your ex-wife?" Kerry said.

"She had custody of Melanie, and I wanted to make sure my daughter was taken care of," Chris said. "Besides, I couldn't let her die alone."

"Is it painful to remember?" Kerry didn't want to press too far. "You don't have to tell me."

"The most painful part was the divorce." Chris slowed as blinking lights directed traffic out of the fast lane to make way for road repairs. Highway work was conducted year-round in southern California, primarily late at night and on Sundays. "It was Lou who wanted out."

"Why?"

"Several reasons—she may not have really been clear in her own mind," Chris said. "Lou was one of those people who peaks in high school. I didn't realize it at the time, of course. She was such a lively person, always up for a good time, then in community college. She didn't even seem to mind when she got pregnant and we had to get married. To her it was just another lark—until, I guess, the reality of dirty diapers and living on a rookie cop's salary came home to her."

"She just left?" Kerry asked.

"She said she wasn't ready to settle down. She wanted to live it up—and she wanted more money than I was making." Chris glared into the night as if the stars were somehow to blame. "We divorced when Melanie was three."

"She lived with her mother?" Kerry tried to imagine what life must have been like for Lou, but she couldn't. In her late teens and early twenties, Kerry had been singularly focused on her career. The possibility of having a baby hadn't even occurred to her.

"They lived like gypsies." Chris's hands tightened on the wheel. "Camping out in her girlfriends' apartments. Lou's father had split when she was a kid and her mother was an alcoholic. You'd think she'd have wanted stability, and maybe part of her did, but when she got it, it stifled her. I wanted to help but I was working long hours myself, and Melanie took up any spare time I had."

"Sounds like you were an involved father, at least."

"I changed plenty of diapers and heated my share of bottles," he said.

"You didn't try to get custody?"

He turned onto the Imperial Highway off ramp. "I thought about it, but how could I take care of a toddler and work such odd hours? Besides, Melanie was the one thing that held Lou together, I think. Their life may have been irregular, but the child was never neglected. I kept close tabs, believe me."

"And then Lou got sick?"

"Breast cancer," he said. "She didn't take it seriously at first. She was only twenty-four. I took care of Melanie during the first operation. Afterward, I remember Lou looking up at me from the hospital bed and saying, 'Thank goodness that's over. Where's the next party?'"

Kerry shuddered. She knew all too well the smell of disinfectant, the discomfort of sleeping in hard hospital beds and the lonely sense of having been cut off from the world. She'd spent a good part of her twenty-first year in and out of hospitals. But I was the lucky one. I lived, and she didn't.

"Then the cancer came back," Chris said softly, "in spite of radiation and chemo. She kept getting thinner and weaker. Her hair fell out and she was nauseated all the time. The thing that makes me so angry is that the last year of her life she couldn't even enjoy herself."

"That's awful," Kerry said.

"So now you know." He turned off the highway onto Brea Boulevard. "I don't want Lou back—not for myself—but I wish she'd had more chance to live."

"And since then you've been raising Melanie alone." Kerry wished they weren't pulling onto the side street that led to her house. She wanted more time with Chris, but she knew he should head home before Melanie got worried. "I admire you."

"That's the part I'm glad about." He pulled to a halt in front of her house. "She's been the best thing in my life."

The way he put it, in sort of a past tense, made Kerry's heart race a little faster. Did he mean Melanie wasn't the only best thing in his life anymore? But this was no time to ask. "You don't have to walk me in. I know Melanie's probably waiting up for you."

"Like an old mother hen," he said. "Jamie had to go visit his grandmother tonight. For once, I wish he'd kept my daughter busy."

He leaned over and kissed Kerry lightly. There was no passion stirring tonight, not with the press of memories and the strain of the evening behind them, but his touch felt natural and right.

"By the way," he said, "if you don't have any other plans, Melanie and I would like you to spend Christmas with us. We leave everything till then—decorating the tree, baking the cookies. That way the day feels really festive."

"I'd love to come," Kerry said. "Thank you."

As she let herself into the house, she realized that Chris had a rare knack for a man: the ability to make a home. Not just to buy a house and fill it with furniture, but to create warmth and closeness and the homey touches that made everything special.

She felt sad for Lou, who hadn't appreciated the man she had while there was still time, but happy for Melanie, who had enjoyed the best of him.

Well, maybe not quite the best. There might still be some of that left for Kerry.

CHAPTER TEN

MELANIE PERCHED ON TOP of the ladder, adjusting the star. Lustrous and many-faceted, it was the perfect crown to the Christmas tree.

"Stop!" Chris called. "The angle's perfect."

"Are you sure? It looks a little crooked from here."

"No, he's right," Kerry said. "It is perfect."

She watched as Melanie climbed down and joined the two grown-ups in surveying the tree. "Okay. Are we ready to open presents yet?" the teenager asked.

Chris laughed. "Don't you even want to see it with the lights on?"

"Oh, yeah. I forgot."

He bent to flick the switch. Rich gems of red, blue and green glowed within the mysterious depths of the fir tree.

"It's so beautiful." Kerry had seen a lot of Christmas trees in her time—in parks and public squares, at fancy homes and apartments—but there was something special about this one. The old-fashioned silk-covered balls and wooden soldier ornaments roused a sense of age-old tradition, of Victorian holidays where the special treats were candles that flickered and sweet, rare oranges from far-off lands.

"You remind me of a kid." Chris started to slip his arm around her waist, then apparently thought the better of it. "Your eyes are as big as saucers."

"Hey, can we open the presents now?" Melanie demanded.

"Speaking of children." Chris winked at Kerry over his

daughter's head. "Sure, go ahead." At Kerry's suggestion, Chris and she had decided to avoid the touchy subject of what to give each other by not exchanging gifts.

"Just a minute. I've got to check the food." Kerry whisked into the kitchen to make sure the ham was browning nicely in its pineapple sauce and to take the potatoes off the fire and drain them, ready for mashing. The salad and cranberry sauce waited in the refrigerator.

Hard to believe it was only noon. After an early morning visit to church, she'd arrived at nine. Since then they'd been busy cooking, hanging mistletoe and decorating the tree.

"Come on!" Melanie called impatiently.

"Sorry." Kerry rejoined the father and daughter in the living room.

Melanie delivered her presents first: for each of them, a beautiful framed photograph. Chris's showed Melanie alone in a sophisticated pose; Kerry's was a striking shot of her beginners' class. Suzie, Tiffany, Rhea, Eileen and the others had been captured as they practiced fourth position, each small face revealing both intensity and something of the girl's individual character.

"Jamie took them," Melanie said. "I got the frames. Do you like them?"

"The best present I could have." Chris kissed her on the cheek.

"This is amazing," Kerry agreed. "Thank you, Melanie. And please thank Jamie for me, too."

"Your turn," Chris said.

Melanie selected the smallest gift first, which was Kerry's present. The jeweler's box revealed a delicate pair of opal earrings in a flower pattern.

"I love them!" Melanie removed the gold balls she'd been wearing and inserted the new earrings. "Thank you, Kerry!"

After exclaiming over a hand-knit sweater from Chris,

Melanie turned to the last present, also from her father. "I've been trying to guess what this is all week, and I'm completely at a loss."

"You need torture yourself no longer," he teased.

Hesitantly, as if almost reluctant to end the suspense, Melanie slipped off the ribbon and removed the paper. As with the other gifts, she folded the paper aside carefully with the bow.

The carrying case unzipped to reveal a video camera. Melanie lifted it out reverently. "Oh, Dad! Gosh, that was expensive. Are you sure you want me to have this?"

"I thought I might get around to taking some footage of you in action," Chris said. "Before you grow up and go away."

Melanie flung her arms around his neck. "Thank you, thank you, thank you!"

Reluctantly leaving the gifts behind, they went in to dinner together. Afterward, feeling stuffed, Kerry lounged back in her seat and closed her eyes. What a day this had been, the stuff dreams were made of....

"Dad?" Melanie said. "Could I go see Jamie? He's going to go crazy over this camera."

Kerry opened her eyes to see Chris frowning. "Honey, it's Christmas."

"I know, but we wanted to give each other presents, too," Melanie said. "Besides, I've never actually been to his apartment even though they just live a few blocks away, and—well, and I've got a gift for Suzie, too, and—"

"Why don't you wait till tonight?" Chris said. "His family might want some time alone together, too."

Melanie's mouth tightened. "Oh, come on. It's the middle of the afternoon. I don't have to spend all day here, do I?"

"You make it sound like a chore."

Kerry sat perfectly still, hating to witness this family quarrel.

"No, it's not a chore, Dad, but I've got my own life, too.

What's wrong with my spending part of Christmas with Jamie?"

His eyes narrowed, as if he wanted to make a sharp retort, but fortunately he bit it back. "Go on, then. But don't stay too long, all right?"

"Thanks." Melanie hopped up and darted into the living room. A few minutes later, video camera and gifts in hand, she vanished out the front door.

"I hate this," Chris muttered.

"Having to share her?" Kerry began stacking dishes from where she sat.

"The whole business. This kid who looks like a juvenile delinquent, the way he monopolizes her time. But I suppose I'm just another jealous father." Chris spread his hands help-lessly. "What do you think?"

"That it's a tough adjustment for both of you," Kerry said. "And that you'll work it out."

"Spoken like a true diplomat." He helped carry dishes into the kitchen. "Let's have some wine."

They settled with their glasses in front of the fireplace, where Chris had built a roaring blaze. For once, the weather outside was nippy enough to need the warmth. Kerry had heard of southern Californians who turned on their air conditioning so they could build a fire, which she considered an incredible waste of energy.

"What are you thinking?" Chris laid his arm along the sofa, brushing Kerry's shoulders.

"About the environment and wasted energy." Kerry smiled self-consciously. "Isn't that romantic?"

"I have nothing against wasting energy, if it's in a good cause." He tilted his head against hers and nuzzled her gently.

"I wouldn't call that wasted energy." It felt completely natural to turn toward him, to let their lips meet. Chris's arm tightened around her shoulders, drawing her closer.

Her mind felt hazy and relaxed. In amazed detachment, Kerry realized her habitual tension had seeped away, leaving her open to the delicious sensation of his mouth exploring hers.

He pulled away and regarded her. "The firelight does wonderful things to your skin. There are so many facets to you, Kerry, like a precious jewel."

And to him, too, she thought. She knew how stern his face could look, but right now it was all tenderness. His brown eyes had the luster of forested glades, layer upon layer of depth drawing her in.

Shyly, she reached up to touch Chris's face, tracing his mouth, his mustache, the curve of his ear. In some ways she knew him so well, but this physical closeness was new to them both. They were entering strange, perhaps alien, territory and yet she had no desire to pull back.

When Chris drew her to him again, Kerry had no awareness but of his hard chest against her soft breasts, his tongue probing her mouth, his passion rousing an answer in her body.

The fire's warmth played over them as they tasted each other, gradually drawing away the clothing that had begun to feel unnecessary and intrusive.

Kerry wanted everything Chris could give, wanted to know him intensely and be part of him even if only for a short time. Even if they couldn't share the same dreams or the same future.

Nothing had prepared her for the fire that raged through her skin and veins all the way down to the core when he united them. Kerry let it consume her, raging freely until all defenses and all thought had burned away to the mellow shimmer of embers on the hearth.

They lay in silence for a while before she said, "A penny for your thoughts."

He shifted position, wrapping his arms around her. "I didn't expect that."

"Neither did I."

"Not just that it happened but that it would be so different from anything I'd experienced before." He stared into the fireplace. "Kerry, I don't know where this is going to take us."

"I wasn't expecting instant commitment," she murmured. "From either of us."

"If I had my way…" His voice trailed off, then resumed. "Well, I don't. The timing—I don't think either of us is ready to cast our tomorrows in concrete."

Part of her wanted to protest that they should be together from now on. But was that really what she wanted? What about dancing, choreographing? What about Melanie's delicate balance as she struggled for independence?

They needed time together to see whether their two worlds might blend, to make sure they hadn't been sucked too quickly into a liaison that was more smoke than flames.

"Play it by ear?" she said.

He planted a kiss on her eyelid. "I suppose we have to. Damn it, I'm not a patient man."

"You don't think Melanie will be back anytime soon, do you?" she whispered.

"She'd better not be," he said, and began caressing her all over again.

"MORE HOT CHOCOLATE?" Mrs. Ezell asked.

"Oh, yes, thank you. It's delicious." Melanie felt a little awkward, sitting here in the middle of another family's Christmas.

Although her own house was no mansion, she could understand why Jamie hadn't been eager to show her his home. The apartment was small, with only one bedroom, which Suzie and her mother shared while Jamie slept on the couch. The paint on the outside of the building was peeling, the exterior stairs creaked, and here inside everything looked clean but shabby.

The furniture wasn't even as nice as the stuff her father had just given to Goodwill.

The tree, decorated with mismatched ornaments and paper angels obviously made in Suzie's Sunday school class, had a scraggly, wistful air. But it was the love that counted, she reminded herself fiercely.

Jamie angled himself across a worn armchair, reading the instructions to the video camera. From the moment she'd walked in, that was all he'd noticed.

Melanie felt a little hurt that he hadn't paid more attention to the Photographers Do It in the Dark sweatshirt she'd bought him. Still, Suzie had more than made up for it in her enthusiasm over her new ballet slippers.

As Mrs. Ezell returned from the kitchen, her daughter nearly bounced right into her. "Sorry, Mom!" Suzie pirouetted away. "Oh, Melanie, they look terrific!" She'd run off to put on her tutu, just so they could witness the effect.

"Yes, they do. That was very generous of Melanie." Mrs. Ezell handed her the hot chocolate. "I don't know if I ever thanked you for helping decorate the costume."

"It was my pleasure," Melanie said. "I wish I had a sister of my own."

When Jamie looked up, he hardly seemed to notice she was there. "Could I borrow this?"

"I guess so," Melanie said. "Although my dad may not like it. But it's mine, after all."

"Jamie, Melanie just got the camera," his mother cautioned. "Maybe she'd like to use it first, don't you think?"

Jamie waved the objection away. "I hadn't figured out what to get you for Christmas, Mel, and this gives me an idea. I'll make a video of you dancing. I can use the lights my mom gave me, the ones that used to be my uncle's. Your dad ought to like that, right?"

"Sure." She felt better. It was sometimes touchy being around Jamie, trying to guess his moods, wondering if he resented the fact that she hadn't let him do more than kiss her. Once he got behind a camera, though, everything changed. The way he studied her made Melanie feel beautiful and special.

"There is something else I'd like to shoot, too," he said. "Kind of a public service project. Okay?"

"Fine." Melanie could see from his expression that he didn't want to go into detail. She wished he would share more with her. Sometimes when they were together it felt as if they could read each other's minds, and then at other times he acted as if he lived on a different planet. "Want to shoot some scenes right now? Of your family?"

Mrs. Ezell's usual worried frown gave way to a smile. "What a lovely idea."

It took only a few minutes for Jamie to get the hang of using the camera and set up his new floodlights. He directed Melanie and Suzie to rehearse a few ballet steps, then shot his mother cutting the apple pie in the kitchen.

"I'm not sure I got the angle of the light right," Jamie grumbled when he was done. "It probably won't look like much."

"We'll have to get a new computer so we can watch it," Mrs. Ezell said. "My old one broke and I haven't replaced it."

"We can watch on my laptop," Jamie said.

"I wish I had one," Suzie muttered.

Her mother bit her lip. Obviously, the budget wasn't likely to stretch that far.

Jamie looked up from tucking the camera into its case. "I've been saving up. I'll buy you one for your next birthday."

"Thanks, Jamie." Suzie gave him a hug.

Melanie wished her father was here. He had such rotten ideas about Jamie. Couldn't he see that Jamie was like any teenager, mixed up at times and kind of a loner, too, but that his heart was in the right place?

He glanced up and she caught her breath. The way he

looked at her was so full of—did she dare use an adult word like passion? A kind of deep hunger that echoed through her bones. How could one boy be so changeable?

He set the camera down. "Okay if Mel and I go for a walk?"

"Sure," his mother said. "We'll save the pie till you get back." Mrs. Ezell didn't make the least bit of fuss. Melanie wished her father would be as understanding.

She and Jamie went out together. The day was still cool and overcast.

"I figured we needed to be alone," Jamie said. "For a little while."

Melanie waited for him to say more, but he didn't, so they walked along in silence.

They hadn't gone far when a beat-up car slowed at the curb.

"Hey! Jamie!" It was his friend Russ, a red-haired boy who looked like a friendly sprite at first glance. Unfortunately, after meeting him a couple of times, Melanie had realized the engaging appearance masked deep-seated hostility and resentment toward the world at large.

"You guys need a ride?" It was Jerry, sitting in the back seat with Phil. The three of them were Jamie's closest friends, although she couldn't understand why. None of them had the sensitivity that hid beneath Jamie's brooding surface.

"Okay." Jamie started forward when Melanie caught his arm. "What's the matter?"

"I—my dad's expecting me back," she said.

He paused. "Already? Yeah, well, I guess you'd rather spend Christmas with Daddy the cop than with a bunch of good-for-nothings like us."

Her temper flared. "Oh? For your information, it wasn't easy getting away! And then you didn't even bother to get me a Christmas present yet. I guess you're the one who wasn't too eager to see me."

He frowned, then waved at his friends. "Some other time," he called. "My mom's got apple pie waiting."

"See ya around!" Russ gunned the engine and the boys hooted as they drove off.

"You don't like them," Jamie observed as they walked back toward the apartment. "Why not?"

Melanie shrugged, hating to criticize his friends. "I just don't. They're not like you, Jamie."

"Maybe you're seeing stuff in me that doesn't exist." He adjusted his loping stride so she could keep up.

"I don't think so. You're special." Heading in this direction, the breeze stung Melanie's cheeks. "You're talented and you get things done. People can rely on you. And you can be really generous, like offering to buy your sister that laptop."

"And?" he teased. "What about sexy?"

"Well, sure." She shifted the weight of her purse against her shoulder, wishing he hadn't brought that subject up.

"I'm not pushing you," he said. "You're only fifteen."

"I'll be sixteen in March." She didn't like feeling like a kid. "Only—I'm not ready. It's too scary, Jamie."

"I'm ready," he said. "But I wouldn't want anything bad to happen to you. I don't want to hurt you, Melanie. I've never met anyone like you and—oh, hell, let's go get some of that pie."

"Sounds good to me," she said as they turned into the apartment building.

TONY HAD TAKEN OVER one of his own Italian restaurants for the wedding. Designed like a Pompeiian villa with pillars and a sunken interior courtyard, the facility had been transformed by thousands of tropical flowers, ferns, hanging plants and even brilliantly plumed parrots perched here and there in the lushness.

"It doesn't feel like New Year's Eve," Kerry said as they

made their way down the courtyard aisle between rows of chairs set up for the occasion. "More like midsummer."

"Tony likes to do things right." Chris waited while she took a seat, then waved half-heartedly to some acquaintances sitting farther up.

Kerry studied the altar set in front. Draped with a richly woven cloth in an exotic paisley pattern, it was surrounded by sprays of calla lilies and birds of paradise. "They must be going to the equator for their honeymoon."

"I hear he's leased a private island in the Caribbean." Beside her, Chris adjusted the bow tie of his rented tux. "Not bad for a kid who used to earn his lunch money working at a taco stand."

"He and Leila certainly have good taste." Gazing around, Kerry flashed back seven years to when she'd dreamed of her own wedding. George would have insisted on something much more traditional, of course. A New York ballroom, lots of roses and baby's breath, ballet dancers mingling with musicians and society patrons.

Funny, she hadn't thought of that for years. Even immediately afterward, during the darkest days of pain and loss, she hadn't wasted any time regretting the wedding. Now, looking back, she felt only relief.

People slid in beside them, and in the front a trio began to play music to a soft Latin beat. "I hope the bride isn't going to conga down the aisle," Kerry murmured.

Chris flashed her a grin and took her hand.

This past week had been special, even though they hadn't been able to spend much time together. With the Romeo and Juliet opening fast approaching, Kerry spent most evenings in rehearsal. And the detective bureau stayed busy investigating holiday burglaries and robberies, shoplifting and mischief indulged in by kids out of school, so that Chris's desk was loaded with paperwork.

Still, they'd managed a couple of dinners together and one stolen evening of lovemaking at Kerry's house.

Studying the man beside her, she wondered how you could know someone so intimately and yet still feel shut out of his inner life. Chris opened to her only in bits and pieces, holding so much inside. But then, didn't she do the same, as well?

Noticing her gaze, he turned to face her and cocked an eyebrow questioningly. "Is my tie crooked?" He tugged at the bow on the rented tux.

"Just admiring your chiseled good looks," she teased softly.

A rustle around them alerted Kerry that Tony and his brother, serving as best man, had entered and were standing by the altar. At the same time, a woman in a colorful print sarong swayed down the aisle, followed by a little girl strewing the floor with rose petals.

"Leila's sister and her niece," Chris whispered.

The music changed, and through the Latin rhythm, she heard the strains of "Here Comes the Bride." Craning her neck, Kerry spotted Leila's tall, elegant figure marching with measured step toward the altar.

She wore a stunningly original dress of white silk slashed from shoulder to waist by an inset made of the same bright print fabric her bridesmaid wore. It looped around her slender waist and then flittered scarflike over the floor-length skirt. There was a gasp of indrawn breath from the crowd, and Kerry suspected that under other circumstances the gown might have been greeted with applause.

With regal decorum, Leila joined Tony at the altar and they exchanged broad smiles. They reminded Kerry of happy children indulging in a long-cherished fantasy.

As the minister began the service, she yielded to a moment of intense envy. Tonight, in splendor and undimmed happiness, Leila and Tony were making their dreams come true.

If it could happen for them, maybe it could happen for Kerry, as well. Maybe.

Except that, sitting so close to Chris and already hungering to be alone with him, she was no longer so sure what her dreams were.

CHAPTER ELEVEN

"WHY THE HELL DID HE have to go and do that?" Chris glared at the newspaper.

"Something up?" Daryl Rogers paused in the office doorway, his latest reports in hand.

Chris pointed to a photograph on the third page. "Our friend Professor Ahmed has gone and given another speech."

"Maybe he figures things have died down enough." Daryl's mouth twisted in concern. He knew as well as Chris that not enough time had passed for anyone to feel safe.

"You'd almost think he wants his wife and daughters harassed." Chris eyed the article glumly.

"What did he say, anyway?"

"Just more assessments of the Middle East situation." Chris had to admit that nothing in the article would stir controversy. But they were dealing with some kind of nuts here, maybe skinheads or other troublemakers who wouldn't need much provocation to resume their attacks.

"Think we ought to warn him to keep his mouth shut?" Daryl tossed the reports onto Chris's desk.

"What? And violate his First Amendment rights?" Chris snorted. "Then somebody's sure to make the police department out to be the bad guys. We'll just have to wait and see what happens."

"Good luck." Daryl wandered out. As the robbery-homicide sergeant, he had plenty of his own work to do. Their hold-up maniac and his girlfriend had hit two liquor stores the first weekend in January. Gunfire at one location had left a clerk seriously wounded.

If only they could catch those guys before somebody died.

Chris rubbed the back of his neck. Tonight was the opening of Romeo and Juliet and he was looking forward to seeing Kerry, even though he suspected she'd be busy backstage most of the evening. He was escorting Melanie, a rare evening together for the two of them.

Damn, she'd practically handed that video camera over to her boyfriend. Chris hadn't gone out and spent all that money to give Jamie a present, yet Melanie had a right to dispose of her property as she wished. The whole situation infuriated him.

He'd have to keep his temper under control somehow. His relationship with his daughter was too important to jeopardize, and he had a feeling these next few months would prove very trying indeed.

THE OLD THEATER in Fullerton had once housed vaudeville, then shown movies for nearly half a century. Now, as the whine of electric saws and the thump of hammers from backstage attested, it was being converted into a home for Alfonso's company.

Kerry propped her feet on the back of the next row and watched the dancers move through their class. They weren't in rehearsals yet and the practice rooms were torn up by carpenters, so the stage was their only place to work out.

Even in leotards and leg warmers, these were clearly superior dancers. Much as she'd enjoyed working with her cast from Romeo and Juliet, much as she looked forward to tonight's opening, Kerry couldn't help noting the difference.

Especially Larisa. She moved with such authority and grace, every line complete, every turn of the head deliberate.

The other dancers weren't quite so stellar but they had the polish and poise that came from experience with a serious ballet company.

What on earth was she going to do? She still hadn't come up with even a glimmer of an idea for a new dance. True, she hadn't said yes yet, but she knew that even if Alfonso wanted to hire another choreographer, he couldn't afford to.

Besides, he didn't need some mediocre work cranked out by a choreographer more interested in the next TV variety special. He needed something spectacular to make the critics sit up and take notice.

The class was over. The performers bowed to Alfonso and wandered off, except for Larisa.

She waited quietly until the theater was empty. Guiltily, Kerry realized she hadn't been noticed here in the back, but she waited to see what would happen.

Larisa rose on point, struck an attitude, then burst into a series of pirouettes across the stage. She wasn't so much dancing as exploding with energy and the love of movement.

Every muscle in Kerry's body responded with the desire to join in. She could feel herself lifting away from the pain, becoming airborne and free, flying through time to a realm where fantasy blended with reality. When Larisa leaped through the air, so did Kerry.

The realities of everyday life fell away from her. Here in the kingdom of the dance, she could move among myths and magic; she could be a swan or a doll brought to life or an ice queen. Anything was possible.

The stage filled with ghostly dancers, an exotic medley in strange costumes. Biblical figures, cats and spirits sniffed around one another, snarling and pouncing and then bounding away.

Music. There must be an orchestra hiding somewhere, because Kerry could hear it clearly. Wonderful swelling music with a modern beat driving its unabashed emotionalism. And then a parting of the chords to reveal a piercingly melancholy tune, slow and haunting.

Larisa danced on, her outburst of energy channeled now into a delicate adagio.

What was this tune running through Kerry's mind? Who were the costumed dancers she'd just imagined?

She closed her eyes and listened to the melody play. Moonlight, no, midnight, something about midnight...

She jerked upright. It was Andrew Lloyd Webber's music she'd been hearing, the theme from Cats. And those people—she could identify them now. Characters from Jesus Christ Superstar and Joseph and the Amazing Technicolor Dreamcoat, Phantom of the Opera and even Evita.

They represented the spirit of the dance, the blending of myth and history and reality. Creatures spilling out of their creative boundaries and taking on a life of their own.

Larisa had slipped from the stage. Looking around, dazed, Kerry realized she was alone in the theater. But not alone at all! She could still see those dancers, her dancers, a cat flirting with a pharaoh, a twisted phantom executing a duet with Evita Perón.

She had it!

Out in the lobby, where the bare floor sported traces of sawdust, she found Alfonso drinking a cup of coffee and reading today's edition of Variety.

"I just had an idea," Kerry said. "I think it'll work."

When he glanced up, Alfonso's face was blank. Then understanding dawned. "You'll do it, then?"

"I'll do it," Kerry said, and couldn't wait to start.

CHRIS HAD NEVER BEEN a big fan of Shakespeare. Actually, the only productions he'd seen were on television, tedious affairs with heavily costumed actors who spoke in gobbledygook.

This Romeo and Juliet was different. He couldn't quite put

his finger on what made it so fresh and so touching. Maybe the sincerity of the actors, or the way they used their bodies to mime out their meaning so the archaic language became understandable. Perhaps it was because the whole production had been set in the 1920s, an era he could appreciate better than the Renaissance.

Beside him, Melanie's fingers drummed restlessly on the arm of her seat. What was wrong with her? Usually she loved any sort of cultural event.

Perhaps she was just waiting for the ballroom scene. Chris hoped it wasn't anything more than that. He was tired of her preoccupation with Jamie, tired of seeing the boy's hostile face confronting him in his own living room.

The dance scene started.

Almost at once, the audience broke into applause, aroused by the energy of the music and the verve of the performers. Every twist of the Charleston was greeted with cheers and clapping, and by the time the scene ended the entire theater had risen to its feet. Even Melanie joined wholeheartedly in the ovation.

But afterward she sank back into her distracted state, reacting only during the bedroom scene when Juliet pleaded with Romeo not to leave yet. Even Chris found himself affected by it.

His thoughts veered away from his daughter to his own tentative relationship with the first woman he'd cared about in years.

Why did it seem as if something were always pulling them apart? Why did their moments together feel stolen, surreptitious, as if they were defying some mysterious fate that wanted to separate them?

She wouldn't stay forever here in Brea, he knew. Not Kerry, with her dreams, her beauty, her sophistication. She belonged in the inner circles of creative artists, somewhere like New York. With a man who owned his own tuxedo and knew all about paintings and music and dance. Damn the man, whoever he was.

Finally the last sad scene was over. Applauding, Chris had to admit he'd enjoyed the performance more than he'd expected, at least when he'd been able to concentrate.

"Kerry said she'd meet us backstage," he reminded Melanie.

Wordlessly, she paced toward the back of the theater. Chris wanted to ply her with questions: Had she enjoyed the play? What had she done at school today? What was she thinking about? But he dreaded the annoyance that would flash across her face. He'd seen it too often these past weeks, as if he were a buzzing pest disrupting her train of thought.

What the hell was happening to his daughter? Wasn't there anything he could do to stop it?

The theater's cramped backstage spilled over with actors and visitors. It took close to ten minutes to make their way down the main hall to the dressing rooms.

"Kerry Guthrie?" he kept asking. Fingers would point, although not always in the same direction.

Finally he saw her, darting out of the women's changing room. She was wearing a midnight-blue jumpsuit. Her new curly hairstyle fell loose around her neck, damp at the edges, and her cheeks were flushed.

Melanie perked up momentarily. "Good going," she called to her teacher.

Kerry came to greet them, with a hug for each. "Did you think it went well? One of the dancers nearly missed her cue. Did you notice?"

"No." Chris felt rather stupid. To him, the performance had looked perfect.

"Good." She beamed at them both. "There's a cast party in half an hour at the pizza place next door. You're both invited."

As Chris was accepting, Melanie said, "I can't. I'm meeting Jamie."

"You're what?"

"You heard me, Dad."

He wasn't sure which upset him most, the rudeness of her response or the fact that, without consulting him, she'd set up a late-night date. "Now, look here—"

"No, you look," she snapped. "I wanted to see Kerry's production. That's the only reason I came. I don't see why I have to hang around any longer."

"Excuse us," Chris told Kerry. "Would you?"

Troubled, she nodded and pointed out a convenient exit.

In the parking lot, Chris confronted his daughter. "I haven't objected to your seeing so much of Jamie—"

"Oh, yes, you have. Every time he comes over you glare at him as if he were some form of insect. His mother doesn't treat me that way!"

"Don't change the subject." He didn't want to let the argument slip away from him. "We're talking about your making a date at eleven o'clock on a Friday night without consulting me."

"So?" Melanie challenged. "What do you think we do, go roll around in the bushes? Don't you trust me, Dad?"

"Of course I do." But did he? "It's Jamie I'm not sure I trust."

"He thinks I'm special. He'd never do anything to hurt me."

"Not intentionally, maybe." Chris wished he could be sure of that. "What do you do at this hour, anyway?"

"Talk," Melanie said. "What do you and Kerry do?"

Chris had to fight off the instinct to tell her it was none of her business. "Kerry and I are adults."

"So Jamie and I don't have any rights because we're kids?" He could see now that the resentment must have been building up for a long time. Whatever had he done to deserve it? Was it wrong to worry about your only daughter?

"Of course you have rights, but I have the responsibility of making sure you're safe," he said as calmly as he could manage. "It isn't easy, Melanie."

"First you wouldn't let me go to New York because I didn't have enough normal teenage experience. Now I'm getting it, and you don't like that, either," Melanie pressed on. "I'm tired of having you breathing down my neck all the time."

"Compared to a lot of parents—"

"Oh, save it, Dad!" To his surprise, he saw tears in her eyes. From frustration? Disappointment? Yet he'd been trying his best not to stifle her these past months.

"Melanie, I don't understand—"

"There's Jamie!" With a cry of relief, she took off across the parking lot, not even pausing for a backward wave.

Chris stood by the exit door feeling like a fool. He didn't see how he could have lived with Melanie all this time and not even suspected the angry feelings boiling beneath the surface.

And what the hell was he supposed to do, abdicate his authority over her? Tell her to go amuse herself at all hours with a boy who would probably abandon her if she ever got into trouble?

Stalking back into the theater, he tried to get his emotions under control. Fortunately, when he spotted Kerry, she was engrossed in conversation with a couple of her dancers and only acknowledged him with a wave.

They walked over to the pizza parlor together, Kerry bubbling with high spirits. Chris kept his mouth shut, not wanting to dampen her evening.

"I'm really nattering away, aren't I?" she said as they walked into the restaurant. "Something special happened to me today."

He focused on her for the first time, realizing that her

enthusiasm came from more than the success of Romeo and Juliet. "Oh?"

"I was watching Alfonso's company work out, and I got this tremendous idea for a ballet," she said. "After all the agonizing I've done, there it was, practically playing itself out in front of me."

Chris tried to imagine how that could happen, but he couldn't. "The only thing I ever saw playing itself out in front of me was a crime scene."

Her free, unabashed laughter soothed some of the turmoil in his heart. "You have such a way of putting things into perspective."

As they waited at the corner to order pizza, he said, "I wish I could be inside your head, just for an hour or two. So I could understand how things look to you."

Intrigued, she reflected for a moment. "And if I could see through your eyes for one day, think how much better I'd understand you, too."

And if he could see from Melanie's point of view, would it all make sense? Would he then be able to restore the happy companionship they'd shared all these years?

A group of theater people made way for them at a long table as they approached with their soft drinks, and there was no more chance that night for intimate conversation. By the time the party broke up at one o'clock, they were both too exhausted to do more than kiss good-night and drive home in their separate cars.

It was nearly two when Melanie came in. Chris, reading a newsmagazine in bed, stifled the impulse to call out and ask where she'd been.

He didn't suppose she'd tell him, anyway.

Listening to the familiar sounds of his daughter in the bathroom and realizing that he hardly knew her anymore, Chris could see that something had to give.

They couldn't go on this way, sniping at each other, both

feeling wounded and misunderstood. Some people might recommend therapy, but he suspected Melanie would resent the idea, and he didn't particularly like it himself. He'd always felt that he ought to solve his own problems.

Which left—what?

Right now, he reflected glumly, he was beginning to wish he'd given Melanie permission to go to New York. Not that she would have left yet, but with that destination fixed in mind, maybe she wouldn't have been so eager to take up with Jamie.

Maybe she was right. Maybe she deserved more trust, more independence than he'd been willing to allow.

The solution that came to him made Chris drop his magazine heedlessly onto the floor.

If Melanie moved in with Kerry for a while, it would remove the immediate conflict. He would also have a chance to see how well she functioned without his direct supervision, since that had been his main concern about letting her trek off to the other coast.

Kerry, of course, would make an excellent chaperon, and the two were already friends. Melanie would even have a ride to and from the studio when she needed it.

He knew that, even if it was only for a few weeks, he would miss his daughter terribly. But she wouldn't be far away. And he could keep track of her.

Mulling over the idea, he finally admitted to himself what scared him most about his changed relationship with his daughter: the possibility that if she became infuriated enough, Melanie might decide to run off with Jamie. It wasn't something he would ever, in the past, have thought his daughter capable of, but these days he couldn't be sure.

Surely she would recognize that letting her stay with Kerry was a sign of trust. Maybe it would even revive her interest in going to New York next summer.

Chris leaned back against the pillows. For years he'd never

questioned that he was capable of raising a daughter properly, at least doing a better job than Lou could have done. Now he wondered. Perhaps a woman would understand her in ways he couldn't.

He only hoped Kerry would agree.

CHAPTER TWELVE

KERRY GAZED AROUND her living room in dismay. She understood that Chris was letting Melanie do everything her own way, from packing to moving, but the place looked as if a hurricane had hit it.

Melanie's idea of packing revolved around the toss-and-carry method—toss her clothes into Jamie's car and carry them into the house.

Cosmetics and beauty aids had been thrown carelessly into one suitcase. The only thing that kept them from rattling and breaking was a large plastic cleaner's bag full of air that Melanie had wedged inside to take up the extra space.

To complicate matters, Melanie acted as if she were moving in permanently. She'd brought along every ratty old stuffed animal she possessed, along with yellowing stacks of dance magazines, a complete collection of Nancy Drew mysteries and a huge, cracked beanbag chair that wouldn't fit in her bedroom and looked atrocious with Kerry's antique-style furniture.

Kerry sighed. Well, she had promised Chris to take his daughter for a month, and she did like Melanie. It was just that she'd grown used to her orderly, solitary existence, and now it was being invaded.

As she stood there trying to figure out how to persuade Melanie to put the beanbag chair in the garage, Jamie panted in under the burden of a large box marked "Costumes."

"She's only going to be here for a month," Kerry couldn't help remarking.

The boy peered sweatily from beneath the load. "I know. The chick's gone crazy."

Those were more consecutive words than Jamie had addressed to her in all the months she'd known him. "I guess she likes to have her things around her," Kerry said.

Melanie staggered in, toting a huge, drooping fern. "Where can I put this?"

"How about the backyard?" Kerry said. "The light in here is murder on plants."

"The backyard?" Melanie shifted the heavy plant awkwardly to one hip. "Put Audrey II in the backyard?"

Kerry eyed the fern. It didn't look like its man-eating namesake from Little Shop of Horrors. "If you don't, you'll have to buy Audrey III pretty quick."

"Oh, all right," the girl grumbled, and staggered out, leaving a drift of potting soil on the carpet.

By the time everything had been stashed away, it was nearly dinnertime. "Here." Kerry hauled her aging vacuum cleaner from the closet. "You hit the living room while I make dinner, okay?"

Melanie made no move to take the vacuum. "I didn't realize you expected me to be the cleaning lady."

Jamie poked his head out of the kitchen, a soda can in hand. "Are you kidding? Look at the mess we made."

Angrily, Melanie kicked at a torn page that had fallen from one of her magazines. "We don't have to clean it up now. I'm hungry."

"Ground rules." Kerry felt as if she were walking on eggs, but she couldn't let herself be intimidated. "I'm glad you're here, Melanie, and I can tolerate a certain level of mess, but I don't want my stuff damaged. That dirt is going to get ground into the carpet if it isn't vacuumed now, and I didn't sign up to be your cleaning lady, either."

"You're not my mother," Melanie snapped.

Even allowing for the fact that Melanie had had an exhausting day, Kerry realized this wasn't an auspicious start. "That's right," she said. "I'm your landlady. If I was your mother, I might give you a break. But you want to be treated like an adult, so I'm treating you like one."

Melanie's mouth was already open to protest when Jamie intervened. "I'll run the vacuum." He thumped his can onto the counter.

"It's not your problem," Melanie said.

"Then quit acting like a baby and clean up after yourself."

The girl glared at him and stalked away to her new bedroom, slamming the door for good measure.

"Whew," Kerry said. "I guess adolescence has hit like a bolt of lightning. I've never seen Melanie like this."

"Me, neither." He sagged against the counter.

"Of course, she is tired." Kerry's back and shoulders hurt, too; she'd spent last night moving things out of the spare bedroom.

"That's no excuse."

His attitude surprised her. "Maybe she's more upset than she lets on about moving out of her own home," Kerry suggested.

"That doesn't mean she has to act like a spoiled brat." Jamie picked up a sponge and wiped some soda he'd spilled on the tile surface. "I don't much like her dad—I guess because he doesn't like me—but he's being cool about this. And I don't like to see her dumping on you. After all, it is your house."

She tried not to show her amazement. Why shouldn't Jamie be a responsible young man, after all? His mother and sister were both people Kerry respected. Still, his words hardly went with his punk clothing and usually sullen air.

Kerry pulled out a pot to boil water for spaghetti. "I care a lot about Melanie. She's a sweet girl and potentially a distinguished ballerina. I suppose as a teacher that really excites me."

"She sure knows how to dance," Jamie agreed.

"Still, she has a lot to learn." Kerry opened a jar of sauce and dumped it into a pan. "Ballet is a difficult and demanding profession. You're always trying to perfect your craft and never quite succeeding. It takes an incredible amount of dedication."

"Whatever it takes, Mel has it."

Hesitantly, Kerry broached a subject that had been bothering her. "I agree, except that lately she hasn't been quite as focused on dance as she used to be. Not that having other interests isn't healthy. But—"

He didn't wait for her to finish. "Ms. Guthrie, maybe you think I want to turn Melanie into some kind of bimbette. Sure, we have a good time, but I think her dancing is, well, as important as my photography. Maybe more, because she's got real talent."

"So do you." Kerry didn't have to feign sincerity.

"Maybe." He shrugged. "Anyway, I don't think anything could ever replace ballet for her. And I wouldn't want it to."

There was a click from the back bedroom and Melanie emerged. "I'm sorry," she said. "I'm real cranky today and I shouldn't have taken it out on you guys."

"It never happened," Kerry said.

A short time later the carpet was pristine again and they were sitting down to a hasty dinner of spaghetti and salad. "This is great," Melanie said. "Honestly, Kerry, I can't tell you how grateful I am."

"Speaking of ground rules," Jamie said, "what are yours? Regarding me, I mean."

Kerry thought for a minute. "I'm responsible for Melanie, so I need to know when she goes out, roughly where she'll be and when she expects to be home."

To her relief, her new roommate made no protest. "I guess that's fair."

"Jamie, you're welcome to visit here, but I'd appreciate it

if you two wouldn't go in the bedroom and close the door. It would put me in an awkward position," Kerry said.

"Okay." He nodded.

"And—just generally, I know you're both good kids, and I hope you'll remember that anything you do reflects on me."

Melanie reached across the table and touched Kerry's wrist. "Honest, I'm sorry I blew up a few minutes ago. You're really putting yourself out for me, and I appreciate it."

Kerry smiled. "I think we're going to have fun."

"Yeah." Melanie beamed back at her, and even Jamie grinned.

It was almost like having a family. All these years Kerry hadn't minded living alone, but she hadn't realized how much she missed having friends around, either.

She was glad she'd agreed to Chris's idea, not just for his and Melanie's sakes but for her own.

"SHE ACTUALLY BACKED DOWN?" Chris dropped a basket of potato chips on the coffee table and sat down beside Kerry. "Good. I was right, having her stay with you. She'd never back down with me."

"That's because I don't have to put up with her temper, and you do." Kerry felt a little guilty, almost as if she were talking behind Melanie's back, yet there was no reason why she shouldn't have accepted Chris's invitation to drop by tonight.

It was Friday, and Melanie and Jamie had gone out, as usual. To Kerry's relief, the first week had gone smoothly. Melanie hadn't even objected one evening when Kerry suggested she stay home and complete her math assignment instead of running around with Jamie.

"I wish I understood her." Chris closed his eyes for a moment. He'd had a hard week, Kerry knew; on top of his usual burden of crime reports, someone had thrown red paint at the Ahmeds' house, although most of it splattered onto the driveway and lawn. "Maybe if she had a mother…"

"That's hardly your fault," Kerry said. "Besides, girls and their moms are notorious for feuding during adolescence."

"Did you?"

Kerry curled up, her knee brushing against Chris's leg. "I was hardly a typical teenager. And my mom—no, we weren't that close. I never would have argued. I was too eager to please her. I kept waiting for the praise as I got better and better as a dancer."

"She never complimented you?" He ran his hand over her foot, massaging the arch lightly.

"Well…" Kerry tried to remember. "I know she was pleased at my success. She did say things like, 'Your teachers say you're doing quite well,' and 'Mr. Carrera tells me you're one of the youngest dancers ever asked to join the company.' But it was all external. All based on what other people said."

"She never took you in her arms and told you she was proud of you?" He rubbed her calf, finding the knots of tension and easing them away.

Kerry shook her head. "Anyway, we never fought."

"But you weren't close, either."

"Melanie doesn't know what she's throwing away." Kerry blinked at sudden, unexpected tears. "A dad who loves her as much as you do."

"We each love in our own way," he said sadly. "And we each perceive love in our own way, too. To Melanie, what I offer is like a leash around her neck. Thank you, Kerry, for helping us."

She rested her cheek against his shoulder. He felt warm and solid.

It was odd that with Chris she felt the kind of security and acceptance she'd always yearned for. Why couldn't she simply forget her nagging, perhaps impossible, ambitions and let herself love him?

Silence hummed between them, full of unspoken thoughts. She picked up his pain, as intense as her own, his own longing for peace with his daughter and for something more. For Kerry?

She lifted one hand to touch his cheek. "Why can't things ever be easy?"

"Because we're so awfully hard on ourselves." He smiled. "We want so much." Their lips met gently. His hand cupped the back of her head, ruffling her hair. After a moment, he whispered, "Speaking of wanting…"

"You, too?" she murmured.

The rest of the evening was remarkably uncomplicated.

KERRY HAD TO DODGE the workmen installing carpet in Alfonso's lobby as she made her way into the theater.

"How'd it go?" Alfonso stopped her just inside.

"Great." Kerry had spent the past two hours meeting with a designer. "He knows where he can borrow a lot of the costumes. They'll just need some refurbishing."

"Good going." Alfonso wiped his face. Although it was only the end of February, southern California was suffering one of its periodic heat waves and the theater's air conditioning hadn't been installed yet. "I hate having to pinch pennies, but that's the reality of it."

"We need to set up a rehearsal schedule." Kerry walked down the aisle with him. Dancers were assembling onstage for class, many of them warming up at a makeshift barre. "You know, we could arrange for you to use one of our studios occasionally."

"Thanks." Alfonso brushed a lock of silvering black hair off his forehead. "Fortunately, our own rooms upstairs should be finished in a week. Now, rehearsals. Can we discuss that later?" He indicated the waiting dancers. "While you're here, want to work out with us?"

"Sure. Just give me a minute." Backstage, Kerry stripped

down to the leotard she still wore from teaching her morning classes and added a pair of ballet slippers from her oversize bag.

Joining the other dancers onstage, she felt a moment's shyness. Although she'd kept in shape, it was a long time since she'd worked out with a real ballet company.

"Positions, please," Alfonso said.

Soon they were working their way through a series of warm-up moves, then leaping in turn across the stage while Alfonso critiqued them.

Next to Kerry, Larisa—after a friendly hello—was all business, concentrating fiercely on every move. It struck Kerry that she herself could relax and enjoy the class, but the younger woman had no time for pleasure. When the company debuted in June, she would be center stage for the critics to attack if her performance was less than flawless.

After some initial stiffness, Kerry was surprised to find that much of her technique came back. She couldn't leap quite as high or turn as fast as in the old days, but she possessed the poise and confidence that as a young girl she'd often had to feign.

The most surprising thing, she discovered as she joined the class in executing a series of steps demonstrated by Alfonso, was that the pain in her legs and hips didn't bother her very much.

Had it really lessened? Or was she simply less tense and therefore putting less stress on her body?

"Kerry." Alfonso beckoned her. Instinctively, from the turn of his body, she knew he wanted to try a lift they'd executed in their performance that splendid, horrible night of her accident. Was he testing her, wanting to see if she still had her nerve, or simply reliving a special moment they'd shared?

Without thinking, Kerry let her body take over. It remembered the steps, the precise angle at which to catapult into his grasp. As he swung her up, exhilaration flooded her veins.

Even while she instinctively completed her line with pointed toes and graceful arm gestures, her heart soared. This was what it felt like, flying, being in control of every muscle and at the same time stretching beyond herself into pure joy.

The class applauded. As Alfonso set her lightly on her feet, Kerry caught Larisa's expression. There was no resentment there, only deep study, as if she were trying to impress into her own muscles every move Kerry had made.

"You were wonderful," the ballerina said when class was over. "Are you sure you don't want to join the company?"

Now that the adrenaline had begun to ebb, ripples of pain ran up Kerry's thighs. "It still hurts too much, I'm afraid."

"But it's getting better?" Larisa asked. "Don't wait too long."

"I know." Kerry headed for the dressing room, her heart pounding faster than usual. She'd loved that moment of triumph, even though it left her limping.

The pain was getting better. And Larisa was right; at twenty-eight, Kerry didn't have much time to play around with.

Examining her freshly washed face in the mirror, she noticed the brightness of her eyes, glowing as if she'd just made love.

Made love. With a guilty rush, Kerry thought of Chris. What would it mean if she went back onstage? She could stay here with Alfonso's troupe, after all....

But she wouldn't. Deep down, she knew that she would never be satisfied with a comeback if it didn't involve New York. That one night she'd been on top in the ballet center of the world, and nothing less would do. Especially not when she had to pay for it in moments of sheer physical agony, and she knew that would be the price.

She wasn't ready to make a decision yet. Maybe after the company's opening in June. If Melanie still wanted to go east to audition, perhaps Kerry would go with her.

And never come back?

Brushing her hair so hard it stung her scalp, she pictured Chris, his face gentling as he gazed at her, his breath tickling across her skin. Their bodies locked together, finding a special world that only the two of them could inhabit.

Neither of them had made any commitment. Both were too much in transition to plan a future. She didn't exactly owe him anything, she supposed, but what was happening between them was hardly casual, either.

Something knotted hard in her chest. She wasn't ready to give Chris up. Would she be, when the time came?

"Kerry?" It was one of the other ballerinas. "Alfonso says he's ready to discuss that schedule now."

"Thanks." She hastily pulled on her clothes. "I'll be right there."

There were too many other things to think about at the moment. She could only hope that, one way or another, her decision would take care of itself.

KERRY RIFFLED ABSTRACTEDLY through the "Arts" section of the Sunday Los Angeles Times. None of the articles interested her today, perhaps because none of them concerned dance.

Or maybe she was distracted by the sunlight streaming in through the window. Or by the unaccustomed silence.

These past few weeks, Melanie and Jamie had taken to spending a lot of time here at Kerry's, cooking together and engaging her in conversation. She felt privileged to be included and was impressed with the genuine affection she could see growing between the two teenagers.

Still, they were only kids. Sometimes they snapped at each other, mainly because Melanie was growing possessive and Jamie insisted on reserving some time to spend with his friends. But generally they managed to work things out with a maturity Kerry admired.

Today, with money Jamie had earned from photographing

a bar mitzvah, the two had taken Suzie to Disneyland. Kerry had turned down an invitation to join them; standing in lines wasn't her favorite thing to do on her day off.

But she felt too restless to sit there reading a newspaper. She wanted something. No, someone.

Kerry picked up the phone and dialed Chris's number. He answered on the fourth ring, sounding vaguely annoyed.

"Yes?"

"Am I interrupting something?"

"Kerry." His tone mellowed. "I was afraid it was something at work."

"I just—" What exactly did she want? "I thought maybe I could make us a picnic lunch."

"Are you sure Melanie won't mind?" He visited his daughter frequently but only for a few minutes at a time, since she still seemed to resent his presence. Neither he nor Kerry—not even Jamie, as far as she could tell—understood why.

"They went to Disneyland."

"I just got out of the shower. I'll be there in, say, half an hour?"

"Perfect." Kerry couldn't help imagining how delicious he must look, still damp from the shower. And what would he be wearing, if anything? Maybe she should suggest he just throw on a bathrobe... "I'll make sandwiches."

"See you then."

Retrieving her picnic basket from the front closet, Kerry thanked her instincts for calling him. They'd had precious little time together since that night a week after Melanie moved in.

Kerry had spent many hours meeting with Alfonso and working out with his dancers, meanwhile observing them and stowing away mental notes that would help with her casting and choreography.

For his part, Chris put in more than his share of overtime between the still-elusive robbers and the Ahmeds. Last week, one of the little girls had left her favorite doll on the front porch; it vanished, only to reappear on the lawn a few days later, hog-tied and badly burned.

Who would do such a sick thing? According to Chris, the child had cried for hours. Worse than that was the psychological stress on the whole family.

Not to mention the fact that a civil rights group had picketed the police station, claiming the officers were dragging their feet on the investigation. What did they expect Chris to do, produce suspects out of thin air?

She was transferring pickles to a plastic bag when the bell rang. Had half an hour gone by already?

Rinsing the juice off her hands, Kerry headed for the door.

Chris stood squarely in the doorway, eyes seeking out hers, his hand reaching for her shoulders to draw her close. The physicality of him struck her like a strong wind.

Without a word, they locked in an embrace that rocked Kerry down to her sneakers. She'd missed him more than she'd realized, a thousand times more.

Now she wanted to make up for lost time, to taste and feel every part of him. Chris himself barely had the presence of mind to step inside and kick the door shut before he carried her into the bedroom.

They made love with pent-up passion, twisting the bed sheets into lumps and knocking pillows onto the floor. This, too, was a kind of flying, but instead of wanting to be in control, Kerry let herself go, burrowing into Chris and urging him on with her own overwhelming desire.

Afterward, they showered together. "It's a good thing I'm not water soluble," Chris teased as he lathered her back. "This is my second dunk of the morning."

"Something about a dripping mustache really gets me." Kerry kissed his upper lip, enjoying the tickle his mustache made against her mouth.

"Mmm." He slid his arms around her slick body. "Maybe we could eat that picnic in bed."

"I hate crumbs," she murmured. "On the other hand..."

By the time they'd dried off, hunger won out over passion. They unpacked the basket and wolfed down its contents in the dining room.

"How's my daughter?" he asked, although he'd seen Melanie only two days before. "She never talks to me."

"She seems happy," Kerry said, "but still unsettled. I think she misses you, although she'd never admit it to herself."

"The month is nearly up." He nibbled at a potato chip. "Do you suppose she's ready to come home?"

"We'll see," Kerry said. "She's welcome to stay here as long as you like."

His gaze locked onto hers. "You're good for her. And for me."

She ducked her head, suddenly shy. "I haven't done anything much."

"Oh, Kerry." His finger touched her chin and lifted her face toward his. "Just being who you are is enough. Sometimes when we're making love I feel as if I can possess you, and then I realize you're like a shooting star. If I ever captured you, tried to hold you against your will, you'd fade and die."

The tenderness blazing toward her brought tears to Kerry's eyes. "You're not that kind of man," she said. "You'd never try to force me into anything."

"No, but you might force yourself." He stared down at his half-eaten sandwich. "Don't ever stay with me out of guilt, Kerry. Or pity. I don't want that."

"I know." But what about love? she wondered. Would she stay with him out of love? And if she did, what would that do to her inner self, to the Kerry who would always be a dancer?

The shrill beep-beep of his phone broke into their mood. With a muttered apology, Chris took the call.

After a terse conversation, he clicked off. "That damn robber and his girlfriend are holed up in a convenience store with three hostages. I've got to get over there."

From a few blocks away, Kerry heard a siren scream by. "Sounds close."

"About a mile," he said. "On Lambert near the freeway." With a distracted kiss, he was on his way.

Kerry cleaned up their picnic and tried again to whip up some interest in the newspaper. It was a lost cause.

She wanted to be near Chris. What could it hurt if she cruised by the convenience store? Maybe the creeps had been arrested by now and the whole thing was over.

Feeling better for having made a decision, she hurried out to her car.

It wasn't hard to find the convenience store; a barricade of police cars blocked off the parking lot. Kerry halted just behind a paramedic unit and an ambulance.

A plainclothesman started toward her; she recognized Sergeant Rogers from the bowling alley about the same time he recognized her. He frowned, then signaled her to stay well back and returned to his post.

She took refuge by a tree, standing near a young man with several cameras dangling from his shoulder and a press card strung on a cord around his neck.

"What's going on?" Kerry asked.

"They've got three hostages, a clerk and a couple of customers," he said. "The negotiator's been on the phone with the robbers and they're making some wild demands—a helicopter, a million dollars, safe passage to Central America."

"What happens next?" She was grateful for the informed company.

He shrugged. "Who knows? They could wait it out, but I'd say those guys in there are pretty unstable. Sometimes you can bore them into submission, but in this case they're more likely to turn violent."

Finally Kerry spotted Chris. He was crouched behind one of the police cars near the front of the barricade, holding a megaphone.

As she watched, he called, "We have the building surrounded. Please come out quietly or we're coming in after you."

A bullet whined out of the building and Chris ducked.

There was a tense pause. Then, inside the convenience store, a woman screamed. "Oh, my God! No, please! Somebody stop him!"

"Go!" She thought it was Chris's voice but couldn't be sure from this distance.

Policemen swarmed across the open parking lot toward the building, Chris in the lead. For a disorienting moment, Kerry thought she must be imagining things. The store looked so ordinary, faced with news racks, its windows posted with advertisements for the state lottery and six-packs of beer. The sun washed the scene with summerlike clarity.

Yet she could hear the zing of bullets, see the glass shatter beneath the impact. One of the policemen fell, clutching his shoulder.

Chris! Oh, Chris, please be careful! She feared briefly that she'd shouted the words aloud, but the reporter next to her didn't react.

What if he was killed? What if she never got to see him again?

From inside the store came shouts and crashes. The reporter edged forward, and Kerry realized he'd been snapping pictures all along.

Finally the thrashing stopped. A uniformed patrolman appeared in the doorway, gesturing to the paramedics to come in.

Ambulance attendants were already assisting the injured policeman in the parking lot. But inside, someone else had been hurt. Who? Not Chris, please, not Chris.

Kerry moved forward through the circle of police cars. She had to know, couldn't bear the suspense another minute....

Two paramedics hurried out carrying a stretcher. In it lay the body of a man. About Chris's height—no, more slender— and he was wearing dirty jogging shoes and ripped jeans. Not Chris...

More people came out of the store. Two officers framed a ragged-looking young woman with long, dirty hair. The robber's accomplice.

Behind them, white and shaken, walked a middle-aged couple and a young man with neatly clipped hair, apparently the clerk. And Chris. Chris was asking them questions, reassuring the woman.

Kerry paused near the edge of the barricade of cars. How could she explain her presence here? Besides, the last thing Chris needed was an intrusion from his personal life. He had work to do.

Unnoticed, she retreated. It was over. Chris was okay.

Yet she had to sit behind the wheel of her car for several minutes before she could turn the key in the ignition. He'd come so close to death....

Kerry started the engine and drove along Lambert. Her concentration was poor, but fortunately there was little traffic on a Sunday.

Gradually the shock faded, leaving an image of Chris leading the charge into the store. Chris, putting himself in danger to save innocent people.

A wave of pride washed over Kerry. How many people were called upon to display that kind of courage? What Chris did might not make him rich like the people at Tony and Leila's party; it might not win prestige in the arts circles that her parents frequented; but she admired him more than anyone she'd ever known.

She only wished, as her nerves calmed and she steered toward home, that Melanie could share these feelings. But maybe that would come in time.

CHAPTER THIRTEEN

"I CAN'T BELIEVE THE RECITAL is only two weeks away." Melanie flicked on the light in the rehearsal studio. "And in less than a month school will be out."

Jamie lounged in the doorway, video camera in hand. "You still haven't said whether you're going to New York this summer."

It was the one issue that separated them, and Melanie knew it was her own fault. Sometimes she wondered at her indecision. After all, she loved Jamie, didn't she?

"Did you have to bring this up on my birthday?" She knew that was cheating, but she didn't want to talk about it now. Not when she was still so unsure of her own mind.

Jamie shrugged. "Suit yourself. Where's Tom?"

"He'll be here." She smoothed down the silver skirt of her costume. "He's never late."

To hide her restlessness, Melanie began warming up as Jamie arranged his lights. She wondered, not for the first time, whether there was something wrong with her. People in love were supposed to forget everything else, weren't they?

So maybe she wasn't in love. Only she couldn't imagine what else she was feeling for Jamie.

Nothing seemed simple anymore after so many years of living for ballet. How could everything have changed so much in one school year?

She would have to decide soon. But even if she chose to go to New York, Dad probably wouldn't let her.

Familiar resentment burned in Melanie's stomach. What

right did he have to control her life? Sure, he'd let her move in with Kerry, but he kept close tabs on her. Like she was still a kid. Like she was a possession or something.

Everywhere she went she heard his imaginary voice in her head, demanding explanations, questioning her judgment. Sometimes, in calmer moments, she had to admit that he wasn't that bad in real life, but other times she felt certain he'd grill her like one of his suspects if he thought he could get away with it.

"Hey, I'm here!" Tom burst into the room, beaming with his usual good cheer and looking terrific in his black-and-silver tunic. Instantly, Melanie felt better. You could always count on Tom to keep things on an even keel.

"Let's get going. I told Russ I'd meet him and the guys at seven." Jamie strode around the room, checking out the lighting angles.

Melanie glared at him, but he didn't notice. That was part of the problem, part of why she held herself back. She hated Jamie's friends. She didn't know what they did when they were together, but she knew she wouldn't like it. Why did he bother with those jerks, anyway?

"I really appreciate this." Tom warmed up quickly. "It'll be great for auditions."

They'd both been flattered when Jamie asked to video the duet they were going to perform at the recital. Although he'd shot rehearsals before, this time they would give a full-blown special performance for the camera.

With Tom graduating from high school, this was the last duet he and Melanie would dance together. She had a keen sense that time was passing and that her childhood was nearly gone. Someday the Leaps and Bounds School and Tom would be only memories. At least she'd have a copy of the tape to look back on.

The question was, Would Jamie be watching it with her?

"Ready?" he called. "Okay, guys. Let's get started."

As soon as the total concentration of dancing was over, Melanie found herself thinking again about how, for so long, she'd lived in the future. Now the present, which she'd always taken for granted, was too quickly becoming the past.

"What's eating you?" Jamie asked as he stopped the car in front of Kerry's house. "You brooding because I'm going off with the guys on your birthday?"

"What do you do together, anyway?" She was in no hurry to get out of the car. In no hurry to let more moments slip forever beyond her reach.

"This and that."

Great answer, she grumped inwardly. "Anyway, I want to take the video camera with me." It was a spur-of-the-moment decision; she just didn't like the idea of his creepy buddies playing with it. "I want a picture of the cake Kerry said she was baking."

"Use your old digital."

"Hey, whose camera is it, anyway?"

Jamie shifted uncomfortably. "Yeah, it's yours. Only remember I told you there's a special project I'm working on? I might need the camera tonight."

Melanie wavered. It wasn't Jamie's fault his family couldn't afford a video camera. And she didn't really need it, after all. "Well, okay."

"Thanks, Mel." He leaned over and kissed her. "I promise I'll preview the duet video tomorrow to make sure it's okay. I should be able to have it copied by the recital." He was having a duplicate made as her birthday present.

"Thanks." Somewhat pacified, Melanie lifted her costume from the back seat and got out.

She paused on the threshold, hearing Jamie pull away. Her father's car was in the driveway, which meant he waited inside with Kerry. It was nice of him to come, she supposed, and he'd probably brought her some present, but not the one she really wanted: freedom.

With a sigh, she trudged inside.

The scent of chocolate cake wrapped itself instantly around her stomach. She'd eaten only a granola bar for dinner, and she was starving.

"Hi." Kerry poked her head out of the kitchen. "How'd it go?"

Melanie hung the costume in the front closet. "Fine. I can't wait to see the video." She bit her lips as her father appeared behind Kerry.

He stood there awkwardly, as if not sure whether to hug her or not. In the end, he stayed where he was. "We were about to attack the ice cream without you."

"Let's eat," Melanie said. "I'm starved."

She dumped her bag in a corner and they tucked into the cake and ice cream. She knew she shouldn't eat too much, but it was hard to be perfect all the time. After some internal debate, Melanie helped herself to seconds.

"Time for presents," Kerry said, glancing at Chris. To her surprise, Melanie realized her dad was nervous.

"If you want," she said. "I mean, it's not really necessary...."

"Here." Kerry produced a package from the living room. "From me."

Inside, Melanie found an oversize volume on the history of dance, with zillions of color illustrations. "Wow! That's terrific." She gave her teacher a hug.

Chris cleared his throat. "Mine's a little smaller." He handed over an envelope.

Curious, Melanie opened it. Inside was one of those typical to-my-daughter birthday cards and two other things: a receipt and a key.

A car key.

"What's this?" she said.

Her father was trying not to watch her reaction too closely, she could tell. "I can't afford to give you your own car, but it's a duplicate key to mine. That receipt is for driver's training. You can start whenever you're ready."

She stared down at the objects. They hadn't discussed getting a driver's license; she'd figured her dad wouldn't like the idea. And here he was offering it to her, key and all.

"Thanks." She felt as if she ought to say more. "I mean, that's fine. I'll do it." She leaned across the table and pecked his cheek.

After they cleaned up, it was time to watch a special dance presentation on PBS's Great Performances. Sitting in front of the TV, Melanie sneaked a glance at the older couple.

Kerry had curled up, leaning against Chris's shoulder. His head was tipped so his cheek rested on her hair.

It made Melanie feel funny. Would she and Jamie be like that in another ten or fifteen years?

She wondered what the future was going to bring, anyway. Would she have children of her own someday? If she did, she hoped she didn't end up raising them alone.

It was hard to imagine having your own kid. Mostly, little children seemed to be a lot of hassle. But what if she had a daughter like Suzie, somebody she felt proud of?

With a sudden, intense pang, Melanie realized that if she had a child she'd smother it with love, fight to protect it, do anything in her power to smooth that little girl's path. To keep her safe and make her happy.

Just like her own Dad was doing.

A lump formed in her throat. Why had she been so angry at him these past few months? Look at how hard he was trying to please her, giving her the car key and driving lessons. And letting her live here with Kerry when he must miss her terribly.

The way she missed him, too.

It amazed Melanie that she hadn't realized it before. Her father was her rock, her security; even while she'd been angry with him, deep inside it had hurt that he let her go so easily. Now she understood that it hadn't been easy at all.

"Dad?" she said.

"Mmm?" His eyes met hers over Kerry's head.

"I think I'm ready to come home now."

He didn't react right away, just looked at her for a while. Then he said, "You're sure?"

"I love you, Dad," Melanie said.

There was a catch in his voice when he said, "I love you, too."

"I know." Nestling into the pillows, Melanie settled down to watch the program.

HE COULDN'T QUITE BELIEVE she was home, even after two weeks. Melanie's stay with Kerry had stretched from one month into nearly three, and during that time his little girl had changed. Or maybe she'd begun changing before then, and he hadn't noticed.

As she carried her recital costumes carefully into the living room, Chris noticed how her face had thinned and how she walked with more confidence. But mostly the difference was too subtle to describe, the beginnings of an adult peace with herself that impressed the hell out of him.

How he loved her. And he was being so careful not to stir up any trouble. He supposed, at this point in her life, there wasn't much influence a parent could wield anyway. You just had to assume you'd instilled the right values early on and hope for the best.

"Your hair looks terrific." Leila had stopped by earlier to pin it up and twist a strand of fake pearls through the light brown locks. "Very sophisticated."

"Thanks, Dad." Melanie laid the two costumes cautiously over the back of the sofa. The silver dress was for her duet with Tom, the purple-and-white puffed-sleeve affair for the gala dance featuring the advanced students. Both looked professional, although he knew she and Kerry had made them. "It was nice of Tony to volunteer his restaurant at cost for our cast party."

"We're going to have a great time," he said, meaning it. "And, honey, if you want to drive to the party with Jamie, that's okay."

"Oh, Dad." Melanie cocked her head at him. "Jamie's sister is in the recital, too, you know, and he should be spending time with her. Besides, I'm proud to be seen with my dad."

He hugged her, wondering where this new rapprochement had come from and how long it would last. "Let's go. We don't want the star to be late."

"Some star." Melanie wrinkled her nose. "But thanks." She adjusted her purse, scooped up the costumes again and led the way to the car.

They were pulling into the parking lot at the high school where Leaps and Bounds had rented an auditorium when the call came over his radio.

A firebombing at the Ahmeds' house.

"Damn," Chris said.

"Was anybody hurt?" Melanie glared at the radio. "Why doesn't the dispatcher tell us?"

"Honey, I've got to get over there right away." He halted in front of the school. "I'll be back as soon as I can but…"

"It's okay, Dad." Melanie picked up her costumes and opened the door. "Jamie's giving me a copy of the video tonight, so you can see the duet later. And I can ride home with Kerry."

"I wanted to be here." This was a special night for her; hell, it was a special night for him, too. But it was a frightening, maybe tragic night for the Ahmeds, and he was needed there. "I wish…"

Before he could finish, a wave of dancers engulfed his daughter, chattering excitedly, and she bobbed off in a sea of eager youngsters.

Grimly, Chris pulled away from the curb, the loving father already mutating into the hard-nosed policeman.

THE FIREBOMB HAD BURNED part of the garage and had filled the house with smoke, causing considerable damage. If it hadn't been for a smoke detector, Mrs. Ahmed and her daughters might have been seriously injured.

"I saw the smoke as I pulled in the driveway," the professor was telling a uniformed patrolman as Chris joined them on the front lawn, stepping over a tangle of fire hoses. "I feared the worst. My God, what could have happened!"

The quiet neighborhood had been transformed into a scene of crisis. Fire trucks clogged the driveway and the street; police cars had been parked helter-skelter, and a paramedic unit was just pulling away, fortunately unneeded.

On the porch, a neighbor tried to comfort Mrs. Ahmed and her two sobbing daughters.

"Did anyone see anything?" Chris asked the patrolman.

He shook his head. "So far, everyone I've talked to was inside, finishing dinner or watching TV."

"This has gone too far." Despite his concern, the professor remained remarkably calm. "I will have to send my family away while I finish the semester. Then, if the culprits are not caught, perhaps it is time we move on."

"I hate to see it come to that." Chris clenched his fists with frustration. With all the modern technology at his disposal, why couldn't he catch one carload of hoodlums? "We'll be going door-to-door this evening, Professor. Perhaps something will turn up."

"We will stay at a hotel." Ahmed gave him the details. "You can reach me there."

"Professor, please understand. We're doing our best. This situation outrages me almost as much as it does you," Chris told him.

"I do understand," the man said. "It is not your fault, Lieutenant."

But he felt as if it were, especially when hours of interviewing people yielded nothing tangible.

It wasn't until he headed home at nearly midnight that Chris remembered he had missed both the recital and the party. All in all, the night had been a total bust.

CHAPTER FOURTEEN

THE LAST TIME KERRY had visited Tony's restaurant in Brea had been for the wedding on New Year's Eve. Then, its Pompeii-inspired decor had been lush with imported vegetation and ripe with flowers.

Now, instead, it echoed with the merry calls of young dancers, who darted from table to table visiting one another beneath the indulgent eyes of their parents. The mood was carefree, as if school were over for the year, even though she and Myron had held the recital a few weeks early to avoid scheduling conflicts.

If only Chris would get here. Kerry glanced at the door again, but although it was almost midnight, there was no sign of him. Whatever had happened at the Ahmeds' must have been serious.

Without him, the evening echoed with hollow moments. She almost felt like going in search of him, but of course that was out of the question. He wouldn't appreciate it, and she'd hurt her students' feelings.

Darn, but she was proud of these kids. In all fairness, despite missing Chris, she'd nearly burst with pride watching the youngsters, noting how much they'd progressed since last fall. Who would have imagined teaching could bring such satisfaction?

She would miss these kids terribly if she went back to dancing. Of course, she could always teach in later years, but these particular youngsters would be grown by then. Some of them were nearly grown now.

Melanie, Jamie, Tom and a few other teenagers sat together at a table covered with Pepsi and antipasto, looking remarkably adult as they bent their heads together. Yet amid the gossip and levity, Jamie maintained a silent, almost sullen, air.

What was eating him, anyway? Suzie had performed delightfully, and the duet had impressed even Alfonso and Larisa, who attended as Kerry's guests. Whatever caused Jamie's recurrent moodiness seemed to have intensified rather than eased tonight.

"More wine?" Leila, holding a bottle of zinfandel, slid into the vacant seat beside Kerry.

"Sure. Thanks." Kerry couldn't help smiling at her hostess. Always beautiful, Leila bloomed as a bride. "Did I introduce you to Alfonso and Larisa?"

"No, but I've been dying of curiosity." With her ready warmth, Leila made everyone at the table feel at ease as Kerry completed the introductions.

As she finished, Myron pulled up a chair. "I'd say our kids done themselves proud."

"'Done themselves proud.' Is that a French phrase?" Kerry teased.

"Really, you both should feel good," Alfonso said. "Especially those two in the duet. Very talented, both of them."

Kerry couldn't help turning toward Melanie and Tom. The girl was making a wry face at Jamie, who didn't seem to notice. "We have great hopes for them."

"And the choreography." Larisa laid her hand on Kerry's arm. "You know exactly how to show off their strengths."

"Let's hope I do as well with more mature dancers." Although she kept her tone light, a familiar wave of anxiety roiled through Kerry's stomach.

Did every choreographer feel this uncertain while mounting a new work? The vision that had struck her at Alfonso's theater had been so sure, so irresistible. It wasn't until later, when it was too late to turn back, that the doubts had come.

Why had she picked something so unusual? A traditional ballet or a modern work in the style of Balanchine might not have been so innovative, but neither would it have left her wide open to attack.

What would the critics say when they saw the elaborate costumes, the mixed and sometimes jarring images? She doubted they'd be enthralled by her choice of music, either. Andrew Lloyd Webber might be immensely popular, but he'd never won much in the way of critical praise.

She cringed inside, imagining the barbs that might be flung her way. Crass commercialism was one charge that might be levied. Chaotic. Overly clever. She could imagine the insults quite vividly, how they would look in print and how they would embarrass her parents.

Not that there would be any validity to the criticism, not in Kerry's eyes. She knew exactly what she was doing, why each step was there, how the characters needed to interact. The tone was intentionally light, even campy in places, but then, that was true of dance itself. Classical ballet was only a few centuries old, but dance went back to the dawn of time. Her pharaohs and cats both had a statement to make, whether anyone but Kerry understood it.

"Where's Chris?" Leila asked.

"An emergency at work." Kerry checked her watch. "I was hoping he'd be here by now."

"Well, I'm sure it's important." Tony came by, and with a wave, Leila bounced up to join him. Watching them, Kerry felt a pang of envy.

When the two were out of earshot, Alfonso said, "What a charming woman. And I like this restaurant. Must be my Italian heritage."

"What is your name, really?" Myron asked.

To Kerry's relief, Alfonso didn't take offense. "Carrera's

my family name, but someone changed it at Ellis Island to Carney. My first name is Alfred, but can you imagine a dancer named Alfred Carney? Sounds like something out of Mad magazine."

"And you?" Myron asked Larisa. He wasn't normally this blunt; wine must have loosened his tongue.

"You think I'd make up a name like Larisa Keller?" She shook her head. "People said I should Russify it. Kellowsky or Kellarnikova. Can you imagine?"

"Larisa Kellarnikova," Alfonso said. "A person could run out of breath trying to pronounce it. Can't you see it now, critics keeling over left and right from lack of oxygen?"

"Not a bad idea," Myron said, and they all laughed.

Their merriment flashed Kerry back to other cast parties, other tables of dancers cracking inside jokes. Maybe soon she'd be part of that scene again.

What had for so long seemed an impossible dream hovered close to her reach now. These past weeks, in between rehearsing Alfonso's company, she'd joined in the classes with increasing dedication.

The pain hadn't vanished; that would be asking too much. But it was no longer intolerable. With proper massage, maybe some pain pills for performances, she thought she could handle it.

Even though, eventually, it might result in additional nerve damage? Even though, under the extra stress of coping with her condition, she might lack stamina, might find herself merely a supporting player instead of a star?

Kerry tapped at the stem of her wineglass. She had to try, didn't she?

If only Chris would get here. More than ever, she needed his reassuring presence. He was the one person she could talk to. Being with him might help to clear her head.

On the other hand, this wine wasn't helping much, and she

had to drive home. The next time a waitress came around, Kerry ordered a diet cola.

An hour later, the party began breaking up. Kerry stretched, feeling the cramp of muscles that had been immobilized for too long. She couldn't remember stiffening up this easily when she was younger. But it wasn't because of her injuries, she tried to tell herself. Or, if it was, she would simply work past it.

Melanie wove through the crowd of departing guests. "Kerry? Can you give me a ride?"

"Of course." There was no sign of Jamie. "You two didn't quarrel, did you? I'm sorry. It's none of my business."

The girl shrugged. "No, we didn't. He's just—I don't know what's eating him tonight. He kind of shoved the disc into my hand as if he hardly knew what he was doing, and then he took off an hour ago looking like thunder."

Kerry wished she could offer some comfort, but she knew better. "Well, let's push off, then. We're both going to be exhausted tomorrow."

When they arrived at Melanie's house, the windows were dark. "Boy, Dad's still out there," the girl said. "I guess I won't get to show him the video tonight."

"Want me to walk you in?"

"No, thanks. We've got dead bolts and burglar alarms— Dad's a real stickler." Melanie hauled her costumes and bag out of the back seat, then paused with the door open. "Listen, Kerry, would you come watch with us tomorrow night? I could fix dinner. About six?"

"You're sure I wouldn't be intruding?"

"Actually, I'd like to have you there. It's kind of like, well, you belong here."

Warmth crept through Kerry. "That's a wonderful compliment, Melanie. I'd be delighted to come."

"See you then."

If she ever had a daughter, Kerry mused on the way home, she'd want her to be just like Melanie.

Maybe she wouldn't be so lonely in New York after all, not if Melanie was there. She might not even mind so much if she couldn't be a star, as long as she could help the younger girl reach her potential.

And Chris... And Chris...

Kerry couldn't finish the thought. She was too tired. But it made her feel better to imagine that after all these years, life might allow her to have her cake and eat it, too.

WHEN SHE ARRIVED at the Laynes' door at six o'clock the next night, Melanie wasn't there.

"She went to the supermarket," Chris said after he'd finished kissing Kerry thoroughly. "Fortunately for us."

"You didn't arrange a flat tire for her or anything?" she teased.

"No, but believe me, I considered it." He nibbled at her neck, unwilling to let go. "Amazing, that a man can want to get rid of his own daughter."

"I have a feeling she'd understand." She pressed her nose against his hair, inhaling the spicy masculine fragrance. "I missed you last night."

"Let's not talk about it." He groaned.

"No luck, I take it." She wiggled past him, letting their bodies touch suggestively. If she had to suffer without him most nights for propriety's sake, she had no intention of suffering alone.

"You shouldn't have done that." He was still holding on to her wrist. "I'm going to have to change the locks, fast."

"Don't you think she might suspect something?"

"Damn. She's getting ice cream," he said. "It'll melt."

They both laughed. "As if we'd really do it," Kerry said.

"You think I wouldn't?"

"Sometimes I wonder." She dumped her purse behind the sofa and wandered into the kitchen. "Where are you hiding the beer?"

"Beer?" He followed her in. "Is that what world-famous ballerinas drink these days?"

"When it's this hot, they do." The May weather was giving an unwelcome preview of summer.

"Coming right up."

Watching him dig through little pots of deli salads to retrieve a beer, Kerry wished she could live right here. She missed him so much when they were apart.

Even if it was only for a few months… But would that be fair to him or to Melanie?

The front door scraped open and Melanie staggered in beneath an overstuffed grocery sack. "Gangway!"

Chris grabbed the sack before it could slide to the floor. "Hey, if I'd known you were going to buy this much I'd have driven you."

"I need the exercise." Melanie rubbed her shoulders ruefully. "Besides, this way I'm really motivated to sign up for those driving lessons."

The easy camaraderie between the two reassured Kerry. She hadn't been sure whether the new truce would last, but things looked hopeful.

The closeness persisted as they all pitched in to make hamburgers, baked beans and salad. The meal took half an hour to prepare and less than ten minutes to wolf down.

"I guess we were hungry." Chris surveyed the crumbs that remained of their efforts.

"I can't wait to see the DVD." Melanie hopped up and began clearing the table. "You don't know how tempted I was to preview it today, but I resisted."

Her father took a deep breath. "Wouldn't Jamie like to join us?" he offered. "After all, it's his video."

With a shrug, Melanie said, "I don't know where he is. Neither does his mom. He hasn't been home all day and he didn't show up at the studio, either. Unless I missed him?"

"No," Kerry confirmed. "Her mother picked Suzie up."

Chris tried not to look relieved. The offer to include Jamie had been made out of concern for his daughter, not out of any particular desire to get closer to the boy. "Let's watch, then."

They settled in front of the TV and began running the video.

The camera work was jumpy and at first Kerry couldn't tell what was going on. Gradually, she realized she was looking at some teenagers clowning around in a garage filled with junk. She recognized them vaguely as the boys who'd picked Jamie and Suzie up once at the studio.

"He must have put some other stuff on here," Chris said.

Melanie frowned. "No, I'm sure he didn't. He was so uptight last night I'll bet he gave me the wrong disc. He's been working on some special project—"

"What's that?" Chris replayed a short section of the DVD. "In the background—what's on the cover of that magazine?"

"It's just junk," Melanie said impatiently. "Let's—"

"That's a swastika." His voice was tight.

They sat silent for a moment, watching. The boys didn't seem to be doing anything harmful, but Kerry made out another pamphlet with a swastika on it, too. Hate material.

"Whose garage is that?" she asked.

"It must belong to Russ." Melanie spoke in small, shocked tones. "That's where they hang out."

"Gasoline." Chris pointed.

"Lots of people keep extra gas—" Kerry began.

"Empty bottles," he said. "Rags."

"Dad—" Melanie's fists were clenched "—it's not unusual to find that kind of stuff in garages."

"Hush." They listened to the chatter on the video, but it was almost indecipherable, slurred words spoken one over another with a background hum from an old refrigerator. Still, once or twice an obscenity broke through, making Kerry wince.

Abruptly, the picture shifted to outside, where the boys were piling into a car, waving beer cans out the windows. Chris didn't comment, but his face was a mask of disapproval. Melanie sat motionless, not even trying to defend Jamie.

"Midsize car," Chris said at last. "Peeling blue, almost gray."

"What?" Kerry turned toward him.

"Nothing."

The scene shifted to a school yard. Youngsters swarmed toward the parking lot, retrieving bicycles and swatting one another with book bags.

"There…" Melanie came to life at last. "See, there's Suzie. It's just a bunch of shots…"

Chris froze the image. Kerry could clearly make out two little girls in the crowd. Two dark-haired, dark-skinned girls.

"Are those the Ahmeds?" Kerry said.

"None other."

The scene changed again, to a tidy suburban home. The same two girls skipped up the driveway, one of them carrying a doll.

"Their house," Chris said.

The picture wavered. Now they were looking at the garage again, at the three boys posing proudly in front of a poster that read Keep America for Americans. One of them—Kerry thought it was Russ—brandished a small-caliber handgun.

"Too bad Jamie couldn't get in the picture, too," Chris said.

"Oh, come on!" Melanie exploded as the video ended. "That doesn't prove anything!"

"No, but it's enough to bring them in for questioning." Chris reached for the telephone.

Melanie gasped. "You can't—Dad! Jamie gave that DVD to me, not the police department. You can't just haul him in—"

Setting the phone back in its cradle, he said, "I'm sorry, Mel, but this is a serious matter. A family narrowly escaped death. What do you expect me to do, ignore the evidence?"

"What evidence?" she challenged. "Some magazines with swastikas on them? Half the novels in the grocery store have swastikas on the cover!"

"Those are historical novels," her father said wearily. "And that wasn't what was in Russ's garage. What are their full names, Melanie?"

"I don't know!" she snapped. "And if I did, I wouldn't tell you!" She jumped up and ejected the DVD, but Chris grabbed it out of her hand.

"I'm sorry," he said. "I have to impound this."

"Impound!" she fumed. "I'm your daughter, not some criminal!"

"Then stop acting like one. And stop defending that—that hoodlum."

Watching the two of them square off, Kerry fought back the impulse to intervene before some permanent damage was done. After all, what could she say? She couldn't believe Jamie would be involved in such vicious goings-on, but the video was damning.

Melanie glared at her father, speechless, then stormed into her room. The door slammed behind her.

Chris rubbed his hand over his forehead. "Why?" he muttered. "Why did it have to be Jamie?"

"Maybe there's some other explanation." Kerry searched her mind for possibilities. "It doesn't actually show a crime being committed."

"No doubt he was waiting for something really big." Chris punched the TV's Off button as if he wanted to pound the remote control into rubble. "I wonder why he missed the fire-bombing?"

"Maybe he didn't know about it," Kerry said.

"Do you honestly expect me to believe that?" Chris slid

the DVD into its sleeve. "We'll have to hope we can worm the truth out of them. At least now we know who they are."

"Are you sure?" Kerry pictured Jamie bending down to give his sister a warm hug. Why would he try to hurt those other little girls? It didn't make sense. "The others, maybe—"

"You're saying he was going along with the crowd? Possibly." Chris retrieved his jacket from the front closet. "But that's hardly an excuse. One thing's for sure. He's not coming anywhere near my daughter, ever again."

Kerry understood how he felt, but didn't Jamie deserve a chance to explain or at least to apologize? "You can't chain Melanie down."

"I've given her plenty of leeway." Chris opened the front door. "Too much, maybe. Will you stay with her?"

"As a shoulder to cry on, sure," Kerry said. "But not as her jailer."

The anger flashing across his face caught her off guard. "Then I want you out of here. This is between me and my daughter. She's going to have to toe the line. My trust has been betrayed, Kerry. Not deliberately, but if she sees that creep—" He left the threat unfinished.

She rose slowly and moved toward the door. "I'm sorry this happened. I can't believe—"

"Believe it," he said. "I've been a cop too long not to accept what I see with my own eyes." He turned and yelled toward the bedroom. "You're on restriction, Melanie, as of right now. No phone calls, no visits unless I approve them. You got that?"

There was no answer.

Reluctantly, Kerry walked ahead of him and got into her car, feeling helpless and uneasy. She loved these two people, and right now they were both hurting. If only she could help!

When tempers calmed, she'd have to find a way.

MELANIE LIFTED HER HEAD when the tapping came at her window. She reached for a tissue, blew her nose with it, then added it to the pile littering the floor.

When Jamie's face appeared, she stared at him for a moment before letting him in.

He loosened the screen and climbed inside. He'd never been here in her bedroom before, and Melanie retreated to the bed, instinctively clutching her oldest, best-loved teddy bear. Right now she didn't know whether she wanted him to stay or to jump off the edge of the earth.

"I know they're looking for me," he said. "I was having this argument with Russ when the police car pulled up. I took off, but his dad came out and grabbed his arm and started demanding to know what stunt he'd pulled this time."

"You gave me the wrong DVD," Melanie said.

"Yeah." Jamie sank into the beanbag chair. "I figured that out this afternoon. I wasn't sure if you'd already watched it. I guess—I guess in a way it wasn't entirely an accident. This has to stop."

"Why?" Melanie demanded. "Why did you do it? Those sweet little girls—"

"You don't understand." For an instant, his face took on the sullen, resentful look he so often directed at adults, but then he softened. "Melanie, I would never want to hurt them."

"Then why?"

"At first, well, the guys were just having fun." He shook his head. "I mean, that's what it seemed like. They did other stuff, too—broke some car windows, stole some real estate signs. Just being rebels."

"They're jerks," Melanie said.

"And I'm a jerk, too?"

"I don't know. Are you?"

He didn't answer her directly. "At first, when Russ got the idea of harassing this Ahmed guy, it sort of made sense. I mean, look at all the trouble those Middle Easterners cause for Americans."

"Two wrongs don't make a right." Melanie wished she didn't sound so stuffy.

"Yeah, but—" He picked up an open bag of tortilla chips and chomped down a handful. "Hey, at first it wasn't any big deal. Only the other guys, they wouldn't let go of it. Like it became this obsession with Russ, and I realized he really might hurt somebody."

He passed her the chips and Melanie took one.

"That's when I got the idea of making the DVD," Jamie said. "I mean, I couldn't turn them in. They're my buddies. I had some vague idea that when they saw it objectively, they'd realize that they were acting like jerks."

"Why'd you take pictures of the little girls?"

"Because they're so cute," he said. "I thought Jerry or Phil at least would call a halt, and Russ wouldn't go on alone. I was trying to stop them, Melanie. It all sounds so stupid now. After you told me yesterday about the firebombing, I realized I'd let it go too far."

"My dad thinks you were part of the whole thing," she said.

"Yeah, he would think that." Jamie stared down at the bag of chips. "I don't know what I'm going to do."

"You can't keep running away. It just makes you look guilty."

"I'll go talk to the cops," he said finally. "After I tell my mom. It's just—Melanie, I want you to believe me. I was trying to make them quit, only I figured I could do it my way. Well, I was wrong."

"I believe you," Melanie said. "But I don't think my dad will."

His gaze met hers. "You're a real special girl."

"He won't let me see you anymore." She felt angry all over again at her father. Just like those crazy parents in Romeo and Juliet, trying to run their kids' lives. And here she'd thought he was finally beginning to accept her as an adult.

Jamie stood up. "I don't want him to catch me here and get you in trouble. I just wanted you to know the truth."

"Whatever they do to you, I'll be waiting."

"No." He paused at the window. "What if they lock me up? I don't want you wasting your life. Go to New York like you planned. I can always find you there."

"But I don't want—"

"Do it," he said, and slipped out the window.

Melanie lay back on the bed and closed her eyes, feeling the tears well up again. But inside, oddly, she felt better.

Jamie had come here because he was innocent. He trusted her, and he cared what she thought. And he hadn't tried to hurt those girls, no matter what Dad thought.

Things would work out all right. The good guys always won, didn't they?

CHAPTER FIFTEEN

WATCHING THE ADVANCED dancers move through their exercises, Kerry experienced a moment of disorientation, as if she were regarding them in a time warp.

Only this week of classes was left. True, most of the teenagers would continue this summer after a two-week break, but not all. And there would be different faces; she'd already accepted a couple of students new to Brea or transferring from other schools.

She would miss this class, its unity, its highs and lows. Teaching made you sharply aware of the divisions of time and how quickly children grew up.

Kerry forced herself to focus on the class, calling out comments as the youngsters moved through a series of leaps and turns.

When you knew a dancer, it was amazing how much you could tell by his or her movements. Tom's leaps echoed with pent-up energy. He'd begun making the rounds of auditions, and she knew he was waiting for results of callbacks.

Another girl, an eighteen-year-old who would be married in August, moved with dreamy distraction. One boy spun with greater precision and determination than ever; he would be dancing the lead roles next fall in Tom's place and was eager to live up to the part.

And then there was Melanie.

As always, her movements and gestures were precise and skilled. Only the fire was missing.

Kerry leaned against the far wall and folded her arms. Just

last week, two days after the explosion over Jamie, Melanie had announced her decision to go to New York. She'd even received her father's reluctant go-ahead. Why then did she look so listless? And why didn't Kerry feel excited and hopeful?

She'd agreed, after consulting with Chris, to accompany Melanie to the auditions. Larisa, bless her, had offered to teach Kerry's classes in the interim.

Certainly Melanie would snap out of her depression by July. If not, the trip to New York, seeing that metropolis for the first time and feeling its vibrant hum, surely would fill her with new purpose.

Kerry could only hope so.

Bella's piano tinkled to a halt. The dancers took their bows and wandered out, giggling and chattering with the restlessness that always accompanied the end of the school year.

Melanie walked out with two other girls, but she didn't appear to be listening to their conversation. Neither did she look at Kerry.

It wasn't peevishness or resentment, Kerry knew. More the result of inner turmoil and a deep unhappiness.

She wanted to reach out to Melanie but restrained herself. The girl would talk when she was ready.

Walking back to her office, Kerry reflected that if rehearsals for the Carrera Ballet weren't taking every spare moment, she'd probably feel pretty glum herself. Frankly, she was grateful for the distraction. Only another week until the premiere.

And then? She stopped at the water fountain for a drink while her thoughts raced ahead of her.

And then July would come. Would she, too, be auditioning during that trip to New York? If so, she'd have to spend the previous weeks in heavy training. The decision needed to be made soon.

After Friday, she told herself. After the opening.

"Kerry?" Chris stood outside her office, looking ill at ease. "Is Melanie done?"

"She's changing."

Despite the bright light of the hallway, his face looked shadowed. "I thought I'd pick her up."

"When's she going to get her driver's license?" Kerry opened the office door.

"She's lost interest." Chris shrugged. "Something about people not driving in New York."

"That's true." Kerry scooped up the pot from her coffee maker. "Like some?"

"I'm about coffeed out." He perched backward on a chair. "Damn, I want this case wrapped up."

She poured herself a cup. "I thought Russ had confessed."

"He has, but he won't implicate his friends." Chris ran his fingers distractedly through his hair, which needed a cut. "We had to release the other three until we get some evidence."

That might not be such a good thing for Jamie, Kerry reflected. If no proof of his innocence came forward, he might escape juvenile hall but his reputation would be permanently tarnished.

Funny, but she'd believed Melanie's story at once, believed that Jamie really had been trying to stop his friends. It made sense from what she knew of the boy's character.

Chris, on the other hand, hadn't believed a word of it. Was that the best story the kid could come up with? he'd demanded, according to his daughter.

Now Chris was saying, "We're circulating photographs of the three of them. There's got to be a witness out there, some motorist or passerby who doesn't realize what he saw. Someone who can place them all in the car at that particular time."

"And how are you holding up?" Kerry asked.

His gaze, when it touched hers, was haunted. "Like hell," he said.

"Armed camp?"

"An armed camp where you love the enemy more than you love your own life." Chris gripped the back of the chair. "Why can't she see it? Why did she have to fall for a jerk like that?"

There was no point in defending Jamie, Kerry knew. Chris had his mind made up on the subject and, given his experience as a policeman, she couldn't blame him. "I miss you," she said.

He released a ragged sigh. "I miss you, too, Kerry, so much I—" He stopped in midsentence. "You haven't said anything about New York, but there's a chance you won't come back, isn't there?"

Kerry sank into a chair, setting her coffee on the desk. "I didn't want to say anything. I still haven't made a decision."

"Do you really think you can dance?"

"I don't know." Suddenly she wanted to confide everything in Chris. "It's just that I have to try. There won't be another chance for me. I'll be twenty-nine in August. Another year or two and it'll be too late to start over."

"So you really have decided, then?"

"I guess so." She hadn't realized it before. "Chris, isn't there some way you could come to New York?"

He spread his hands helplessly. "Melanie would hate having me around. Besides which, police work isn't something you transfer in and out of so easily. I've got nearly fifteen years invested here. Another five and I could take early retirement. In New York I'd have to start from ground zero. I'm not sure I'm up to that."

The unspoken sentiment behind his words was easy to guess. If Kerry chose dancing over him, he'd merely be tagging along at her heels, a stage-door Johnny hanging around waiting for a spare moment. That was no way to build a life together.

"This may be the worst mistake I've ever made," she said miserably. "It's just a compulsion I can't shake."

"You still need to prove yourself, don't you?" Chris regarded her steadily. "For your own sake, or for your parents?"

"I wish I knew," she said.

He turned as several students flurried by in the hall. "I'd better go if I'm going to catch Melanie."

"You are coming to the premiere Friday night?" She stood up when he did.

"Of course." He reached over and gripped her shoulder. "Whatever you do, Kerry, I'm behind you. I want you to be happy."

When he walked out the door, she had to bite her lip to keep from calling him back.

THE DAY OF THE PREMIERE, Kerry nearly canceled her afternoon class with the advanced students. But that wouldn't be fair to them, she told herself firmly as she drove to the studio after a late lunch.

Besides, there was nothing left for her to do at the Carrera Ballet. The dress rehearsal the previous night had gone a bit roughly, but that was considered good luck. It was too late to change anything; the dancers needed a good warm-up this evening, and that was all.

If she didn't go to class, she'd spend the afternoon worrying herself sick.

The minute she walked into the rehearsal room, Kerry knew something exciting had happened. The air buzzed with it.

"Well?" She regarded a knot of students.

"It's Tom!" one of the girls said. "He's got a job!"

Kerry looked around and spotted him at the piano, joking with Bella. "Tell all!" she demanded as she approached.

His handsome young face split in a grin. "Man, you were right about waiting till summer! The timing's perfect!"

Kerry gave him a playful poke in the side. "If you keep me in suspense any longer, Tom Hadley…"

"I surrender!" He held up his hands. "It's a new musical. We're opening in August at the Music Center and then we hit the road till next spring."

"And then?"

"We open in New York!" He grasped Kerry by the waist and swung her around. "New York!"

Catching her breath, she said, "And exactly what sort of part are you playing?"

"Well, it's only in the chorus," he conceded as he set her down. "But I get to understudy the supporting lead. It's a terrific role—lots of spectacular dancing!"

"What about singing?" Bella said.

"That, too." He winked at her. "I've been working with a vocal coach this semester. He says I've got a good natural voice and my technique is really coming along."

"That's wonderful." Kerry's spirits lifted; she truly wished Tom the best.

"Melanie!" Tom darted forward as the girl entered the studio. "Did you hear?"

She managed a weak smile. "Congratulations. I'm really pleased for you."

"It just goes to show," he announced, "that dreams do come true. Yours will, too, Mel. You'll see. Next summer we'll both be stars in New York!"

Her mouth clamped into a thin line. Tom didn't seem to notice as he spun away to accept more congratulations from his friends, but the misery in Melanie's face was too clear to miss.

It was time to start class, and Kerry tapped her students to order with her stick. Yet throughout the next hour, she observed Melanie closely.

Her dancing lacked spirit. If she auditioned like this, she wouldn't be accepted to anything.

But that wasn't what really mattered. The important thing was that if she felt this way, going on with her plans would be a terrible mistake.

As the others sauntered out, Kerry signaled to Melanie. "Can I talk to you for a minute?"

The younger girl came obediently but she didn't meet Kerry's gaze.

"You don't really want to go to New York, do you?" Kerry asked.

Melanie shook her head.

"Then why did you say yes? Just to get away from your father?"

Sad brown eyes looked up at her. "Jamie told me to go."

"Jamie did? Why?" Kerry stared in surprise.

"He doesn't want me to waste my talent." Melanie sagged against the wall. "Only it doesn't mean anything anymore."

A deep pain twisted through Kerry's heart. So many years invested together, so many hopes... But it was Melanie's life. "You don't want to dance anymore?"

"Oh, yes!" Melanie straightened. "I couldn't give it up. But Jamie wants to study filmmaking in college. He thinks he could get a scholarship to U.C.L.A. I could study dance and acting. I'd stay here in L.A.—I don't know—Jamie and I would work something out together."

A voice deep within Kerry wanted to cry out, You have a talent other girls would kill for—you can have the dreams I've lost. Everything lies ahead of you. For God's sake, don't throw it away!

But then she would be speaking for her own sake, and she wasn't Melanie.

"You have to do what feels right for you," she said slowly. "We grown-ups have a way of projecting our hopes into young people that we care about. It's hard for us to stand aside when they choose a different path. But sometimes we have to."

Melanie threw her arms around Kerry and gave her a long hug. "I was so afraid—I couldn't talk to you—I knew how disappointed you'd be, how much you've counted on this."

"You would have gone to New York to please me?" Kerry asked.

"Well, partly," Melanie said. "It's okay if I don't?"

"Of course." Kerry restrained herself from asking about Chris. He certainly wouldn't push Melanie to leave; the problem was, how would the two of them survive in one house? "You're coming to the opening tonight, aren't you?"

"Of course." The light died in Melanie's face. "With Dad."

"I'll see you then." Kerry watched thoughtfully as the girl left.

She'd forgotten about Bella until the pianist paused beside her. "It's so complicated to be young. I'm glad I'm past it."

"I hope I feel that way in a few years," Kerry admitted.

"Things will work themselves out," Bella said, "as long as people listen to their own hearts."

After she left, Kerry went to stand at the barre. She ought to step up her practice beginning now, but her knees didn't want to bend. Her whole body felt stiff and inflexible, but it wasn't from physical pain. The hurt she felt was for Chris and Melanie and herself.

"Miss Guthrie?" The quiet masculine voice came from the side door.

"Jamie!" Kerry turned toward him. "How are you?"

Ignoring her question, he hurried into the room. "I came by to get my sister and I wanted to give you this." He handed her a DVD. "I can't give it to Mel. If her dad saw it, he'd think she'd been seeing me on the sly and he'd get mad. But I thought maybe later you could give it to her."

"Later, you can give it to her yourself," Kerry said.

"Maybe." He stood reflected in the mirror, a duplicate picture of misery. "He's out to get me, her dad. He'll find some way to send me to juvenile hall. Hell, maybe I deserve it."

"I don't think so." Kerry tucked the disc into her skirt pocket. "I'll take good care of this."

He studied his hands as if they were works of fine art. "And I wanted to say—well, thank you. For what you've done for Suzie and Melanie. And me. You really act like you trust me. I hope I haven't let you down—oh, shoot."

Without another word, he stumbled out of the studio, embarrassed by his own frankness.

Kerry stood there alone for a while, feeling the DVD in her pocket as her thoughts collided and roiled with images of the two teenagers and of Chris. Then slowly the solitude calmed her and her thoughts drifted to the days ahead.

She really should be taking classes with Alfonso. That was what she'd do during her two-week break, of course.

Except that now, since Melanie's change of plans, Kerry would be going to New York alone. Struggling alone, sacrificing alone, without anyone to share her hopes and disappointments. Without anyone else to root for, anyone whose own successes could compensate for any setbacks Kerry herself encountered.

She wished she felt sure it was worth it.

CHAPTER SIXTEEN

KERRY WATCHED THE VIDEO as she slipped on her designer gown, the one she'd worn to Tony and Leila's party.

The camera work was much smoother than on the video of Russ and the boys; clearly Jamie had planned his angles and maintained better control over the lighting.

After a minute, she forgot about the technical aspects as the duet came alive on her TV screen. Most of all, Melanie bloomed, dancing for the camera, dancing for Jamie, and he managed to capture every nuance of her silky, youthful exhilaration.

How had he done it? Dance rarely filmed well, even when done by professionals. As she took out the DVD, Kerry wished Chris could see this.

Collecting her beaded evening bag, she decided to take the disc along with her tonight. It belonged by rights to Melanie, and surely Chris couldn't object if he knew it had come directly from Kerry.

She hurried out to her car, muttering curses at the high heels that sent quivers of fire through her unaccustomed leg muscles. The darn things were nearly as crippling as another car accident.

Although it was early, the parking lot at the theater was already filling up. Women in long dresses and men in tuxedos descended from their cars, along with a scattering of less formally dressed students.

This certainly wasn't New York, or even the Los Angeles Music Center, but she knew from Alfonso that some prominent critics would be here tonight, as well as dance enthusiasts from across Southern California.

Stark terror engulfed Kerry as she shut off her engine. What if they hated her work? What if she failed?

Until this moment, she had always considered her choreography as a backup career, something she could turn to if all else failed. Now, suddenly, she had to face the possibility that she might not be good enough at it.

Damn it, she loved this work, this piece of imagination and nonsense that she'd entitled Of Cats and Pharaohs. It had vitality, spark, originality.

But her judgment hadn't been proven. What had she made before? Only some dances within rigid limits for musicals, brief moments that faded into the overall flow of an evening. Not showpieces. Not works that were judged individually.

The temptation to flee nearly made her turn the key in the ignition, but Kerry forced herself out of the car. She had to stay and face whatever was coming. She owed her dancers that much.

Entering through the stage door, she found the dressing rooms brightly lighted and filled with nervous movement and sound. The air smelled of makeup overlaid with flowers.

"We're sold out!" Alfonso, wearing the blue-and-gold tunic and tights for the first, traditional piece, appeared at her side in the hallway. "I wish I could be out front!"

"I hope I haven't let you down," Kerry said.

Her former teacher regarded her sympathetically. "Nerves getting to you?"

"I think I'm going to throw up," Kerry said.

"Go watch from the lighting booth," he advised. "Then at least you won't have to make polite conversation."

Thanking him, she made her way to the narrow staircase, little better than a ladder, that led to the booth high above the rear of the auditorium. The technician glanced at her knowingly and indicated a vacant folding chair.

From here, the stage looked impossibly far below and the audience merged into one shifting blur. Chris and Melanie must be down there, Kerry knew. She wanted to see them, but it would have to wait. Right now, she couldn't deal with anything except her own paralyzing fear.

Thank goodness I don't have to dance tonight.

True, she'd suffered from stage fright a few times, but nothing like this. When she'd danced, her performance had represented the accumulated efforts of the choreographer, her teachers and her partner as well as herself. But tonight her work stood alone. She and no one else was responsible for its success or failure. Even if it was portrayed at its very best, it might still be rejected.

Kerry shivered, remembering bad reviews she'd read of other people's creations. Critics seemed to enjoy using their wits to skewer and slash.

The house lights dimmed. Kerry sat back, willing herself not to torture her already tightly strung nerves. There was nothing she could do now.

The opening ballet proceeded smoothly. Larisa and Alfonso worked well together, and the supporting dancers had been honed to a unified, technically excellent team.

Kerry drank some coffee from a paper cup, generously offered her from the technician's pot, during the brief intermission. Next came a modern story ballet by Antony Tudor, a sure crowd pleaser that showed off the talents of some of the other principal dancers and received a good measure of applause.

Was it only Kerry's imagination, or did the audience below radiate restlessness during the second intermission? Were they bored or merely anticipating the centerpiece to follow?

Among them, she knew, were Myron and many of her students. Naturally, they would offer support no matter what happened. But they were only a few among the hundreds who packed the refurbished auditorium.

And then it was time.

The lights came up, blue spots picking out the cats as they crept onto the stage. Then a huddled figure darted out—Alfonso, as the phantom of the opera.

Kerry leaned forward, her damp palms clasped together, mentally cuing the dancers. Now the pharaoh, then Mary Magdalene from Jesus Christ Superstar and—at last—Larisa whirling across the stage as Evita.

Then a strange thing happened.

Kerry forgot about being the choreographer. She forgot about the audience and the critics and even Chris and Melanie watching below.

She became Larisa.

It was Kerry, lost in the moment, soaring and leaping, caught in a magic world of colored lights and exotic creatures. There was no pain, no physical awareness, but instead an exhilarating weightlessness.

And then she became something more, a consciousness that transcended mere bodies. She touched a thousand stages, a thousand premieres. Petipa, Nijinsky, Balanchine, Robbins, Ailey, Tharp; she could feel their blood pulsing in her veins. The vision that had touched her mind months before had carried her into a new world that only they could understand.

It was a world that transcended individual performances. A ballerina might grow old; the ballet never would. A dancer could claim only so many nights, so many audiences, but the dance went on forever.

Here was the freedom Kerry had longed for, the wonder of flight without the grueling long hours of working out, the pain of recurring injuries that all dancers suffered, the unremitting fear as age crawled into her bones. Why hadn't she seen it long ago?

She came out of her daze to discover that the ballet had reached its blazing climax, and then, before she was ready for it, the music ended. The theater rocked with cheers and applause.

Kerry closed her eyes, feeling the air vibrate with energy. With approval.

Below, the dancers took their bows. Flowers flew onto the stage, materializing as if from nowhere. Cries of "bravo!" echoed up to the lighting booth.

With a start, Kerry realized the audience was calling for her. "Guthrie! Guthrie!" Who had started the chant, she would never know, but others picked it up. The applause turned into a rhythmic clapping.

"You'd better get down there," the technician said. "I'm not sure how much this building can take."

With a stiff nod, Kerry fumbled down the narrow staircase. In the wings, the stage manager caught her arm and piloted her out onto the proscenium.

Standing between Alfonso and Larisa, she made a deep curtsy. It was impossible to make out individual faces in the dark mass before her, but right now it didn't matter. People were on their feet, stomping and clapping. All of them. Where were the critics? They wouldn't take part in this ovation, would they? In vain, Kerry searched for seated figures scribbling scornfully on little pads.

Alfonso caught her hand and led her forward—just as he'd done that night in New York, the night of their triumph. Cheers washed over her.

Finally, embarrassed when the applause refused to abate, Kerry indicated the conductor of the small orchestra and directed the clapping toward him.

The stage manager must have caught her pleading look, because at last he closed the curtains. The ovation continued for a minute or two, muffled by thick velvet, then faded away.

"Wow." Alfonso gave her a hug. "They loved it!"

Were those the same words he'd used that long-ago night

just before her accident? It seemed to Kerry that, at last, they'd come full circle.

She leaned against him, feeling dizzy. "I had a lot of friends out there."

"That wasn't a polite reception," he chided. "Besides, the critics were on their feet, too."

"You really think...?" Kerry paused to accept the congratulations of the dancers, and to compliment their work. "Everyone was splendid tonight."

"I was the first—" Larisa beamed at her "—the first one to dance your Evita."

The implication that Of Cats and Pharaohs would be performed again by other companies stunned Kerry into silence. She would not be one ballerina but many, each new and fresh, reborn through her ballet. It was far, far better than the goals she had set for herself long ago as a child, when she could see no further than her own small self.

Walking out through the wings, catching her breath in one welcome solitary moment behind a fold of curtain, Kerry felt a huge burden lift from her shoulders and flutter into the dimness. Yes, she would always love to dance for the sheer joy, but she didn't need to devote her life to it.

She wanted to see Chris right now more than anything in the world.

He would come backstage, of course. That was where Kerry headed now, through a hallway crammed with well-wishers.

There! She waved and Melanie, her face shining, waved back.

Chris turned. Through the crowd, she felt him reach out to her in a new way, as if tonight's experience had changed him, too.

"Chris!" Nodding politely as compliments flew toward her left and right, Kerry made her way through the crowd. "Did you like it?"

"It was more than that." His arm slipped around her waist,

drawing her close. "I felt like I was inside your mind. I didn't understand everything, not intellectually, but I felt it. It all made sense to me."

"It was wonderful!" Melanie leaned over to kiss Kerry's cheek. "I'm so proud!"

"Someday you'll dance Evita," her father told her.

Instantly, Melanie's expression closed up like a withering flower. She hadn't told him yet that she wasn't going to New York, Kerry realized.

"Let's go celebrate," she said to distract the girl. "Ice-cream sundaes all around, my treat."

They were making their way toward the stage door when Kerry saw someone else signaling her, someone as small and delicate as a bird. Suzie.

"Hi! Hi!" The little girl bounced up and down.

"Suzie!" Kerry waved back.

"That was the neatest thing I ever saw!" Suzie cried. Behind her, Mrs. Ezell smiled warmly.

And then, behind the woman's shoulder, Kerry spotted a dark, brooding face. Jamie had come, too.

She felt Melanie tremble beside her. The way the two of them looked at each other across the hallway sent shivers down Kerry's spine.

"Let's get the hell out of here." Chris caught his daughter with one hand and Kerry with the other, and a moment later they emerged into the June night.

Things couldn't go on this way between two people she loved so much. Kerry knew that neither of these two hard-headed people would open up to each other unless she intervened.

But how?

The DVD. Maybe that would give her an opening.

"I'll tell you what," she said. "I'll pick up some ice cream and toppings, and let's eat it at my place. I've got something I want to show you."

"Sure." Chris, his mouth still pressed tight, steered Melanie to the car. "We'll meet you there."

Oh, God, what am I doing? Kerry wondered as she drove home, stopping off at a convenience store on the way.

It was risky, interjecting herself between father and daughter. She might succeed only in alienating them both.

Emerging from the store with her purchases, Kerry took a gulp of night air and looked up at the stars. To have come so far, only to lose Chris now?

Because tonight, for the first time, a life with him seemed possible. She hadn't given up her dreams; they'd simply changed along the way without her realizing it, and at last she'd awakened to the truth.

But she had to take the chance. She couldn't make a fresh start with this heartbreaking estrangement standing in the way. Besides, she owed it to Melanie, whose dreams were still so tenuous and vulnerable.

Kerry reached home to find Chris and Mel waiting on her porch, the silence thick between them.

"I hope you both like chocolate ripple," she said as she opened the door. "With caramel topping and nuts."

"Sounds great." Chris escorted them both inside. "What was it you wanted to show us?"

"You'll see." Kerry caught Melanie's quizzical glance as the younger girl joined her in the kitchen, but she turned her attention to preparing the sundaes.

When her guests were seated in the living room, Kerry set her dish down and turned on the TV and the DVD player. "Okay," she said. "Here goes."

Chris shot her a dubious look, as if he'd guessed what she was up to and didn't quite believe it. Kerry stared down at her ice cream, feeling like a traitor.

The images of Melanie and Tom came on-screen. Oh, no, Chris wasn't even looking at it. Please, please let him at least give it a chance, she prayed.

And he did, at first reluctantly, then with growing fascination. Melanie's face, too, lost its initial grim expression and softened as she watched.

"Is that really me?" she asked when the video was over. "I always look so stiff in pictures."

"Chris?" Kerry asked gently.

His mouth twisted with anguish, and it was a moment before he spoke. "My beautiful daughter," he whispered.

"Dad!" Melanie said, but Kerry waved her to silence.

Finally Chris said, "I'll give the boy one thing—he's got talent."

"I'd say there was more than talent guiding that camera." Kerry swallowed hard, awaiting his reaction.

Melanie couldn't wait any longer. "He loves me, Dad. I know you think he's just a punk but—"

Chris stared straight ahead at the now blank TV. "Possibly he does care about you. But there's another part of his life, Mel. Maybe it didn't touch you. Maybe it never would have. But we can't ignore it."

"I'm not going to New York, Dad," his daughter said. "I'm going to stay here and finish high school and go to college. I'll still dance, but I want to be near Jamie."

"You're so young." His voice was achingly gentle. "You can't see it yet, but the decisions you make now will shape the course of your life. You'll never come back to this point again, Melanie."

"I won't want to," she said. "I'm doing the right thing."

"I can't let you see him." Chris clenched his hands together as he met her gaze. "I'm sorry."

"You don't want to understand, do you?" Animated by fury, Melanie jumped up. "You think I'm so stupid I can't judge him for myself, don't you? If that's the way you want things, fine. You're still the boss till I turn eighteen, but not one minute after!"

She started for the door, waving away his attempt to reach

for her. "I'll walk home, if you don't mind. Good night, Kerry. Thanks for trying to help."

The door slammed behind her.

"Oh, no." Chris sank back down on the sofa. "And I thought things couldn't get any worse."

Kerry poked listlessly at her melting ice cream. "I meant to help, but instead—I'm sorry, Chris."

"And how exactly did you think that would help?" His eyes were dark, hooded. "Did you expect me to fall apart with admiration, to say this kid who terrorized an innocent family can have my daughter with my blessing because he happens to possess a little talent?"

Kerry's chest squeezed painfully. "Can't you give him the benefit of the doubt? He says he made the video to try to persuade the boys that they were wrong."

"And meanwhile a woman and two kids nearly got killed," Chris snapped. "Sure, he'll probably get off. We haven't found the witness we need—maybe we never will. But I saw that family, how terrified they were. Their whole lives have been changed because of this. Do you think I'm going to believe a weak sob-sister story that he thought some half-baked video was going to change everything?"

"Chris, please. Did you see how hurt Melanie was? She needs you. She doesn't want this quarrel anymore—"

"I appreciate your concern but what happens between my daughter and me is really none of your business." His jaw clenched, holding back more angry words. "No, I don't want to fight with you. Just stay out of this. Do you understand?"

She nodded wordlessly.

He stopped halfway across the room. "Congratulations again on your dance. It was—something special."

"I wish—" But she wasn't sure what she wished just now.

"Good night, Kerry." He went out, closing the door quietly behind him.

She leaned back in her chair, sorting through the argument, wondering where or how she could have diverted it. But perhaps that wasn't possible.

What happened next would be up to Chris. She'd done everything she could.

HE HARDLY SLEPT THAT NIGHT. It didn't help that, in the next room, Melanie, too, was tossing and turning.

Had he lost them both, his daughter and the woman he loved? Because he did love Kerry; there was no denying that. In a funny way he even admired what she'd done, confronting him with Jamie's DVD. Taking the bull by the horns. It wasn't her fault it backfired.

He wished it wasn't so damn hard to sort out his feelings.

Tonight, seeing the dance she'd created had been a new experience. Chris had felt himself swept into another world, an existence incredibly far removed from the real one he lived in. It had been as if he were inside Kerry's imaginings, inside her body, moving and dreaming with her.

He couldn't bear to lose her. She was part of him now. And he knew that she loved them both, Melanie and him; that was something he'd never expected to find in a woman.

Now what the hell was he going to do about it?

By the time he finally fell asleep, it was nearly two o'clock. When he awakened it was after nine, and Melanie had already gone out.

To the dance studio, probably. Today was the last day of classes before the break; no doubt she'd want to see her friends and work out some of her frustrations at the barre.

He had to do something, Chris reflected as he went to fix breakfast. Maybe if he could prove Jamie was not guilty, Melanie would concede her father wasn't entirely an ogre. And if, by any slim chance, he could clear Jamie's name...

Chris wolfed down his cereal in record time.

CHAPTER SEVENTEEN

THE LAST CLASS OF THE last day of spring term. Even Bella had a faraway look in her eyes as she dutifully played the rehearsal piano.

Although there were no windows in the rehearsal room, it seemed full of light to Kerry. Perhaps because the ghosts were gone.

No longer was she haunted by the memory of classrooms past, of childhood dreams that had never come true.

This morning's review in the Times had confirmed her wildest hopes. It qualified as a rave, and Alfonso had called to say the company was extending its performance schedule to meet the ticket demands.

He requested another new ballet in the fall. There would be other invitations, too, he assured her; she would probably be approached by some of the top companies. And he planned to look into the possibility of taping Of Cats and Pharaohs for a public television airing. Kerry's head buzzed with the possibilities that lay ahead.

Without Chris, it would all ring hollow. But she believed in him, that somehow he would find a way back to her. The love she felt was too deep, too lasting, to allow for any other outcome.

She trusted him in a way she'd never been able to rely on her parents or George. Trusted him to be honest with his own heart and to care deeply enough about her to keep seeking a path that would bring them together.

If he didn't find it, she would. Somehow.

In front of Kerry, the beginners' class didn't look so much like little girls anymore as they executed their plié at the barre. Only eleven, they were already trading pigtails and ponytails for permanents, tracing their childish mouths with lipstick and beginning to grow breasts and hips.

Kerry sighed. Today she had to face the most difficult task of the year: deciding who would go on and who must be cut from the class.

Giving herself a momentary treat, she watched Suzie work out. There was still room for improvement, of course, and next year's transition to dance en pointe would be a major challenge. But the girl displayed the kind of poise and line, the lightness and charisma, that augured well for the future.

Another Melanie? It was certainly possible. This time, Kerry's hopes wouldn't be invested in her to the same extent. Still, a teacher always lived part of her life through her students.

Most of the other girls had made enough progress and shown enough talent to continue, although they weren't likely to become stellar ballerinas. Still, they might use their ballet in other ways—in musicals, for example, or as a foundation for modern dance.

There were only two she would have to cut. Kerry dreaded it.

When the class was over, she asked each of the girls to come, one by one, to her office. She saw the looks of dread they exchanged, and her heart contracted.

In her office, Kerry handled most of the girls quickly. "Congratulations," she would say. "We look forward to having you back next term."

Then it was Rhea's turn.

To Kerry's dismay, the child burst into tears when Kerry told her she wouldn't be returning. "But why not?" the girl begged. "I love dancing."

"I know." Kerry leaned across her desk. "Rhea, you just

can't bring yourself to take it seriously, can you? To put in those long hours, to concentrate."

"I will!" The girl's eyes widened. "Please!"

"I have something for you." Kerry reached into her desk and pulled out a couple of fliers. "Auditions for children's theater and for a children's mime troupe. I think you'd be terrific at it, Rhea. No one can be the best at everything. You'll never be a ballerina, but you could be an actress someday."

"You think so?" Rhea sniffled.

"I'm sure of it."

The child managed a weak smile. "Well, actually—I mean—I dream about being a ballerina, but I guess I don't really like all that hard work."

"You'll go to the auditions?"

Rhea nodded. "Thanks, Miss Guthrie."

"Let me know how it turns out. Good luck." Kerry exhaled deeply as the girl left.

Tiffany breezed into her office, having already changed into a designer T-shirt and jeans. The girl's chin was lifted defiantly.

"I've been meaning to tell you," Tiffany said before Kerry could start. "My mom found a new ballet school for me in Newport Beach. They put on four productions a year with full costumes and everything."

"That sounds terrific," Kerry said.

"So I won't be coming back," the girl added, unnecessarily.

"We'll certainly miss you."

"Have a nice summer, Miss Guthrie." Tiffany flounced out.

Well, that was a relief. Kerry greeted the last two girls with their good news, and then her work was over.

She closed the office and went down the hall to Myron's studio, where the advanced students were taking their character dance class. Today's specialty was a Scottish reel, and everyone except Melanie seemed to be enjoying it. The students kicked up their heels and launched themselves through the figures, and Myron stood by grinning, not bothering to correct anyone.

When he saw Kerry, he angled over to her side. "Quite a year," he said. "So. When do you leave for New York?"

"I don't." She shrugged sheepishly. "It was a crazy idea and you knew it, didn't you?"

"I hoped for the best," he said kindly.

Kerry watched the youngsters dance for a while, saddened by the spiritless way Melanie wove through the reel. To Myron, she said, "Maybe we could use Larisa, though, if she's willing—as a guest instructor. It wouldn't hurt the kids to get a fresh point of view."

"Agreed." Myron studied her closely. "You're not upset? This change of heart seems awfully sudden. Or does it have to do with last night?"

"Yes and no," Kerry said. "I suppose it's been building for a long time. Things just came into focus."

"Your new ballet is brilliant." Myron returned his attention to his class. "Tom! You keep that up, you're going to pull a muscle!"

"Sorry." The boy grinned impishly and toned down his cavorting.

The dance came to an end. "Okay, everyone." Myron clapped his hands once. "See you in two weeks. Except Tom. Good luck on your tour!"

The students bowed and trouped out, whooping and chuckling together. Melanie was trying her best to fit in, Kerry could see, but the girl drooped like a flower left out of water.

"Hey!" Kerry greeted her at the door. "You look like you had a rough night."

"I hardly slept at all," the girl admitted as they walked down the hall together. "Kerry, I can't stand it. I don't know what I'm going to do."

"Maybe I can help."

At the sound of the masculine voice, they both glanced up in surprise. Neither had noticed Chris's approach.

"Dad!" Melanie bit her lip. "I don't need a ride. I can walk."

"I have something to say to you both." Chris guided them toward the Green Room. "This won't take long."

"Oh, all right." Melanie trudged along as if to her own execution.

Kerry tried to read Chris's expression, but it was impossible. He looked tired but not as tense as he had these past few weeks. She could almost swear he was repressing a smile.

Inside the lounge, he directed them both to a couch and sat down facing them. "This morning I decided to make one more stab at finding that witness, the one I've been so sure must exist."

"The one who saw Jamie in the car," Melanie muttered. "Right."

"Well, I found him."

Kerry felt the girl tense beside her. Neither of them could speak.

"He's a gardener who works for several of the neighbors." Chris rested his elbows on his knees. "He doesn't speak much English and he's wary of police, which is why he hasn't come forward before."

"And?" Kerry pressed.

"He saw Jamie make that video of the girls a few weeks ago," Chris said. "And he saw the car the day of the firebombing."

"I don't care!" Melanie's head snapped up. "He's lying! Jamie wouldn't—"

"Jamie wasn't in the car," Chris said.

It took a moment to absorb the impact. "You mean Jamie's in the clear?" Melanie said.

"That's right." Her father's mouth twisted ruefully. "I guess

I should have trusted your judgment, both of you. We'll be picking up the other two boys this weekend. We'll need Jamie as a witness, but that's all."

"Does this—does it mean I can see him again?"

Chris nodded. "I'm sorry, Mel. This whole mess—it's just that I want to protect you. I love you so much."

She reached across to clasp her father's hands. "Oh, Dad, I've been so miserable. It was so unfair. But I'm really proud of you. You didn't have to go out there today, on your day off, and find that guy."

"I had to find out the truth," he said.

"Can I call Jamie?" she asked. "Maybe I could meet him for a Coke."

When Chris nodded, Kerry said, "Use the phone in my office. You deserve a little privacy."

"All right!" Melanie bounced to her feet with more energy than she'd displayed in weeks. "See you guys later!" She breezed out of the room.

After a quiet moment, Chris said, "I owe you an apology."

"For what?"

"For telling you that what happened between me and Mel was none of your business." He gazed at her levelly. "I couldn't have been more wrong. You're the best thing that ever happened to either of us."

"You know what?" she said.

"What?"

"I'd kill for something to eat. Something with lots of fattening calories and tons of condiments now that I don't have to worry about staying in tiptop shape."

"You don't?" Chris said.

"I'm not going to New York." Kerry stood up. "Oh, maybe for a few weeks at a time. Alfonso seems to think I'll be in demand as a choreographer. But this is my home. Now and for at least the next five years."

"What happens in five years?" He moved close to her, so close that she could feel his breath whisper across her neck.

"Somebody might decide to take early retirement, and then who knows where we'll want to go?" Before he could reply, Kerry whisked out the door. "Your car or mine?"

"Ladies' choice," he said, and followed.

BREA'S BEST WAS PACKED with an odd assortment of Saturday diners—families with little kids, biker types, two old ladies with blue-white hair tucking into the biggest hamburgers Kerry had ever seen and three teenage girls setting a new world decibel record for giggling.

"Everything on it," she told the man at the counter.

"This is where it all began." Chris feigned a dreamy expression. "Our first meal—"

"Our first argument," Kerry reminded him.

"Something about my daughter."

"It figures."

They collected their order and carried it to a table. "You hardly touched your food, as I recall," Chris reminded her.

"Force of habit." She attacked the hamburger and didn't come up for air for several minutes.

"Tell me something." He downed a french fry. "Is a jungle really necessary?"

"For what?"

"Weddings," he said.

Kerry hadn't thought that far ahead. "I don't think it's required, no. Does this mean—"

"I'm not taking any chances on you changing your mind," Chris said.

His hand clasped hers across the table. Unfortunately, they nearly overturned her soft drink in the process.

"Oops." Kerry rescued it barely in time. "Can we leave the details till later? I'm more the let's-elope-and-throw-a-party-later type, myself."

"Oh, no," Chris said. "If we're getting married, we're going to do it right."

This didn't feel quite real. Were they actually sitting here in a hamburger joint discussing their wedding? Vaguely, she recalled that George's proposal had been presented over a carefully planned dinner at one of New York's finest restaurants.

She liked it this way a heck of a lot better.

"Okay," she said. "Maybe Leila will help. And Melanie. You know she wants to go to U.C.L.A. with Jamie?"

"He's going to college?" Chris waved his hand. "Forget I said that. I'm always underestimating that kid, aren't I?"

"We'll just pound you over the head when you get out of line," Kerry teased.

He groaned. "I can see it now. With my wife and my daughter teamed up against me, I don't stand a chance."

"Just remember that," she said.

"We'll have to even things up a bit." Chris set down his hamburger. "Or—I guess with all that traveling you'll need to do—and I suppose I am kind of old to start over again, but—"

"Are you hinting that you want a baby?" Kerry asked. "I thought the woman was supposed to say that."

"I've always wanted a son." Seeing her expression, he added quickly, "Or another little girl. Whatever we get. Or maybe one of each."

She wiped her hands on her napkin. "In that case, maybe we'd better go home and start practicing."

"Sounds like the best idea I've heard all day," he said. "Let's get out of here."

So they did.

Fall in Love with...

MEN
in UNIFORM

MUBPA10

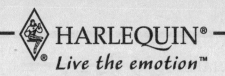

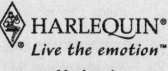

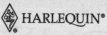

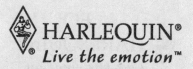

HARLEQUIN®
INTRIGUE®

BREATHTAKING ROMANTIC SUSPENSE

Shared dangers and passions lead to electrifying romance and heart-stopping suspense!

Every month, you'll meet six new heroes who are guaranteed to make your spine tingle and your pulse pound. With them you'll enter into the exciting world of Harlequin Intrigue— where your life is on the line and so is your heart!

THAT'S INTRIGUE—
ROMANTIC SUSPENSE
AT ITS BEST!

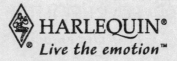

HARLEQUIN®
Live the emotion™